A SEA'S TITHE

SILVER SEA TRILOGY
(BOOK ONE)

A SEA'S TITHE

SILVER SEA TRILOGY
(BOOK ONE)

KATALINA BRYANT

To my mom and dad,

*For never giving up on me and supporting this book through
everything. I couldn't have done it without you.*

CHAPTER
One

WITH EACH CRACK OF THE WHIP, HER BODY TIGHTENED IN PAIN AND the ropes pulled taut against her wrists. Tears ran down her face, but they went unnoticed in the rain.

She looked up through her soaking hair to see the king watching, dry underneath his pavilion. His golden eyes followed the whip as it flayed across her back once more.

The people of Ascen watched in silence, sympathy written across their faces. The girl made eye contact with a small boy holding the hand of his mother. His face was blank, completely unbothered by the scene playing in front of him.

So this is what we will teach our children to be like, she thought, *desensitized by cruelty*. She had lost count of how many times the whip's sting had lashed out, but it didn't matter. She could feel the executioner's hesitation, but by the king's command, the deed would be done.

The girl clenched her teeth in pain and tasted blood in her mouth. She wanted to scream, but the king would just laugh and continue to have her whipped. It took all she had not to sag in relief when he raised his hand to stop the executioner.

The ropes were untied and she collapsed on the ground, mud squeezing through her fingers. Blood dripped down her body, warm against the rain.

Black boots, *the king's boots,* entered her vision.

"Lift her up," he said.

She was lifted by the arms. Her head hung limp from exhaustion. Using his thumb and forefinger, the king grabbed her chin and forced her gaze to meet his. The gray sky was bright behind him, blinding her as she looked at him. All she could see was his hair, as light as the golden crown he wore.

"Have you learned your lesson, filth?"

She shifted her head away from the sky and stared for a moment, searching his face for an inkling of remorse. His face was kept clean shaven, and not a speck of dirt could be seen upon it. She spat in his face and watched the blood and saliva drip off his chin.

"Have you?" she asked.

Her head was knocked to one side with a sharp sting.

"Take her back to the castle."

The girl was thrown back into the caged wagon with the other criminals. They were just as beaten down and dirty as she was, but they dared not look at her.

She turned away from them and crawled to her corner of the wagon. She kept her back away from the sides and grabbed the rusted bars to keep herself steady as the wheels squelched across the wet ground.

Hundreds of years ago, the people used to throw rotten food at the criminals. Now, they couldn't afford to waste any food, rotten or not.

THE STRAW SHE STOOD ON DID NOTHING TO KEEP THE STENCH OF excrement and rotting flesh away. The others locked up with her were huddled together to stay warm; she stood alone.

Footsteps sounded, and the iron door opened with a squeak. Ryn, the head of the guard, held the gate open for her while an entourage waited by the foot of the stone steps.

"Let's go," he said.

She didn't look up as she was led away. One of the other prisoners tried to crawl past, but the guard knocked them over with his foot.

The guards led her through the main halls to an ornate wooden door. The guards stationed there opened the door and threw her in. She landed in a heap on the floor. Groaning, she sat up and rubbed the hand-shaped bruises that littered her arms.

The stone floor was cold, but Aesara didn't notice.

A soft face appeared in front of her, and she plastered a smile onto her face.

"'Ello, Carina. Howrotoay?" Her words slurred together, the pain and blood loss causing her mind to fog, but Carina understood.

"I'm doing well, Your Highness," she said. She carefully removed her chains and lifted the princess from the ground. She led Aesara to the bath. "Can you lift up your leg for me?"

Aesara's head lolled to the side a bit, the question taking a moment to register. "Mhm? Oh, yes." The princess sunk low into the warm water, watching the color shift from clear to a murky red. "You're always so gentle, Carina. A true miracle worker of Gi'v, did you know that?" Her mind was clearing as Carina let her magic seep into her skin. It left no sensation, but its healing effects were always obvious.

"Thank you, Your Highness, but I am simply doing my duty. Try to hold still."

Aesara let out a small hiss as the sponge was placed on her raw back, waking her from her exhaustion. She wanted to take the whip to the king, her *dear father*, and see how well he liked it, if it truly showed the power he thought it did.

"My apologies, Your Highness."

"You can call me Aesara," she said, using her finger to swirl the dirty water.

"No, Your Highness, I cannot. Lean forward for me."

Aesara did as she was told and leaned forward. She told Carina every day to call her by her name, and every day, Carina would refuse. Aesara couldn't remember the last time someone had used her name without a title attached to it. She liked to imagine how it would be when someone finally did, if it would be a man saying it sweetly, if it would be pretty on their lips.

"What was your crime this time?" Carina asked, breaking her thoughts.

Aesara scoffed. "I tried to free a prisoner. For once, it was a crime I might actually commit."

"You shouldn't speak in such a way. If King Ciran heard you—"

"He'd what?" Aesara interrupted, attitude dripping from her lips. "Have me whipped again? Don't make me laugh, Carina. My father is a coward. Had he the choice to face the heavens and admit to his crimes, he would wear his crimes like jewels and walk backwards into darkness." She sank lower into the water. "He is not a king. He's a monster."

"Yes," Carina whispered. "He is. Come now, let's get you dried off and wrapped up. An infection is the last thing you need."

Aesara liked watching Carina sew the lashes closed. It was somewhat satisfying seeing how flawlessly she wiped the blood and continued her needlework, pure concentration etched on her face. She avoided looking at the actual sewing, as it made her nauseous, but she could always see the blue glow from Carina's magic.

Magic wasn't something to be trifled with. It was dangerous at the best of times and could be catastrophic if it got out of hand. Aesara thought Carina handled herself well; she didn't have the strength to fully heal all her wounds, but she had enough to take most of the pain away and close them.

In a moment of vulnerability, Aesara had asked her once if she could get rid of the scars, but those were something she would have to bear for the rest of her life.

Aesara laid her head down and closed her eyes, trying to rest instead of thinking about the lingering pain. Flashes of green and laughter filled her mind as she dozed. Aesara ran in her dreams, a child chasing the hems of a gown. She almost had them in her grip when a sharp knock sounded at the door, shattering the pleasant vision.

She raised her head slightly, still groggy.

Aesara stood up slowly so as not to disturb the freshly sewn wounds, using the vanity as a support. She winced as her skin pulled tight against the new scars. Aesara stared at herself in the mirror. Dark circles encapsulated her eyes, and her cheeks were sallow. She would eat like royalty and her form would fill out again until her father found a new crime for her to have committed.

The knocking continued.

"Yes?" she called out.

"His Majesty requests your presence."

"I'll be down in a moment." Her peace never lasted. He always wanted something, needed something. She wished she could run away from it all sometimes.

Aesara sighed. *But what good would running do?*

She walked to her wardrobe. "What color shall I dazzle our guests with tonight? How about blue for sorrow? Hmm…no." She threw the dress onto the bed. "Red for anger? Murder? Destruction? Perhaps green for envy?"

Carina walked toward her. "Your Highness? Is everything all right?"

Aesara spun around. Choosing what to wear always delighted her. It was one of the few things she could control, and so she'd learned early on what colors meant to the public eye—what colors would enrage her father the most.

"I know what color I'm wearing. Help me change."

CHAPTER

Two

AESARA WALKED DOWN THE STAIRS WITH A BOUNCE IN HER STEP. HER hair was done ornately, several strands wrapped around the weighted tiara. The king waited for her at the bottom of the stairs, watching a footman adjust one of his cuffs. Her shoes clicked on the stone floor as she walked to him. Lanterns flickered firelight in the hallway, casting an orange glow.

"Good evening, Father," Aesara said. Her heart raced as she waited for him to see her, a mix of excitement and fear.

"You're late," he said without looking up.

"My sincerest apologies. Carina had a bit of trouble helping me."

"Black? You've chosen to wear black?" Her father had finally looked at her, face hard.

Aesara smiled again. "I'm simply mourning for our queen. I will never forget her sacrifice to me."

Though the comment was made out of spite, Aesara's heart hurt for her mother. Ten years had passed since Aesara was a child, sick with the Rose Fever. Queen Siofra refused to let anyone else take care of her daughter, and as predicted, caught the Fever herself. Aesara had survived; Queen Siofra had not. Aesara touched the ring hidden beneath her corset. It had been a parting gift, the last thing she ever received from her mother.

Knowing her father could not lash out at her in front of so many people, Aesara pushed the thoughts of her mother away and took triumph in the way he gritted his teeth and said, "Of course. As is understandable, my daughter."

She used to treasure it when he claimed her. Pride would swell in her chest, and she would feel herself stand a little taller. Now, she wanted to run, hide, sink into the ground. She wanted to be anywhere that wasn't with him. Her mother's death had taken a toll on everyone, but her father had taken it the hardest.

"Your Majesty, Princess Aesara," Ryn said upon entering the hall. "The lords are waiting." His sword clinked against his armor as he walked to them.

"Thank you, Ryn," King Ciran said, glaring once more at Aesara's black gown.

The dining hall was lavish, even for a king. Gold decorated the room everywhere—in the candle fixtures, the picture frames, even in the table setting. Large windows were on either side, one overlooking the front courtyard and the other overlooking the garden.

"Ah, so you've finally decided to grace us with your presence!" The lords stood with drinks in their hands, toasting as Aesara and her father entered.

"Lord Buckley," Aesara said with a wide smile plastered on her face. "You're looking well. It's been too long since we've seen each other. Tell me, what news have you brought us?"

She hoped he'd brought actual news. The lords were her only way of learning about what happened outside the castle. She could study maps and legends, but she knew nothing of the real world around her.

He bowed to her in greeting. "Well, my son is of age to start courting as of last month."

Aesara grabbed a glass of wine from the table and took a swig, fighting the urge to grab the entire bottle. That wasn't exactly the newsworthy event she was hoping for. While she had nothing against his son, she wanted the chance to find love herself, even if that hope was futile in her father's castle.

"I'm sure you'll find a viable candidate soon," she said, swallowing the dry wine and nearly choking. She wished the kitchen had chosen something sweeter.

Lord Buckley opened his mouth but was cut off by another lord. They often interrupted one another. It was to be expected in a room full of men, each one more impatient than the other.

"We are not here to discuss courting and marriage. We are to discuss war." Lord Avery was a coarse and large man. Though he wasn't the most pleasant to be around, he was Aesara's favorite lord. *He always had news.*

"War?" Aesara asked. She clutched the glass tightly in her hand. Though the relationship between the kingdoms of Gilan were strenuous, there hadn't been an outright war in a long time.

They each controlled something unique, something that the other lands would want.

Tecrane controlled the growing of Tack, a plant that produced the common drug known as greenroot. It was a powerful drug and, though Aesara wasn't proud that it would one day be hers to control, it meant Tecrane still had some power. North of Tecrane stood Eshenia. Their fabrics and threads were sought across the world. Even as a princess, Aesara only owned one Eshen gown. More than that, Eshenia dabbled in witchcraft, sacrificing their own people to pagan gods.

Aesara hated going to their lands. It had always left her with a slimy feeling, as if someone had made malice into a liquid and bathed her in it.

To the east, Sodaya controlled the Crystal Coves. The crystals thrummed with magic; possessing even one would allow a Common to use magic. As long as the Coves stood, Sodaya would hold the most power.

It was that fact that made Aesara's heart drop when Lord Avery spoke again.

"Sodaya has threatened war, Your Highness. A crow with blood on its wings came from their king." He turned to Aesara's father. "How do you intend to respond, Your Majesty?"

"We cannot afford a war," Aesara said before the king could answer. She took a step forward, slamming her glass onto the table. The wine sloshed against the glass, some of it spilling from the top. "A war would decimate our city, our kingdom. The people barely have enough to get by as it is. For a war, we'd need—"

"It is *not* your decision to make," her father interrupted, glaring at her. "Last I recalled, I remain on the throne, not you." His voice was a lethal calm, threatening more than war on Aesara.

It never crossed her mind to bow down. "You cannot truly be thinking of going through with it." She turned to Lord Avery. "How long ago was this?"

Her father did not take lightly to the disrespect. "Silence! You have no power to judge what is right for Tecrane. You don't even know why they're threatening war."

Anger boiled in her veins and her skin heated. Though strange, the feeling was becoming increasingly familiar as she got older, and her emotions controlled her actions more than her head.

"I don't need to know why when I can already tell you that we will *lose*."

The lords remained silent, watching the scene unfold.

The king stared at Aesara for a moment before snapping his fingers and calling for Ryn. The captain entered the hall moments later, bowing to the king before taking his command.

"Escort Princess Aesara out of here. She and I will discuss respect when I am finished with the lords."

Aesara had always thanked G'iv that her mother had been blessed with magic and not her father. She could only imagine what King Ciran would do with even more power.

Aesara clenched her fists but let herself be led from the hall. It would do her no good to argue anymore; her father no longer saw reason. She managed to catch Lord Avery's eye and he nodded, just for her to see.

Shut out from the dining hall, Aesara stormed through the endless hallways until the lanterns' oils were dying, casting long shadows everywhere. For ten years, she had not been allowed outside the castle walls except by her father's command. She knew the twists and turns. Where the stone dipped and where it rose. She could traverse the halls blindfolded and never trip.

Aesara used to run through the halls, watching the lanterns for her bedtime. Her mother had the oil containers marked with a small line; when the oil had reached the line, Aesara was meant to return to bed.

Aesara stopped in front of one, trailing her finger across the etched line. The oil was well beneath the line. The dark used to haunt Aesara; she would watch every corner with a diligent eye, seeing monsters that weren't there. She learned long ago that the real monsters did not hide in the dark. They walked in the light, wearing crowns of gold.

Ryn followed her, but she didn't mind. He was one of the few who understood her. She walked beside the lantern to look out the window. The city beyond the walls was dark, the people no doubt resting from another hard day plowing dead fields. The only light came from the port, where a single ship was docked.

She frowned at the sight. Ships weren't often docked in Ascen anymore, but occasionally she would see one. Aesara imagined running to it and sailing away. She imagined traveling to the different kingdoms, exploring their lands with no title but her name. She imagined a lot of things, but everything still seemed *wrong*.

Aesara didn't know her path. She prayed for guidance, but sometimes the answer she was given wasn't always clear.

"Why do I feel so useless?" she asked, stretching out her shaking hands. She looked at the ship again and thought about boarding it once more. She didn't know where it was going or where it came from, but she didn't know that she cared.

"Your time will come, Your Highness," Ryn answered from behind her.

Aesara looked at him. "And if you're wrong?"

"Then may Gi'v welcome us home," he said, smiling.

Ryn was averagely handsome. Aesara stood a little taller than most women, a trait taken from her mother. She met most men just beneath eye level. Ryn was no different. His blond hair was neatly combed back as it always was, and he stood stiffly, as if he never relaxed.

Aesara often wondered if her father would have her marry him, but nothing was ever spoken about a marriage of any kind despite Aesara being well of age at seventeen.

"Do you think I'll ever marry?"

Ryn blinked, taken aback by the question. "Your Highness?"

Aesara shrugged. "Most women my age are married by now. Are you married?"

"No, Your Highness, I'm not." Blush bloomed across his cheeks.

Aesara chuckled. He could fight, plan battles, and train, but the second she asked about marriage, he blushed like a schoolboy.

"Pick someone nice. Make sure they'll be good to your children." Aesara grew quiet, whispering, "You don't want someone cruel."

Ryn reached for her, breaking his position and taking her by surprise. Aesara looked at him in shock as he grasped her elbow.

He had never touched her before. Not like that.

"I...you're nice," he said, refusing to meet her eye.

Aesara smiled sadly, removing his hand from her gently. "Do not choose so quickly and do not choose me. I am broken, Ryn. *I* wouldn't even pick me."

Ryn was silent for a moment. "Do we ever really choose?" he asked thoughtfully. "G'iv guides us throughout our lives. I imagine

He would guide us to who we're supposed to be with, wouldn't you agree?"

"It's a nice thought," she agreed. What she didn't say was that she didn't know if G'iv had anything that good in store for her. She would consider herself lucky if she married outside Ascen. There were lords all around Tecrane, but Aesara's luck didn't run that far. Lord Buckley's son might be the best option for her, unfortunately.

Aesara let their conversation fade, having nothing else to say. She stood there, watching the stars until the moon was at its highest. *Would the stars look the same outside of Ascen, outside of Tecrane?* It was something she often wondered and feared she would never know.

"Do you think he's in his room?" she asked. She didn't bother saying her father's name. There was only one man she avoided like Rose Fever and Ryn knew it.

Ryn looked up and down the empty halls. "He must be at this hour, Your Highness. I don't imagine many people are up and about."

"I pray you're right."

When they reached her room, the guards opened the doors for them without question.

"Carina," Aesara called. "Are you there?"

"She will come later."

Aesara stopped in her tracks, and her heart threatened to beat out of her chest.

Her father stood next to the window, looking over the city. He still wore his full regalia from dinner, his sword and knife strapped to his belt. His crown gleamed in the low firelight, and a spark of anger ignited in Aesara. How she hated that crown. It used to be a symbol for hope, for the people, but now it only meant power for *him*.

"Hello, Father," she said, running her fingers through the plaits in her hair. She kept her fingers busy to conceal the way they shook. "I wasn't expecting you so late in the evening."

"Your disrespect tonight will not be tolerated again."

"Of course not. Ryn, you may go." Whatever her father had planned, Ryn did not need to bear witness.

He turned to leave when her father stopped him.

"I may have a need for you, Ryn. Stay. Aesara, with me."

Aesara stiffened when her father grabbed her by the elbow, in the same place Ryn had just touched so gently. He led her to the vanity and sat her down with a kindness Aesara had not seen from him in ten years. Fear held her in a fierce grip.

King Ciran untangled the rest of the braids and brushed her hair, tugging softly on any knots he came across and humming a soft tune. The brush looked small in his hands, and Aesara sat rigid, hoping his hands stayed where they were.

"Your mother used to sing that song," he said finally. "She'd sing it every night to you before coming to bed. I've since forgotten the words, but I remember the tune."

Aesara remained silent. *She remembered the words. She would never forget them.*

"You look so much like her, you know. Except your eyes." She felt his gaze on her, but she kept her eyes downcast, counting the grains in the wood. She did not want to give him anything to use against her, to anger him further. Despite his calm demeanor, she had no doubt anger lurked beneath like a dragon in a dark cave.

He paused brushing her hair and tilted her chin up to look straight in the mirror. His face was soft as he looked at her before he resumed brushing.

"Your mother hoped you'd have my eyes. When she looked at you..." He set the brush down and opened the drawer.

Aesara didn't look away from her father's face. Where he had hard lines, hers were soft. Where he was tall, she was average. Where he was aggressive, she was peaceful.

A flash of silver caught her eye, but before she could react, her father yanked her hair tight and chopped it off with the scissors. Aesara yelled, leaning as best she could to avoid ripping hair from her scalp.

Long strands of brown dropped to the floor as he hacked at her hair. Aesara yelped and squirmed, trying to get away, but her father was stronger than she was. When he was satisfied with his work, he tossed the scissors onto the vanity and blew out a breath, composing himself.

Aesara looked into the mirror to see her hair, uneven and short. Her hands shook as she reached up to touch it. She had loved her long hair; she had such fond memories with it.

Eyes watering, she spun around to face her father. "*Why? Father, I don't*—"

He launched forward and grabbed her by the face, slamming her down onto the vanity's surface. He brought his knife to her face and stroked her skin from her eye to her chin.

"She was a gentle soul…" His eyes became unfocused as he spoke, and his grip on the knife loosened for a moment.

The cold edge of the knife tickled her skin and Aesara twitched, bringing his attention back to her. She wanted to scream at herself for her mistake, but she didn't need to. He pressed the knife into her skin and sliced downward. The blade stung as it cut deep into her flesh.

As Aesara screamed, her father spoke, the words lost in her pain. "Your mother had to heal you, her precious daughter. Even as she lay sick, dying, she praised *you*. You, who killed her!"

Blood ran down Aesara's face, and she struggled to get away. She finally managed to get her foot pressed against his torso and pushed as hard as she could. He fell away, crashing into her full-length mirror. It shattered on the floor, glass shards scattering on the stone.

Aesara held her face, unable to see clearly out of her left eye. The salt from her tears stung as they flowed freely, mixing with the blood dripping from her skin. She backed away toward the window as her father slowly rose.

He shook his head and rolled his shoulders before adjusting his clothes. He took a deep breath and faced Aesara. Backed against the window, she had nowhere to go.

She lunged for a piece of the broken mirror and brandished it in front of her. Her heart pounded in her chest. Her father had hurt her through others many times, but this? This was something beyond either of them.

Her father held his hands up in surrender, her blood smeared across them. Aesara wanted to use the broken mirror. She wanted to lash out, hurt him the same way he had hurt her, but her body wouldn't move. She was frozen in place.

"It's all right. It's over now. I'm done," he said softly, as if to soothe a child. "Let me see."

He pushed away the mirror shard and reached for Aesara's other hand. The shard clattered to the floor, a poor excuse for a weapon. She flinched and stared wide-eyed in fear, unable to move away. Her father shushed her and carefully lifted her hand from her face.

He stroked her mutilated skin lovingly. Smiling, he whispered, "Perfect," and turned away. He stopped in front of Ryn, who stood perfectly still, a mask of indifference spread across his face. But if Aesara looked close enough, she could see the horror in his eyes. King Ciran handed him a letter before leaving the room, shutting the door with a gentle *click*.

CHAPTER
Three

CARINA SAT IN FRONT OF AESARA, CLEANING UP HER WOUNDS AS A Common would; the king had banned Carina from using magic this time. Ryn stood solemnly behind her, clenching the letter in a tight fist.

Aesara looked at her reflection in one of the mirror shards on the floor. *Her mother had loved her long hair.* She'd loved to braid it and do intricate hairstyles, some beautiful and some silly. It had been one of their favorite pastimes together.

"Can you fix my hair?" she asked Carina, eyes watering with memories.

"I will do the best I can."

Aesara watched Carina's hand as she opened the vanity drawer and took out the scissors her father had used. Her eyes didn't leave the silver metal until they disappeared from her view.

Carina snipped Aesara's hair so it was all one length—much gentler than her father did. The strands floated delicately to the floor. Aesara cried quietly. As Carina finished, Aesara looked at Ryn, who refused to meet her gaze.

"What does it say?" she asked.

Ryn shook his head. "I don't—I don't want to say."

Aesara stood and approached him. He tried to back away, but he was pressed against her bedpost. She grabbed the letter with shaky hands and opened it, skimming its contents.

"Your Highness, don't." Ryn tried to stop her, but she moved the letter out of his reach.

Her heart stopped for a moment.

Carina took a step toward Aesara. "Your Highness?"

Aesara laughed, the sound burning her throat. "You don't have to call me that anymore." She tossed the letter onto her bed. "I've been sold. I'm nothing more than a part of the crew of *The Promisea* now. I'll probably be thrown overboard before we even make it a league out to sea." She continued to laugh; she couldn't help it.

Carina stood in front of Aesara and grasped her hands. "Whether you are dressed as royalty or a beggar on the streets, you will *always* be the princess to me," she said, tears forming in her eyes. "I have taken care of you since your mother brought you into this world, and I will not see you as anything other than the royalty you were born as."

Aesara stared at Carina, still giggling, before she broke down, her laughter turning into sobs. She collapsed to her knees, tears streaming down her face. Carina sat with her and held her, stroking her hair.

"It's okay," Carina whispered. "Everything will work out in the end. Gi'v has a plan for us all."

Aesara shook her head. "I can't...I can't do this. Carina—"

"If anyone can do this, Your Highness, it's you. You are stronger than you know."

Ryn fidgeted next to her. "I am to take you to the port tomorrow morning. You've been…you've been sold as a…" He swallowed, unsure, before continuing. "You've been sold as a bastard son."

Aesara touched her hair and more tears welled in her eyes. "Before I am escorted, allow me one thing."

Ryn and Carina watched the halls as Aesara knocked at Lord Avery's chambers. The door opened a crack, Lord Avery's face barely illuminated in the dim light.

"Princess? Is that you?"

"Pardon my intrusion, my lord, but I'm afraid I'm out of time."

The door opened wider. "If the king has done something, it is out of my hands."

At times, Aesara had wished so desperately that Avery had been her father. But now, her fate was sealed.

"I wouldn't dream of asking you to go against the king. I simply have one question for you."

"And what would that be, my princess?"

"What are our odds?"

Lord Avery stepped out of his chambers and leaned toward her, looking under her cloak. Aesara did not hide her face or the wounds her father had dealt. Lord Avery searched her eyes. For what, Aesara wasn't sure. Whatever it was, he must have found it because he answered her.

"We are going to lose."

CHAPTER
Four

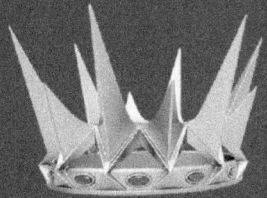

THE RAIN HAD STOPPED, BUT DARK CLOUDS STILL LOOMED OVERHEAD. Aesara gazed at the sky, blinking away tears. A tender hand guided her into the carriage.

She sat down on the bench, facing Ryn. She gave him a small smile, but he stiffened and looked away, unwilling to meet her eye. Aesara sighed and fidgeted with the hem of the shirt she wore. She liked her dresses and her corsets—liked the way they made her feel. She didn't like the shirt and pants. They hung loosely on her and didn't do the curves she had justice. Aesara not only looked like a boy, but she felt like one, too.

"I don't know how you wear this all day," she said, trying to ease the tension in the carriage. "It's so itchy."

Ryn half-smiled at her. She waited a moment to see if he'd say anything, but when he didn't, she gave up on talking and dropped her hand to the worn velvet seat. Threads hung from the bench and dark spots stained the cloth in areas. The rest of the carriage matched its worn interior; the black paint chipped on the outside and the moth-eaten curtains were drawn on the inside. Nothing about it seemed of importance.

Aesara chuckled humorlessly, shaking her head. *A carriage of no importance for cargo of no importance.*

At the crack of a whip, the carriage started, rocking side to side as it moved across the drawbridge and into the city.

Aesara peeked outside the window to see people minding their business, completely uncaring of the world around them. Everyone who walked the streets were filthy with torn clothing and dirt layered on their bodies. She bunched her shirt in her fists, seething at the sight. When she tried to move the curtain further, Ryn pulled her away from the window, shaking his head.

She leaned her head back, trying to gain composure of the fire burning inside her.

King Ciran sat tucked away in his castle, eating lavishly, living lavishly, and doing *nothing* to help the people closest to them. Aesara closed her eyes, trying not to feel completely and utterly helpless.

They wound their way down through the streets and to the port. It used to be bustling with tradesmen, fishermen, and visitors. A couple small fishing boats floated next to a single trade ship, but there would be no fish to find in the banks this close to Ascen. There were no crops. Without crops, there were no insects. Without insects, nothing for the creatures of the water to eat. It was a vicious cycle.

As the carriage came to a stop, Ryn finally spoke. "I am sorry about this. I wish there was *something* I could do."

Aesara leaned forward and grabbed his hand.

"Survive. Survive the king so that there may be a queen."

SHE AND RYN APPROACHED *THE PROMISEA*. THE SHIP WAS LARGER than it appeared from the castle window. Aesara wanted to run, but there was nowhere for her to go and nowhere for her to hide. They were stopped by a large man that Aesara was sure could easily rip her in two. Ink and piercings lined his ebony skin, and when he spoke, his voice came out in a thick accent Aesara didn't recognize.

"What is your business?" he asked.

Aesara wanted to shrink under his gaze.

Ryn handed him a letter with the Virral royal seal. Aesara would recognize it anywhere; the two-headed falcon with a sword through its chest had defined her life.

The large sailor glanced at the seal and then motioned for them to follow him onto the ship. Sailors ran back and forth, preparing to sail. Aesara swayed with the ship, unnerved by the loss in stable ground.

For a moment, Aesara couldn't think. Her breaths became as erratic as the sailors moving around her and the world blurred through her one good eye.

Her footing slipped and she landed on one knee. Her palms scraped against the grains in the planks, rough compared to the smooth wood at the castle. Ryn lifted her and guided her forward. He whispered something, but a sharp ringing overtook everything.

It was too much. Everything was too much. She wanted Carina. She wanted to be back in her room. She wanted—her thoughts stopped abruptly. *No.* She would not falter so quickly.

She sucked in a deep breath, letting the fresh air fill her lungs and clear her mind. Her hands shook, but she curled them into fists and pressed forward.

She was brought up to the helm to a man who could only be assumed to be the captain. He shouted orders from his pedestal, making the sailors run faster to prepare the ship. Aesara tripped over her own feet, stunned.

He had tanned skin and hair so dark it seemed black. Golden ringlets wound in small braids framed his face. His anthracite eyes met hers briefly and her heart skipped a beat. She hadn't even spoken a word to the man and already her body was responding.

Ryn stopped as the inked man walked to the captain's side.

"Who is this, Byrd?" he asked, his voice deep like the ocean he sailed. It rolled over Aesara, a relaxing sound despite the situation she was in.

Byrd handed him the letter and said, "I believe this is the king's payment, Vance."

The captain ripped it open and scanned it quickly. Aesara couldn't help but have a desire to read it herself. How much was she really sold for? How much did her father deem her worth?

Aesara turned her head to the left slightly to get a better look at the captain. His clothes were nicer than those around him, considering he had more clothes than them anyway, but he and his crew were all surprisingly clean. He wore a loose-fitting linen shirt tucked into brown pants. A red coat laid across the railing the captain stood next to, the color accentuating the pigment in his skin.

The ship itself was not nearly as clean. Grime caked the deck, making it black more than brown. Aesara's shoes stuck as she walked, and she could only imagine what had been spilled over the years the ship had been in use.

"So it is," Captain Vance said, interrupting her inspection of her surroundings. He folded the letter and put it into his coat pocket before stepping up to Aesara and scrutinizing her from head to toe. "Not much of a thing, are you? Just goes to show what royalty can handle, eh?"

The sailors laughed before the captain waved a hand at Ryn, shooing him away. Ryn released Aesara and left, his boots thudding against the deck. He hesitated for a moment—*just* a moment. Aesara wanted to beg him to stay, for a friendly face to be with her. But she said nothing and let him go.

As he walked away, Aesara's body grew heavier with dread by the minute.

"You know how to work a ship, boy?" the captain asked, stepping into her space.

Aesara answered simply, "No." She didn't like her personal space being invaded and wanted the situation over with as soon as possible.

He moved swiftly and shoved her against the railing, her back leaned over the edge. A dagger was placed against her throat, and Aesara decided that she had had enough of men and daggers.

"I think you meant, no, *Captain*," he said.

Aesara glared at him, the heavy feeling in her gut replaced with anger. "Go ahead and kill me, *Captain*. It's what my father wants anyway, and that's all you're good for, isn't it? Following the king's orders like a dog?"

The captain took the handle of the dagger and slammed it into her cheek. She rolled over as a wave washed against the ship, spraying her in the face. The salt water seeped through her bandages, creating a stinging sensation. Aesara took a shaky breath and faced the captain once more.

"Get him a mop and a bucket. He'll be swabbing the deck until it's sparkling, and I don't care if it takes all night." He raised an eyebrow as if daring her to challenge him.

Aesara scraped her boot against the grimy deck. She made no face, but she spoke before she could stop herself. "I think it'll take more than a night," she grumbled under her breath.

"What was that, boy?" The dagger pointed at her once again.

She held her chin higher. "I said, 'I think it'll take more than a night.'"

The captain walked toward her and placed the dagger on her bandages, just enough so she would feel its presence. Aesara held her breath, the delicate motion terrifying her more than she was willing to show.

"With an attitude like that, it's no wonder you got this. You need to learn to pick your battles because, right now, you're losing all of them."

She knew she was. But she never knew when to stop. And right now, what was the point in stopping? If he didn't kill her now, he surely would when he found out that she was a girl. A dark part of her hoped he found out sooner than later.

Aesara shook her head, chasing the hellish thoughts away. The world around her was already so cruel, there was no need for her to think such distressing thoughts about herself.

The captain leaned closer, his scent washing over her. He smelled of sea salt and spice, a warm scent that sent her mind on a much different path. One she wasn't sure G'iv would be proud of.

The captain dropped the knife, drawing her attention back to him, and walked to Byrd, whispering something before yelling, "Cast off!"

Aesara watched him walk away, her heart racing from fear and the closeness of him.

The sails were released, and with a lurch, the ship moved away from the dock. Aesara stumbled and gripped the railing. With each push of the tide, her home drifted away. She had never been away from home, at least not by way of sea.

Byrd laughed at her and slapped her on the back. "You best find your sea legs, or this will be a miserable journey," he said.

Aesara grimaced. She couldn't tell if he was making fun of her or trying to be funny to lighten the mood. Whatever his tone, Aesara was sure this was to be a miserable journey anyway.

"And where are we going, if I might be so inclined to ask?" she asked, doubtful she would get a straight answer.

"Sodaya. The captain has business there."

"I suppose I'm the business?"

Byrd only stared at her in response as another crew member ran up the stairs to bring him the mop and bucket.

"Better get working," he said, handing her the cleaning supplies.

She wouldn't be getting answers anytime soon.

CHAPTER
Five

AESARA SIGHED AS SHE LEANED AGAINST THE MOP HANDLE. THE SHIP was well out at sea; only the water surrounded them.

She decided the stars did look different on water. She didn't know if it was the way the water reflected their light or just that she was entirely exhausted from the day. Water dripped from the mop and onto her boot. Only a quarter of the deck "sparkled," and she had been cleaning all day. *At least it was starting to look brown instead of black.*

She dropped the mop into the bucket and set it against the railing before letting herself rest next to it. Placing a hand over her bandaged eye, she grimaced. She would endure, but, by Gi'v, *it hurt.*

"An eye for an eye and a tooth for a tooth," the captain said, walking up to her.

Aesara quickly grabbed the mop, gripping it tightly. She hadn't even heard him coming, a mistake she wouldn't make again. The captain leaned against the railing, watching her.

"For whoever harms me," she said, "I will not harm them in return. Hatred only stirs hatred and strife. How would that make me any better?" Her mother had taught her early in her childhood that people would get what was coming to them, that G'iv had a funny way of working sometimes. Years later, Aesara still believed it.

"Sounds like a bunch of fancy words that don't really mean anything," he said, rolling his eyes.

Aesara loosened her grip on the mop and faced the captain, taking in a deep breath. She'd never met someone who was able to irritate her so easily.

"Perhaps they are empty words to you, but I will stick by them. I don't want revenge for myself. What happens to me doesn't matter. It is what happens to my people that matters."

The captain laughed. "*Your* people? You really believe that?"

"Right now," Aesara said, looking across the vast ocean, "all I can do is believe." She had been alone at the castle and she was alone here. But at least at the castle, she had Ryn and Carina, people to confide in. Aesara wasn't sure if she would consider them *friends*, but she missed them terribly.

The captain followed her gaze before facing her once more. "If you don't do anyone else harm, what good are you?"

Aesara snapped her head to him. *Of all the inconsiderate things!* "I beg your pardon?"

"Clearly you don't know how to fight back."

Aesara kicked the bucket of dirty water into the captain's shins before bringing the mop's handle straight into his stomach, causing him to double over. As he did, she brought her knee to his face just hard enough to knock him onto his back.

He rolled onto his side, groaning. Aesara smiled at the sound and felt a swell of pride that she hadn't completely lost her skills.

"Just because I actually have morals doesn't mean I don't fight back," she stated, standing a little taller. The captain stared at her before barking out a laugh.

"You are not what I expected, Adequin." He stood and stretched, rubbing where Aesara had struck him. "If I did not have a need for you, I would suggest we take you back and place you on the throne; but alas, I am but a humble captain with morals long forgotten."

"It's never too late to get them back," Aesara suggested.

The captain took a step toward her, his demeanor suddenly serious. "I will get them back, *Selen Od*. Unfortunately, your blood will be the price."

Aesara's grip tightened on the mop's handle, the wood slick with her sweat. The Silver Language of G'iv slipped off his tongue sweetly, and though Aesara recognized its sound, she didn't know what the words meant.

She was familiar with the language; she had studied it for years. *So, how was it that she didn't know?* That frightened her more than the threat upon her life.

"I don't fear death," she whispered.

The captain stepped even closer, an inch from her. His looming figure reminded her of her father standing above her at the whipping post, glaring down at her as blood poured from her back. Her body felt heavy as the memory washed over her.

"Tell me, then, what *do* you fear?"

Aesara jutted her chin out, trying to appear unmoved by his actions. If she could stand against her father, she could stand against the stranger, handsome as he was. "Nothing."

The captain quirked an eyebrow up and smiled. He stepped away and put his back to her, walking to the captain's quarters.

"If I were you, boy," he called out, "I would be careful of what I said. Because if someone told me they weren't afraid of anything, well, I'd be damn curious to see if it was true."

The moment the door slammed shut behind him, Aesara's body gave out. She crumbled to the deck, her heart racing and lungs gulping in air as if she were stuck inside a box.

"Oh, G'iv," she said to herself. "I can't do this. I can't."

She gripped the ring on her necklace tightly, the silver metal leaving an indentation in her palm. Beneath her, she felt the thumping of music in the hull.

There was nowhere to go. She had no room to escape to. Carina was not here to guide her. Ryn was not here to…

It was unlikely she would ever see them again. It was unlikely she would, or could, ever return to her way of life before. Aesara swallowed. In one hand, she held her mother's ring. In the other, she gripped the ship's railing and pulled herself up. The wind blew across her face, and she tasted the salt in the air.

It was calm tonight. There were no waves crashing against the ship, just a gentle sway in the breeze. The sea was black in the night; she could see nothing beneath its surface.

She had survived the day, but what if the captain was right? What good was her survival?

Aesara looked at Captain Vance's closed door. Her father had sold her to him, and his intention was to use her in Sodaya. For what purpose, she didn't know. Her wounds throbbed and it felt as if the scars laced around her body tightened. They were a permanent reminder of her tortured life.

Maybe it wouldn't be so bad to do something for herself, even if it was only for the briefest of moments.

She grabbed the ropes and pulled herself onto the edge of the ship. Her balance wobbled as the ship rocked on the water.

She may have done nothing, but if she could stop Captain Vance's plan, perhaps that was *something.* And then…and then she could see her mother again. She would like that.

Death had never scared her. She had predicted it would have greeted her sooner in life. *If it would not come to her, then she would go to it.*

She jumped with her mother's smile in her mind.

The warm memory was ripped apart by the frigid sea. It seeped through her clothes and deep into her bones. Though there were no waves, the current beneath pulled her under. Aesara did not fight it as the moonlight began to disappear.

She wondered if her mother would be disappointed in her, if G'iv would still accept her when she arrived at His feet. This was not a heavenly way to die, Aesara knew that much, but maybe He would grant her mercy. She had to hope that He would—*or push her forward in life.*

It was that thought that made her realize how much her lungs burned for air, how much the freezing waters hurt her skin. Unable to control herself, she opened her mouth. Panic set in. Water rushed inside and she began to choke. Her body wanted to fight, but Aesara fought against herself.

No! Let the water have me.

Above her, lanterns flickered, and she could hear shouting.

Good, she thought, *let them know what has become of their prize.*

She couldn't stay awake much longer. The sea would claim her soon, and she would go home to her mother. For a brief moment, the thought seemed wrong, but Aesara didn't have time to dwell on it. The sea dragged her farther down, and Aesara's eyes drifted closed, uncaring of the world above.

CHAPTER
Six

In the dark, Aesara reached for the green light in front of her. Her mother stood beyond it, reaching back. *If she could just get a little closer...* She was almost there.

A shock like a bell rang through her, and the light started to pull away. *No!* She was almost there. She had almost felt her, hugged her.

Aesara awoke with a start, her mother's ring burning into her chest and the green light still pulsing in her mind. She rolled onto her side, coughing up salt water. It stung as it rushed out of her nose and mouth. Aesara gasped for air.

She stared at the floor, noticing a dirty spot she'd missed. Her clothes stuck to her uncomfortably, the salt making the material starchy. Aesara could feel the eyes of the sailors on her, could feel their questions, but they did not deserve her answers.

A hand touched her shoulder. The captain crouched in front of her, water dripping from his hair and clothes. Together, they made quite the puddle.

"Come with me," he said. Gripping her underneath her arms, he lifted her up.

The crew parted for them as they headed toward the captain's quarters. Aesara kept her head bowed, the silence of the crew deafening. She shook in the captain's warm arms—whether it was from the cold or nerves, she couldn't tell.

Thoughts of what to say ran through her head, but nothing seemed right. Lying and saying she fell would make her look foolish. Telling the truth and saying she jumped would make her look weak. *But was it weak if you had the world's weight across your shoulders?*

The captain tugged her arm, forcing her out of her thoughts.

"Don't you all have jobs to do?" he barked. In mere seconds, the sailors scrambled to disappear.

Upon entering the captain's room, Aesara was blasted with warmth. Firelight illuminated the large place from candles and lanterns. A desk sat in the center of the room with trunks of all shapes and sizes lining the walls. Blankets and cushions were scattered atop one of the large ones.

The captain guided her there, telling her, "Sit here." He dug around in another, pulling out dry clothes and handing them to her.

Aesara took them, her hands still quivering.

"Thank you," she said, her voice meek. She hated the way it sounded, but the cold still wracked through her body, and she wasn't sure she had more in her to sound tougher.

The captain took the wooden chair from behind the desk and placed it in front of her. He sat, watching her with an unreadable face.

"You want to explain what the hell that was?" His voice was sharp, and Aesara flinched. The warm air that was a comfort now felt suffocating.

"I don't owe you anything." Aesara wanted out of the room. She would take the scrutiny of the crew over the captain's biting tongue.

He scoffed. "Oh, no. You don't owe me anything. Just your life! If I hadn't heard you fall—"

"I didn't fall," Aesara said, interrupting him. She raised her eyes to meet his. "I didn't fall," she said again, her voice a whisper.

There was a brief pause, and for a moment, Aesara wondered if he understood what she meant. He stood, shoving the chair away from himself. He paced the room, frustration leaking in every step. Aesara gripped the bundle of clothes tightly in her hands, trying to make herself appear smaller.

"I have a plan for you," he said, finally facing her. "I need you *alive* for it to work."

Anger burrowed its way into Aesara, replacing the cold. For most of her life, she'd crafted her words carefully; but without her father lingering, without the crown atop her head, she found the words fell from her lips with ease.

"You need me? Well, you should have thought of that before you worked with my father. Before you threatened me. You need me, I don't need you, *Captain.*"

He took a deep breath. "All right. You want an apology, is that it? Fine. I am sorry for how I treated you." He walked and stood in front of Aesara, caging her in. The position was intimate, and Aesara's breath caught in her throat. "But if I must tie you down and lock you in here, by all that is Silver, I will. Do you understand?"

Aesara spoke before she could think about what she was saying. "Then I suppose you had better get some rope."

The captain opened his mouth to speak when a knock sounded at the door. "What is it?" he snapped.

"Sorry to disturb you, Captain," a muffled voice said through the door. "But we've got a trail."

Captain Vance stood up straight, towering over Aesara. He glared at her before walking over and yanking the door open.

"Show me," he said. The door slammed shut behind him, and the voices faded as they walked away.

Aesara let out a heavy breath, her muscles loosening. She had never been more thankful for an interruption.

Rope? G'iv, what was she thinking? She needed to learn when to keep her damn mouth shut.

She looked down at the clothes in her arms and quickly started to change, lest the captain returned quicker than she hoped. They hung loose on her smaller frame, but they were dry and covered her. Though the binding around her chest was still wet, the dry clothes felt nice. Wet spots had already appeared on the clothes from her holding them, so she could only hope the captain didn't notice the binding underneath.

No sooner had she finished adjusting herself did the captain walk back in. Aesara didn't believe in luck, but even she could admit the timing was perfect.

She spun around and faced him. "What trail?" she asked in a way of greeting. *So much for keeping her mouth shut.*

"The none-of-your-business trail. Ever heard of it?" He walked to the map spread across the desk and looked it over, confusion etched on his features.

The ship began to sway underneath Aesara, though this time it wasn't because of the water. It was just then that she realized how long the day had been, how spent her mind and body were.

"Where am I to sleep?" she asked.

The captain pored over the map still, reaching for a quill.

"Captain Vance?" she asked again. Aesara didn't want to get on his nerves or anger him further, but she really would like to sleep. Whether it was on the deck or with the other sailors, she didn't care. She needed somewhere to rest.

The captain snapped his head up. "Did you say something?"

Aesara squeezed her eyes shut and opened them again, trying to keep herself awake. "Where am I sleeping?"

He pointed offhandedly to a cushioned bench by the window. "There. I'd rather keep my eye on you in case you decide to go for another midnight swim."

"Not everything I do has an ulterior motive, you know," she said, facing away from him with a huff. Despite her annoyance, she was thankful for the soft place to rest and the solitude it provided her against the prying eyes of the sailors.

The captain grumbled something under his breath, too low for her to hear. As her eyes closed to the sound of the captain's quill, Aesara's thoughts drifted over the day's events. Just that morning she had been in the castle under her father's scrutiny, and despite all that it had taken to get her here, Aesara couldn't help but feel just a little bit freer.

CHAPTER
Seven

SHE WOKE WITH A JOLT, CLUTCHING HER EYE, HER FATHER'S FACE still lingering in her mind, her dreams turned to nightmares. She took a deep breath and peered out the window. The sea sparkled in the sun, the waves a blinding and soft reminder of where she was.

Bowing her head against the warm glass, she whispered, *"Tmes visith fi."* She liked the sound of the Silver Language. It rolled off the tongue like honey and sent a shiver down her spine.

"Ol Gi'v slei vizh."

Aesara jumped, startled by the captain. He leaned against the door frame nonchalantly, his hand clasped loosely around a piece of bread. The rings around his fingers glistened in the sunlight, catching Aesara's eye. She liked the way his hands flexed. The way they curled loosely around the bread, she could see the strength he held. He had the ability to protect or destroy. Aesara could only wonder what he would choose.

Aesara's fingers found their way to her ring once more, the movement not going unnoticed by him.

"What's with the necklace?" he asked, moving further into the room.

"I thought you weren't religious," Aesara countered, dodging the question. She didn't share its history lightly, and certainly not with a roguish captain.

He chuckled and tossed her the bread before sitting at the desk. He leaned back in the chair, propping one leg over the other.

Aesara cringed inwardly. She thought the position disrespectful when talking, though it did look comfortable.

"I said I didn't have morals; not once did I say I wasn't religious, *Selen Od.*"

"You've called me that before," she said, taking a bite out of the bread and ignoring his propped boots. "I recognize the Silver Language, but I don't know what that means."

A small smile curled at the ends of the captain's lips. Aesara chewed slowly, the bread suddenly hard to swallow as he leaned forward.

"Let's play a game. A truth for a truth."

Aesara eyed the captain warily. "How do I know you're telling the truth?"

"How do I know you are? It's a fair price, Adequin. Are you playing?"

Adequin. Aesara hated the name. Every time he said it, it left a sick feeling in her stomach, as if he knew her secret—as if he was toying with her. Aesara wanted to scream her truth and her lies.

Instead, she said, "I'll play."

"Excellent! I'll go first." He moved about the cabin, searching for something. "What's around your neck?"

Aesara curled her fist tighter around the ring, as if concealing it would make the question any less real. She didn't like how he knew what questions set her on edge, what words made her uneasy.

"It's my mother's wedding band. It's all I have left of her."
Before the captain could give her a witty remark, she continued,
"What does *Selen Od* mean?"

"It means Silver One. Why wouldn't the king claim you as
prince? Even a bastard is more of an heir than a daughter."

Aesara frowned, his question completely going in one ear and
out the other. "Silver One? No one's been named that since...well,
since G'iv sent His soldier in the beginning—before everything.
Why would you call *me* that?"

Captain Vance smiled mischievously. "Ah, ah, ah. You have
to answer my question first. Why didn't the king claim you? Why
keep the daughter?"

Aesara huffed and sat a little straighter. "Maybe it's time the
kingdom had a queen again."

"Maybe you're right." The captain chuckled. "Go on, ask
your next question."

Aesara opened her mouth and almost repeated her earlier
question when something else struck her mind, something that
mattered more than his riddle with the Silver Language. "What
trail did you find last night?"

The captain stilled, his hands frozen on the clasp of an ornate
trunk. He dropped them to his sides and turned to her, a scowl on
his face.

"The game is over."

"What? But it's only just started!" Aesara rose from the
window seat and took a step toward the captain. "You said a truth
for a truth. I gave you mine."

The captain turned away, stalking toward the door.

"Fine," Aesara called after him. "I change my question. Why
are you such an ass?"

In a flash, the captain was no longer in front of the door, but
leaning over Aesara. His scent affronted her, clouding her anger.
His dark eyes bore into hers, something fierce burning within them.

"Because if I'm not, who will be?"

He raised his hand toward her. Without thinking, Aesara shied
away, shielding her left side. Her eyes were squeezed shut, but

when no blow struck, she slowly opened them to see the captain looking at her curiously.

Never breaking eye contact, he moved his hand forward slowly. He grasped the ring around her neck and examined it.

"This is real silver. I suggest you hide it unless you want it stolen." He dropped it as if it burned him and, in two long strides, created as much distance as he could between them.

Aesara let out a breath, finally being able to breathe. He had such passion with everything—the way he acted, spoke, even moved. Aesara wondered what it would be like to have him turn that passion toward her.

He opened the door and stepped out. The captain, however, didn't close it.

Aesara took the opportunity to look across the deck. The crew bustled about, working on the ship as it needed. At least, she could only assume. Aesara knew a great many things, but she didn't know where to begin in how to run a ship.

Her eyes caught the red coat of the captain as he made his way to the helm. Byrd waited for him there. They linked their arms, pulling the other toward themselves and bumping shoulders. Aesara had never seen a greeting like that before. It was much more casual than the ones at the castle.

In fact, everything was more casual—the people, the clothing, the greetings, even the way they spoke. Aesara took a step further out of the cabin, keeping to the shadows but wanting to see more of this world.

"We don't bite."

Aesara jumped, putting a hand to her chest to try and calm her racing heart. She looked to her left to see a young man. Though, Aesara wondered if man was the right term. He looked younger than her. He wore a simple sleeveless tunic and cropped trousers. His feet were bare, but he wore a straw hat that Aesara believed could have seen better days.

"Sorry," he said, raising his hands. "I didn't mean to scare you. You're Adequin, right?"

Aesara nodded, not trusting her voice.

"My name's Six." He held out his hand. Aesara eyed the grime and filth caked on his palm with disdain before figuring that was something she would have to get over and shaking his hand.

"Nice to meet you," she said, making her voice as deep as she could.

Six smiled. "It's always nice to get a new man on board. Sometimes the older ones get a little…grumpy."

Aesara looked across the deck. "Yeah," she agreed. "I can see that." All the older crewmates looked worn down and tired, as if they were just waiting to be called upon by G'iv. Aesara wondered if maybe they were.

"Don't think too harshly on it." Six slapped her on the back, pushing her into the sun. "Or them. They've been on *The Promisea* for a long time, at least since Vance has been captain."

Aesara stared at her feet and grimaced inwardly. She had wanted to explore alone, but it would seem Six had no intentions of letting that happen. He walked forward, pointing out the different crew members, what they did, and how long they'd been on the ship. Aesara followed along, nodding but not really listening. She wanted *off* the ship, there was no reason to remember anyone's history but her own.

"I just joined the crew a few months ago, myself. My dad wanted me to learn how to man a ship, and what better way than on *this* ship?" Six kept moving, but Aesara's thoughts snagged on something he said.

"I take it *The Promisea* is a popular ship, then?" she asked.

Six paused, staring at her with wide eyes. "Only the best! It's been through wars and battles and storms! Not to mention, it has the most legendary captain."

Aesara took a step closer. She didn't care about the crew, but information about the captain? That was something she could use.

"What can you tell me about him? I have to admit, I'm not exactly well-versed in the ship's history."

Six opened his mouth but quickly snapped it shut when a shadow fell over the two of them.

"If you want to know about the captain, maybe you should ask him."

Aesara clenched her teeth in annoyance. "Maybe I did and he was too much of a bastard to answer," she said, turning around and glaring at said captain.

The ship fell silent, and Aesara could feel their eyes on them. She hadn't meant to say it in front of everyone, but the words slipped out before she could think.

Six placed a hand on her shoulder, pulling her back slightly. "If I may, Captain—"

"You may not."

Six immediately released her, whispering, "I tried."

Aesara wanted to smile at him, let him know that she appreciated his help, but that would have to wait.

Captain Vance took a step forward, once more invading Aesara's space. "I am not a forgiving person. If you think I'll treat you any differently because of who you are, you're wrong."

Aesara wanted to scoff. No truer words had ever been said to her. "I don't expect you to. So, do whatever you're going to do and let's get it over with."

What her father did to her hurt, yes, but it was the waiting that Aesara hated the most. Always being unsure of when the pain would come, what it was that he was going to do. Aesara liked knowing, and her father knew that.

Captain Vance stared at her before smiling. "You've got nerve. You might just survive longer than I thought."

With that, he walked away. The rest of the crew went back to minding their own business, though Aesara caught the smiles on some of their faces. Six clapped her on the back, congratulating her for beating his test.

Aesara blinked. She didn't know what test Six was talking about. She had simply spoken out of experience, but, she supposed, they didn't know that.

Aesara smiled back at Six and let him finish showing her the ship.

IN THE SUN, AESARA FIDGETED. SHE HAD NEVER HAD TO HIDE HER body before and now she had to do it every day. She managed to hide between the many barrels of ale and rum to re-bind herself, but her constant fidgeting was beginning to be noticed. Aesara needed to find a way off the ship quickly.

After the morning of their game of truths, Aesara spent most of her time with Six, watching the captain from afar. Six reminded her of a puppy, always happy to be around and willing to do anything you asked. There were days they were separated, when she was tasked with the occasional cleaning job or he had to do his. Aesara still wasn't entirely sure what he did. He had explained it to her once, about being in the crow's nest, watching. Watching for what, she didn't really know. When night fell, Aesara would return to the captain; and in the morning, she was free to roam about.

Today, Aesara was alone. Six was high up in the crow's nest and no one else had been nice enough to befriend her. She breathed in the salty air and sneaked a glance at the captain on the helm.

His eyes stayed forward, never straying. *Good.*

She pushed herself off the railing and made straight for his cabin, hiding herself in between and behind other sailors moving about the ship. In an easy few seconds, she was alone inside.

Aesara felt a little bad for what she was doing. Not because of the captain, but because of Six. He was a good friend, and she didn't want to do anything that might bring him harm. So, she decided she needed to move fast.

She pulled out several drawers in Captain Vance's desk, finding nothing worth her time.

"Come on, come on," she whispered to herself. "There must be something."

But there was nothing; the drawers were empty.

"Dammit! How could there be nothing?"

Aesara felt around some more. Just wood—wait. Her finger caught on a small latch.

Click.

The bottom of the drawer lifted, revealing a stash of papers. Aesara pulled them out, laying them across the desk. They were maps.

Aesara spread her hand across the maps, laying them flat. She couldn't read a sailor's map, but she could read the handwritten notes scrawled across them.

"'Dead end…turned left…disappeared…found—killed half of the crew.' What killed half the crew?"

Aesara shuffled the maps and found similar notes. But none of it made sense.

"Oi! Where'd Adequin go?"

Aesara looked up with wide eyes. She raced against the captain, stashing the maps in their secret compartment and putting everything else back. Her heart beat against her chest as his footsteps sounded closer.

He was at the door, but there were still papers on the desk.

No, no, no. She needed more time.

Her ring warmed against her chest and a large wave rocked the ship to the side, knocking the sailors and captain down. Aesara looked out the window. The sky was clear, and the sea sat still.

She wasn't about to question it now. She shoved the papers back in their respective drawers and threw herself on the window seat just as the captain walked in.

"What are you doing?" he asked.

Aesara shrugged, trying to act bored despite the panic in her body.

The captain walked forward, standing in front of the desk. Aesara's eyes darted down.

One of the papers was sticking out.

She jumped up. "What's it like, being the captain of a ship? Is it hard? Could you teach me? I've always wanted to learn. Do you think I could learn? I'm a pretty good listener when I want to be." She threw question after question, pushing her way toward the desk. She could only hope it would distract him long enough for her to fix the paper. She sat as the captain had nights prior, legs propped. She hated herself for it, but it was the best way to conceal the map.

"Stop, stop, stop!" he yelled, waving a hand at her.

"What?" she asked, feigning innocence.

"They whisper."

Aesara frowned. "Who whispers?"

"The lost souls." Captain Vance walked to one of the trunks, the one he almost opened the morning of their game, and clicked open the latch.

Cold air rushed out, causing Aesara to shiver. It smelled different, as if it had been trapped there for years, unopened and unused. Aesara exhaled, trying to push the scent from her nose. The captain reached in and pulled out a long object shrouded in black cloth.

He set it down in front of her. When she reached forward, looking at him expectantly, he nodded. She pulled the cloth off to reveal a sword. Its pommel was a brilliant silver with a single glittering gemstone in the center. Aesara wanted to call it a black gem, like an obsidian, but the color seemed to shift as if it were *alive*.

Aesara stilled.

"They whisper," she repeated, her voice barely audible. Fear rose in her, and the paper sticking out of the desk left her mind—it didn't matter now.

Captain Vance trailed his hand along the sword, tracing the stone. "So, you know it?"

"Yes, I know it. And I know you, *Reaper.*"

CHAPTER

Eight

THE CAPTAIN SMILED, TEETH GLEAMING.

"You shouldn't go through other people's belongings, Adequin. It's rude."

Aesara licked her lips. The panic that had dissipated was slowly worming its way back under her skin. "Better to ask forgiveness than permission."

Captain Vance *tsk*ed at her. He unsheathed the sword and held it straight, hovering his hand against its razor edge. Aesara felt a bit like she was being held against its edge as well, her life dangling over a precarious cliffside—one shift, one breath, and she would tumble over.

Sweat formed on Aesara's brow as a clap of thunder shook the ship. The sun entering the room disappeared as storm clouds blocked out its light.

"What's your name?" he demanded.

Her mouth went dry at the question and her hands trembled in her lap. For once, no words spilled from her mouth. Aesara didn't know what to do. She had imagined this moment since she stepped foot on the ship, but she had imagined it with a *normal* captain, not the Reaper.

"I asked you a question, imposter."

Aesara bristled at his accusatory tone. "*I'm* not an imposter. Adequin is an imposter." As she stood, the wind whistled sharply outside the window. "I am Princess Aesara Virral of Tecrane, sole daughter and heir to the Virral throne. You will refer to me as such."

The captain pointed his sword at her. "And if I don't?"

How *dare* he?

A wave crashed into the ship, almost knocking it onto its side. Aesara and the captain were flung into the wall. Aesara cursed as a chest stabbed into her ribs, promising bruises in the morning. Glass lanterns shattered on the floor and the captain's collectibles rolled about, loose from their confines.

"By all that is Silver!" the captain exclaimed, struggling to get up. He dislodged the sword from the planks, the wood rotting where it had been implanted, and stormed to the door.

He swung back around to face Aesara.

"Stay here."

He ran out, the flood on deck flowing its way into the room. The door swung on its hinges, the wind pushing it back and forth violently.

Aesara groaned as she pushed herself up. The ship rocked side to side in the storm, throwing Aesara to and fro. She slid against the desk, smacking her head into its thick wood.

Blood dripped down her neck, the feeling familiar to her. She shook her head and rose, lunging for the swinging door. She caught its handle and managed to get on the deck.

It was chaos.

Sailors ran in every direction. She couldn't hear over the wind and the screaming. Rain pelted her face and she squinted, trying to make out where the captain was. The storm had come so suddenly. The captain had never explained what to do in a storm. In fact, no one had explained what to do.

Where was he? She couldn't find him.

She spun in a circle.

"Captain?" she called. "Where are you?"

She couldn't breathe. He knew her secret. What if he told everyone? What if he was rallying them to kill her now? She needed to find him.

"Captain Vance?"

Hands grabbed her by the shoulders and twisted her around. It was him.

"What are you doing out here? Get back in the cabin!" The captain immediately turned away and started commanding his sailors. Not to kill her, but to sail the storm.

The cabin?

"Why?" she called after him. "So I can wait for you to kill me?"

He stalked toward her, irritation in his every movement. He pinched her jaw between his fingers. "If you don't let me do my job, we're all going to die."

Anger and fear built up inside her like a fire, the ring against her chest burning just as hot. But before she could say anything, a wave bigger than any that had come before welled up beside them.

"Hold on!" was the last thing the captain said before it crashed into the ship. Wood splintered, and Aesara was swept up in the commotion.

Water pressed against her chest, and she struggled to swim. She opened her eyes and kicked to what she could only assume was up. Her head broke through the ocean's surface, and she gasped for air only to be pushed back down by another wave.

Her hands flailed for something to grab—anything. She prayed this wasn't a punishment for jumping and reached again. By G'iv, her hands found a rope. She gripped it tight and pulled. It cut into her palms, red staining the blue water, but she didn't let go.

The rope moved on its own, and she landed on the deck. Choking, she looked up to see Six, his eyes worried.

"The captain?" she asked.

Why she was worried about him, she didn't know. *If he perished, it would save her trouble, wouldn't it?*

Six and the rest of the crew avoided her questioning gaze.

"Where is he? Where is Captain Vance?" Aesara pushed them away, looking over the edge of the ship. The storm still raged on, and she could hardly see through the rain.

"There!" Aesara pointed.

Just barely, she could see his head bobbing up and down in the water. She looked back at the crew. They stood, their heads bowed.

"Aren't you going to help? You helped me!"

"The captain is...different," Six said, fidgeting.

"Weren't you saying how legendary he was? Oh, never mind!" Aesara didn't have time to think about what he meant. If they didn't want to help, she would do things as she had always done them. Alone.

Aesara grabbed the rope, nearly dropping it from the blood and water on her hands. She tied it around the main mast and then around her waist.

Six grabbed her forearm before she could jump. "Why are you helping him?"

Aesara thought as her ring pulsed against her chest. "Because no one else will."

She leaped into the water, immediately being pulled under the crushing waves. She pushed herself to the surface, searching for the captain once more.

There!

She kicked forward, praying she would reach him before it was too late. She was almost there. Just a little farther.

"Captain!" she called. Water flooded her mouth and she spit it out, trying to stay afloat.

"Captain Vance!"

She swam farther until she was yanked back at the waist. *She had no more rope.*

With wide eyes, she called to the captain again. "Swim to me! I can't go any further. Hurry!"

There was no way to tell if he had heard her. As his head disappeared, a sinking feeling filled her stomach.

"Captain! Where are you?" She kept kicking at the length of her rope, searching. "Captain!"

He sprung up in front of her, gasping.

"Captain!" She grabbed ahold of his torso and started to swim back to the ship.

Aesara panted. She was already so tired, and now she had to carry twice her weight.

"C'mon. I need you to help me. Kick."

The captain mumbled something, but she couldn't hear him.

"What? I just need you to swim."

He laid his head on her shoulder, his lips right next to her ear. "Breathe. Calm down. You're making it worse."

Aesara gaped at him.

"I'm saving your life, you ungrateful little sh—" A wave pushed them under and Aesara struggled to keep hold of him.

When they resurfaced, his eyes were open and fully aware.

"Aesara, was it? Look at me," he said. "*You* are causing the storm. Your emotions. You need to calm down."

Aesara frowned. "What are you talking about? We need to get you back to the ship."

She started to swim when he pulled her back to him. He pressed her against his chest, wrapping one strong arm around her middle. He kept them both afloat, kicking against the current.

He whispered low in her ear, "What's your favorite color?"

"This is hardly the time—"

"Just answer."

Aesara huffed. "Green."

"Green? That's it? So, like the algae growing on my ship."

Aesara made a face. "Ew, no. If you must compare it to the sea, the moss. I like dark green, so rich in its hue that you feel as if you could dip your hand in it and it would come out covered in the color. There's a tree in the castle gardens; it flowers once a year, but it always stays a beautiful green. My mother loved that tree. She raised it from a sapling."

She was rambling. She knew she was, but the color made her think of so many things—so many *good things*.

"Did your mother take you to the tree often?" Vance asked.

"It was our favorite spot. She would read to me, teach me, even take naps with me there." Aesara smiled at the memory. "Mother was a mage. She had natural magic. She would make the roses bloom in winter for me sometimes. Just for a second, though. She said they needed their time to rest. She said I might inherit it, but…"

"Why'd you stop?"

Aesara tilted her head up. "Why do you care about all this?"

Vance smirked and motioned toward the settled sea. "Because I think your mother was right."

CHAPTER
Nine

Aesara stood at the edge of the ship, hands clenched tight against the railing. A single white cloud drifted across the blue sky, the sea calm beneath it. After the storm, Vance had talked to the crew about her. Those who didn't want to work with a woman were free to leave the next time they docked, but most didn't seem to mind after learning she was a mage.

Aesara was grateful she didn't have to wear the binder anymore, but more than that, she was grateful Six still wanted to talk to her.

She took a deep breath and with one hand, she pulled out her mother's ring and inspected it. Despite the slight tarnish in some areas, it was still worth more than some people's lives.

"Queen Siofra was a fierce woman. Not many could keep up with her." Vance leaned his back against the railing, his face tilted toward the sun. "We were all surprised when she passed."

"You speak as if you weren't a child then."

"I wasn't."

"But how? You don't look much older than me."

Vance smiled, his hand gliding to the hilt of his sword. "I have been a captain for a *long* time, Princess. I didn't choose this life any more than you did. The sword chooses you; it is not just a blade, it is an extension of you—your soul, your life, your *death*. It sees, it conquers. You bend to it."

Aesara eyed him warily. "That is not how the stories go."

"No? And how do the stories go?"

"I...well..."

"Go on. I haven't been able to shut you up since you boarded, but when I ask for a story you go silent?"

Heat bloomed across her cheeks. She turned her head away. Usually her hair would fall, shielding her from prying eyes. Though she missed the comfort of it, the breeze blowing through her cropped hair felt nice.

"My mother told me it as a story to keep me in bed at night. She said the blade was forged at the Black Rocks outside the Crystal Coves. Red stained the stones and flooded the sea. It was a massacre with a single survivor. The Reaper." She glanced at Vance. "The first Reaper, I mean. He searched among the bodies for survivors only to find his wife and son amongst the dead. He pleaded with G'iv to bring them back. G'iv did not answer him. A witch did.

"She rose from the sea and let him cry, collecting his tears to salt her waters. She promised him a gift if he would give her his tears. He too quickly accepted. She presented him with a sword, a glittering black gem in its center. It would keep the soul of anyone he killed, never allowing them to escape their humanity." Aesara looked at him to see if she was telling the story right, but his face revealed nothing of what he thought. "With it, he was unstoppable. It never shattered, never dulled, and it never missed.

He spent years wandering the land, trying to find the man who commanded his family's death. When he finally found him, he was old and wrinkled. There wasn't much of a fight left in him. The Reaper didn't care. He raised his sword and in one fell swoop, killed them both. As he lay dying, he heard his wife's voice, calling to him, but as the witch had promised, his soul would never leave the stone. With his soul trapped, the sword returned home to the sea only for another to find it. But it always ends the same. The sword *always* returns to the sea."

"Hmm."

Aesara glared at him. "That's your only response?"

"Forgive me, Princess. What response were you expecting? A less scary tale?" He eyed her.

"A more gruesome tale, then."

Aesara scoffed. "I don't know what I was expecting. Certainly not the truth."

Vance paused for a moment. And then, "Morana."

Aesara snapped her head up. "What?"

"The witch's name. It's Morana." He shifted to his side, facing her. "She found me when I was still part of the crew, trying to gain any sort of experience on a ship. My captain at the time had led us into the Black Rocks. Like most pirates, he wanted to go after the most powerful treasure, but the bastard didn't know how to navigate it. Our ship was ripped to shreds. Those of us that survived the crash held on to scraps of wood, praying to a god we didn't believe in that we would make it out."

Aesara's heart clenched at his words.

"That was when Morana found us. Killed the captain right then and there. Said that if anyone challenged her and won, they would go free. They all tried; they all failed. Then it was just me. I didn't want to challenge her. At that point, I didn't even want to live." Vance shook his head, laughing dryly. "I don't know if she gave me the sword because she thought it was funny or because she saw something in me. But now I'm bound to it, and it's bound to me until either I perish, or she does."

"Vance, I…" Aesara set a hand on his shoulder. "I'm sorry."

"I was going to kill you, you know?" He motioned toward the sword. "When they told me that you weren't a male. I don't know what use I have for a woman aboard my ship. But then you made that storm."

Aesara wrapped her arms around herself, doubt creeping into her mind. "I don't even know how I did that, Vance. I don't know if I could do it again."

The words slipped from her mouth. She wanted—no, *needed*—to survive, but to make promises she couldn't keep? She thought of Ryn's face as he left her aboard the ship.

Vance stepped closer, invading her space. It made her heart thump against her chest, but she didn't feel the scared panic that was becoming all too familiar. This was a different kind of nervousness.

"What if I helped you? Aesara, I'm a Common, stuck in an endless cycle. I just want it to end. Help me. Please."

Her stomach fluttered at the way he said her name. No one had ever said it like that before—so openly, so tenderly, so *desperately*. She took a step back.

"What would you want me to do?"

He smiled, something to behold in the sun.

CHAPTER

Ten

AESARA WANTED TO GO HOME. SHE MISSED HER BED. SHE MISSED HER bath. She missed her clothes. Most of all, she missed the way she could be alone. On the ship, she was surrounded by people. Some nights were quieter than others, but someone was always there, lingering.

The clothes she wore hung from her frame, but Aesara didn't complain; at least they were dry. Though, nothing on the ship was ever *really* dry. The wind held onto moisture, and it seeped into everything aboard the ship. Even the food had a salty taste.

Aesara sighed, hanging her head. Vance had helped her clean up her eye and rewrap it. It was healing well, considering her environment. Thankfully, Vance had asked no questions. Aesara wasn't sure she was ready to answer them.

Six stood beside her, giving her company. Aesara was grateful for the companionship. He never pried, never invaded her space, he was just there. In a way, he reminded her of Ryn.

"My dad always liked that one," he said, interrupting her thoughts. He pointed at the stars dotting the night sky. Aesara followed his finger to the dog-shaped constellation, Kingo.

"Kingo? Why's that?" she asked.

"Dad always wanted a dog like him, but we always got the runts. They were good dogs, but there was always something they were bad at. Musty couldn't wrangle the sheep for nothing, and Jackie bit at the chickens too much. We had one, Rebel"—Six whistled.—"*loved* the water. Always found him playing in it. Of course, Dad always found me playing with him, too."

Aesara laughed at the image of a young Six and a dog playing in the water, getting yelled at. She imagined it was quite the mess to clean up.

Six stared at her in shock.

"What?" she asked, a smile still on her face.

"Nothing, I just…well, I've never heard you laugh."

Aesara thought about it. "I suppose it has been a long time." She bumped her shoulder into his. "Thank you."

She looked up at the sky again, searching for her favorite constellation. It was called The Harbinger, a figure wielding a sword in one hand and an olive branch in the other. It was based on *Selen Od*, G'iv's first soldier. She pointed it out to Six. "That one is my favorite. My mother showed it to me when I was a little girl and it quickly became my favorite, though I never did figure out what it was the harbinger *of*." She shrugged. "I suppose I'll never know now."

Stretching her arms out straight, she flexed her fingers. Green sparks flew out, just for a moment, making her and Six jump.

"So, magic, huh?" he asked, leaning against the railing.

"Yeah, *magic*." She blew out a breath and dropped her hands. "Magic I don't know how to use."

Six smiled at her and held up his hand, revealing an extra finger. "They call me Six 'cause of this, and I just got it to wiggle about a year ago. Had it for eighteen years and it took me seventeen to figure it out. You'll get there."

Aesara smiled and reached forward, tracing around the sixth digit. Despite his boyish looks, he was older than her. It didn't really matter, but knowing the small truths about him made her feel closer to him. "What's your real name?"

"Not one worth remembering; besides, I like Six more." He placed his hand on her shoulder, a comfortable weight. "You'll find yourself eventually, Aesara. Until then, try not to think about it too hard."

Aesara opened her mouth to speak when the door to the captain's quarters slammed open, banging into the wall. Vance stormed out, Byrd following quickly behind. Aesara watched carefully, her curiosity piqued.

"It is a mistake, Vance, and you know it!" Byrd yelled. "We made this deal with one thing in mind—"

"You think I don't know that?" Vance interrupted Byrd, spinning on his heels to face him. "You think I don't remember? I was there, Byrd!"

Without realizing what she was doing, Aesara took a step forward, out of Six's comforting embrace.

"You were there, but I'm starting to wonder which head you're thinking with."

Vance scoffed at the accusation. "I'm thinking very clearly, thank you. I'd appreciate a little more confidence after all we've been through."

Aesara had a sinking feeling that the conversation was about her, though that didn't stop her from listening. Six tugged on her, trying to get her to leave.

"Aesara," he whispered. "We should go."

She swallowed, suddenly nervous at being caught, and nodded. She turned to follow Six and cringed as the board she stepped on creaked loudly.

Vance and Byrd stopped, both turning to them. Aesara smiled weakly and gave Vance a little wave.

"We go through with the original plan," Vance hissed. He turned away from Byrd and made his way to her. "What are you doing out so late?"

Byrd scowled and stormed down the stairs to the crew's quarters. Aesara never did understand why Byrd had such a problem with her, but that would be a conversation for later.

"What were you two arguing about? It seemed serious." She paused briefly. "Was it about me?"

"Don't worry about it. Let's get you to bed." He nodded at Six, who nodded back and followed Byrd. Aesara didn't understand the unspoken words, but she hoped she would in time.

Vance pressed his hand into the small of her back, guiding her into his cabin. Aesara took one last glance at The Harbinger before the door shut behind them.

THE SUN BLAZED DOWN ON THE DECK. SWEAT DRIPPED FROM AESARA'S brow from both the heat and concentration. In front of her, Vance had propped up a book on top of a barrel. Her job was to knock it over without touching it.

She breathed heavily, her hands shaking at the attempts.

"By all that is Silver!" she screamed, letting the tension go. "I can't do it."

Vance leaned against the railing, watching her. He bit into an apple, some of the juice dripping down his chin. "You'll get it. Keep trying."

Aesara stomped to him, snatching the apple from his hand and taking her own bite out of it. It was deliciously sweet and cold compared to the weather. Vance raised a brow as she crouched, still chewing on the apple.

"Do you feel better?" he asked.

"No," Aesara mumbled. "My mother used to grow groves of trees. Flowers bloomed right in my bedroom! How is it I can't even knock a single book over?"

Vance lowered himself next to her. His shoulder pressed up against hers, the warmth comforting despite the heat.

"Maybe you're thinking too hard about it. Stop trying to be what she was and be what you are."

Aesara sank lower, letting her legs stretch out in front of her. She raised the apple to be at eye level. It was bruised on one side— just a small little dot, still completely fine to eat, but the spot was there all the same. The product, to most eyes, would be considered damaged.

Aesara rubbed her thumb against it, thinking about the many scars etched across her body. Would she be considered damaged? Beneath the apple, her palm glowed softly in a brilliant green, and when she brushed her thumb across the bruise once more, it was gone.

She handed it back to Vance. "Here. Undamaged."

"Look at you," he said, smiling.

Aesara laid her head against the railing, turning it so she could look at the water. Gentle waves lapped at the sides of the ship, keeping them at a steady pace.

"How often do you stop for supplies?" Aesara asked, keeping her voice as even as possible.

Vance chuckled, leaning his head back and draping an arm over his eyes. "We won't need to stop for at least another few weeks. You're stuck out here whether you like it or not, Princess."

Whether she liked it or not? Logic told her she shouldn't like it. She should hate it after everything she'd been through. But the other side of her, the one not run by logic, was what made her nod stiffly and put as much distance as she could between her and Vance.

She scrambled down the stairs to the hold, the dark and damp area inviting compared to the deck. The area was empty except for her. She trailed her hand along the countless barrels and crates.

Vance was right. With this much cargo, they wouldn't need to stop anytime soon. Not unless something happened to it.

Making sure to stay silent, Aesara hauled a crate of potatoes to the side. She slid her hand along the wall, the moss and algae sending shivers across her skin. She pushed against the wood, looking for any weak spot.

Aesara fell forward as her hand broke through the rotted wood. She crouched low and poked her head through the hole she'd made. Pulling her head back in, she dumped the crate into the water below.

For a few weeks, Vance had said. Aesara smiled as she dumped another crate. *Try a few days.*

CHAPTER
Eleven

"YOU'RE AWFULLY QUIET," VANCE SAID, HANDING HER A PLATE OF hard bread and cheese.

Aesara dipped her bread in her water before taking a small bite. She had rolled a barrel in front of the hole, but the lack of food would be noticed soon. The thought made her stomach ache, and it wasn't from hunger.

Six sat next to her, watching her with furrowed brows. She needed to get a grip before they truly suspected her.

"Maybe I don't have anything to say," she said finally.

"I find that hard to believe." Vance took a seat next to her, not bothering to dip his bread in water. Aesara cringed. To have been at sea for so long…

"How can you eat bread like that? Doesn't it hurt?"

He ripped off another piece. "Bread lasts longer than the fruits and vegetables. We'll eat it for weeks on end if that's what it takes before we get to another port."

Aesara twisted her face in disgust. "That's not any way to live."

"We're not all spoiled princesses."

Silver flashed in Aesara's memory—the blade cutting across her skin. "No, of course not," she whispered.

Vance eyed her, frowning. He opened his mouth only to have a crow caw interrupt him.

Aesara snapped her head up. "Was that a crow?"

"Crows fly all the time," Six said. "It's nothing to get excited about."

Aesara stood, knocking her plate to the floor. "No, you don't understand. It could be from my father. Or Sodaya. I need to find it!"

She scrambled across the deck, looking into the night. She cursed the dark sky and the crow's black wings. The crow cawed again. Aesara ran to the other side of the ship.

"There," she yelled, pointing. "Give me food. An apple, bread, anything!"

"I'm not wasting my food on a bird, Aesara."

Despite the shudder that ran through her when he said her name, Aesara glared at Vance.

"Fine," she spat. "I'll do it myself."

She snatched the cheese from her fallen plate and waved it in the air. She clicked her tongue, trying to get the bird's attention.

Its wing dipped slightly, but it kept straight.

"No, no. Come back! Please!" Aesara reached out a hand before slumping against the railing. "Please," she whispered.

The wind blew across her face, and she watched as the crow flapped its wings against it. Maybe Vance was right. She should stop trying to be her mother and try something different, something her.

Aesara flung out her hand once more, the wind brushing coldly against it. A wave of green light pulsed from her. The wind picked up, and the crow cawed just as wildly, struggling to fly against the torrent of wind. In mere moments, it was brought down to the ship.

"Catch it!" Aesara called.

She ran to it as Vance clutched its body, holding its wings securely. It screeched and pecked at Aesara's hands as she unwound the small metal canister tied to its leg. She made sure to wipe the blood off her hands before taking out the letter within.

"Well?" Vance asked. "Was it worth all that?"

For a moment, Aesara's heart stopped in her chest. She wanted to crumple the letter, rip it, burn it—anything to make the words disappear. She paced back and forth, back and forth. The wind whipped at her hair, but she paid it no mind.

"What's wrong?"

Aesara ignored Vance. She didn't know what to do. Did she demand to be taken back? If she did go back, what good would it do? She couldn't stop her father the first time, how would she be able to stop him a second?

"Aesara, what did the letter say?"

In an instant, everything stopped. No wind, no screeching of the crow, no pacing.

The letter burned in her hand, its presence a shadow in her mind.

"My father is going through with the war," she said. "My people are going to die."

CHAPTER
Twelve

VANCE PINCHED THE BRIDGE OF HIS NOSE, SIGHING. "ABSOLUTELY NOT."

The crow sat in a cage, unblinking. Vance's sword laid across the desk, holding the letter down, the ink glaring up at Aesara.

"Please, Vance. I can't sit back and do nothing."

"Good thing it isn't your choice." The words stopped Aesara. For a moment, it wasn't Vance talking, but her father.

Vance swiped the letter and folded it, moving toward the crow, unaware of the turmoil raging inside her. "Believe it or not, I didn't get you for free. I *paid* for you."

Aesara shook herself of the memories and ran in front of him, blocking the cage from him.

"Whatever you paid, I can get it back! What was it? Gold? Silver? Please, I have already agreed to help with Morana!"

"I traded him for my service, Princess. He gave me you for my *sword.*"

Aesara blinked. "He…he what?"

Vance leaned forward, making himself eye level with her. "You wanted to know how much you were worth? There you go. Now, move. I am putting this letter back on that stupid bird and we are sailing on."

Aesara let him push her out the way, her head still reeling. She wanted to deny it, say her father would never do such a thing. But that would be a lie. That sounded exactly like something King Ciran would do.

The crow squawked in its cage, its wings flapping violently. She squeezed her eyes shut, willing the tears to go away. A wave rocked against the ship, sending Aesara slumping against the desk.

For a brief moment, the smooth wood reminded her of the way she would lay against the floor as Carina healed her. The ship swayed again, and Vance's sword slid against Aesara's hands.

Instinctively, she grabbed it. She had never touched it before, and she gasped as it writhed beneath her palms. Looking at it, it was completely normal, but she could feel them—*the souls.*

They moved in a sickly, slimy way. Whatever magic created this, it wasn't kind.

"Do you feel this all the time?" she asked, standing up, sword still in hand.

Vance glanced her way before turning his attention back to the crow. "Always, Princess. You just feel their presence. I hear them, too. Constantly whispering. Begging. As if I could change their fate." Vance laughed dryly. "As if I'd want to."

Aesara frowned, his words settling uncomfortably in her stomach. "Why not help them?"

"Because they don't deserve it," he snarled. "You don't understand who's in there."

Aesara's grip tightened on the sword. The souls continued to move like ink spilling over a page.

"You're not a god. This fate…this isn't right."

Vance eyed her. "Give me the sword, Aesara." He held out his hand, his attention fully on her.

She held it tighter, backing away. "There must be a way to free them. Without their physical forms, they'll be returned."

"Returned? There is no returning. Once that sword takes your life, it belongs to the blade. Now, hand it over."

Aesara glanced at the crow and then at Vance's outstretched hand. "Help me stop the war."

"Have you lost your mind? Truly? You were given up for my part *in* the war!" Vance took a deep breath. "Besides, where would you run off to, anyway? If you haven't noticed, we're still out at sea."

Aesara smiled and took another step further. She bumped into the wall of the ship, the latch to the window digging into her back. Reaching behind her, she unlocked it and flung the window open. She thrust her hand outside of it, dangling the sword above the waves. She had *never* forgotten they were at sea.

Vance froze.

"I assume there are consequences to losing a magic sword a sea witch gave you?" she asked sweetly.

"For someone who prays as much as you do, you're quite wicked. Bring the sword inside; we'll talk about this."

Aesara stretched her arm further, flexing her fingers across the scabbard. "We'll talk about this now. Help me or I'll drop it."

Vance rubbed his face, groaning. "Fine! I will help you, just bring the damn sword inside." He paused. "Please."

Aesara smirked, feeling triumphant. She brought her arm back in, holding the sword with both hands on either end.

"Go on, Captain, take your sword."

He scowled and stomped forward. He gripped the sword in the middle and pulled. Aesara let the bottom fall out of her hand easily but kept her hold on the sword's grip.

Vance pulled the scabbard off. He looked at the empty scabbard with wide eyes and then at Aesara.

The sword was heavy in her hands and the souls made her shudder. They slid across her skin like oil and Aesara wanted nothing more than to drop the blade.

"Aesara…" Vance warned.

"You didn't really think I was going to hand over my only leverage, did you?"

"Put the sword down. You can't handle it."

Aesara scoffed. "I know how to use a sword."

"Not this kind. You have my word I'll help, just put it down."

Aesara opened her mouth to tell him off, that his help was unnecessary, but she never got the words out. His figure blurred in her vision. Her head began to pound like a drum, low and steady. The air grew heavy around her, and her breathing picked up.

"What's happening?" She swayed, her grip loosening on the sword. It clattered to the floor.

Aesara followed quickly, collapsing onto the wooden planks.

Vance rushed to her side, pulling her onto his lap.

"What did you do to me?" she asked, struggling to breathe.

She saw Vance's lips moving, but a sharp ringing overtook her. Her world went black.

AESARA GROANED AS SHE AWOKE. A SPLITTING HEADACHE TORMENTED her, and the blinding sun only made it worse.

"Glad to see you awake."

"What do you want, Vance?" Aesara sighed, refusing to look at him. "Come to gloat? Tell me I should've listened to you? That I'm worth as much as a piece of metal?"

The cushions dipped as he sat in next to her. "No, I came to check on you. How are you feeling?"

"Just perfect. I have a headache from hell, my people are being sentenced to death, I'm worthless according to my father, and I can do absolutely *nothing.*"

"You're not worthless. When I told you of the sword, you called me the Reaper. You were half right. I don't bother correcting people most of the time, but the sword is the Reaper. I am only its wielder. Your father traded you for something beyond this world. Something only magic could make."

If her head wasn't pounding as much as it was, she would've scoffed, or rolled her eyes, or smacked him—maybe all three.

"A father shouldn't trade his daughter for anything, let alone a magic sword. Besides, what would he do with it? It's not like he's wielding it." Aesara paused, a frown crossing her face. "He's not wielding it. So, what *is* he doing with it?" She swiveled so she was facing Vance. "What were the full conditions of my father's trade?"

Vance shrugged. "He wanted to try and use it. I let him, but he passed out just like you did. I didn't care to know more than that."

This time, Aesara did roll her eyes. "Of course, you wouldn't."

"Why should I? I can hear the bloody thing. When I can't hear it, I'll worry."

"Have you tried—"

"Yes."

Aesara blinked, her train of thought cut short by his interruption. "But I didn't even finish."

"Doesn't matter. Whatever you were going to say, yes, I've tried it. I've tried everything from magic to taking it to a blacksmith. The damn thing won't even get hot, let alone melt."

Aesara sucked her teeth, rising from her seat and pacing the floor.

Vance shook his head at her. "Princess, I don't know what you're expecting to get out of this. Your father is a Common. He doesn't have magic. You do, but not the kind that made this. Neither of you can wield it. Whatever you're thinking, stop it."

Aesara glared at him and raised her chin higher. "No."

"You are annoying. The worst."

"Yes, thank you. Father is magicless, I have the wrong kind. What magics did you try?"

Vance waved his hand nonchalantly. "Oh, elemental, runes, binding, even went to a necromancer to try and figure it out. None of them could do anything against it."

"What about its creator?" Aesara smiled as Vance tensed. *So, there* was *something he didn't try.*

"Its creator," Vance said slowly, "dabbles in dark magic. Even I wouldn't risk that, *Selen Od.*"

Aesara straightened her back, trying to appear unafraid. Dark magic was not something to take lightly. It was a magic you had to take by force. Her father being interested in something created by it made her heart thunder with fear and worry.

"Where would we be able to find the creator, Morana, you said?"

Vance stared at her blankly for a moment before bursting into a fit of laughter.

"What?" Aesara asked. "Stop laughing!"

"You reluctantly agreed to help me find her, now you want to find her on your own without any training?" He laughed again. "Forgive me, *Your Highness,* but that's funny."

He was right. She couldn't go after Morana now. "But," she said, interrupting his laughter. "I can go to the source of her power. All magic comes from the Crystal Coves, right? Even dark magic."

Vance stopped laughing, eying her warily. "Yes, but that's on Sodaya's borders. Your enemy? Or have you forgotten that, too?"

Aesara stuck her tongue out at him. "No, I haven't forgotten. I don't need to go there straight away. Sodayan ships travel all the time. Their wine is sold and traded across all the lands. If I could get onto one of their ships—"

"Woah, woah, woah. No way. Do you know how dangerous that is?"

Aesara raised an eyebrow as a challenge. "I thought you were the Reaper."

"Yes, but I'm not an idiot."

Aesara eyed his sword, once again latched to his hip. "Tell me, Captain, do you possess magic yourself? Or is it just the sword?"

Vance growled, grabbing the sword protectively.

Aesara smiled. *Just the sword, then.*

"You promised to help," she pointed out.

"Fine! And just how do you suppose we even find one of their ships? We don't know their routes."

Outside, a seagull squawked.

"No," Aesara said. "But the birds do."

CHAPTER
Thirteen

FINDING A BIRD WAS EASY ENOUGH; FINDING THE RIGHT BIRD WAS harder. Hummingbirds didn't often fly across the sea, but occasionally there were lovers that were separated. The birds would need to rest and take refuge on any ship. The birds were neutral. They did not pick and choose sides as the people that sent them did.

When Aesara was a child, she had asked her mother once what kind of bird G'iv would send to them.

"Oh, I imagine a crane," Siofra said, smiling. "Can you see it, Aesara? All white feathers gleaming in the sun." She pinched Aesara's cheek. *"It'd be as big as you!"*

Aesara giggled, swatting her mother's hand away. "Would it carry me away, Mama?"

"Oh, most certainly. It would grab you like this"—She grabbed Aesara underneath her arms and tossed her up.—*and take you to the heavens!"*

The room began to glow in a vibrant green as the wind lifted Aesara out of her mother's arms and spun her around the room. When the wind finally died down, Aesara fell into her mother's arms once more.

"You'll be there, too, right?"

Siofra kissed her head. "Of course, my darling. I will always be with you."

Aesara smiled fondly at the memory, releasing the small hummingbird in her palm. It zipped across the sky, its multitude of colors flitting in the sunlight.

"You sure this will work?" Vance asked.

Aesara was becoming used to him always being there, hovering. Though she knew it was just to keep an eye on her, she liked to pretend he was there for her and only her. It made the company less obtrusive. At least, that's what she told herself.

"Yes," she said. "It'll work. It's a traditional Ascenian name. I highly doubt a Sodayan ship will have anything like it. And when they don't, the bird comes back to us."

Vance scoffed. "I think you rely on the birds too much. We'd be better off just trying to find the ship on our own."

"Doubt all you want, Captain. I have faith."

When night fell, Aesara feared Vance had been right. Her legs were beginning to ache from how long she had paced the deck, waiting for her hummingbird to come back.

"There's no shame in trying again tomorrow," Six said, handing her a small stack of bread, meat, and cheese. Though it wasn't the freshest food, Aesara found the miniature sandwiches cute.

Vance leaned against the railing, watching them and chewing on a makeshift toothpick. He frowned as Aesara took the food from Six and turned away, giving a little huff of annoyance.

Aesara tilted her head curiously. "What's up with him, you think?" she whispered under her breath, leaning close so only Six would hear.

Six chuckled. "Nothing I'd worry about. You should know by now he gets in moods."

Aesara rolled her eyes with a smile. "Oh, don't I."

She looked back at Vance and caught his eye. Before she could react, he tore his gaze away. Aesara shook her head; she had more to worry about than the feelings of men. The night sky still only held the moon and stars. The hummingbird was nowhere to be seen or heard.

"I suppose it isn't the worst thing if I try tomorrow, right?" she asked softly.

Six placed his hand on her shoulder. "It beats staying out here all night. I think Dirk is in the nest tomorrow, so I can be down here with you."

"Thanks, Six." Aesara hadn't thought she'd find a friend, especially not on *The Promisea*, but she was grateful she had. It made holding on that much easier.

Just as she started toward Vance's cabin, she heard a small chirping. Without thinking, she ran to the edge of the ship. She could just barely see it, but it was there—the hummingbird.

Aesara's heart soared, and she thanked G'iv for staying with her. She held out a hand and the bird landed on it gently. Aesara stroked its back softly, letting it rest.

"You did well," she whispered. "Thank you."

Vance pushed off the railing and stood behind her, looking over her shoulder. "Good job," he said. His warm breath fanned her cheek and Aesara could smell a hint of alcohol.

"It did well, yes," she agreed, trying not to think about why he had been drinking.

Vance brushed his finger along the side of her cheek and over her bandages, pushing a lock of her growing hair behind her ear. Aesara did not stiffen as she usually did. There were no memories of her father flashing through her mind. Instead, she found herself leaning back into his touch, seeking the warmth his body radiated.

"I wasn't talking about the bird, Princess."

His words made her heart jump and beat faster. "Oh...thank you." She wanted to say more, but her mind and mouth weren't connecting, as if she had been the one consuming alcohol.

Vance's hands fell to his sides, but Aesara wanted them around her. She wanted all that she had never been able to have. The pink cloud fogging her mind blew away the second Six cleared his throat.

"I don't mean to interrupt, but the bird might want food and water?" he suggested, looking everywhere but Aesara.

Vance grumbled under his breath as she stepped away.

"Yes, you're probably right. Thank you." Aesara marched past both men, head down so that neither one would see the blush painted on her cheeks.

The moment the door shut behind her, she released a sigh, sinking against the door. The hummingbird glided onto the desk and watched her with beady eyes.

"Don't look at me like that," she mumbled, pushing herself up. "All these feelings are so new. Ryn was the closest I've ever been to a man, and he felt more like a sibling than a lover."

She tried to imagine kissing Ryn and nearly gagged. He had been there for her through so much, and now that she had been around Vance, she didn't think she could ever see Ryn as anything more than a brother.

"I've found myself in quite the predicament, wouldn't you agree?" Of course, the bird said nothing. Aesara placed a cup of fresh water in front of it, allowing it to drink. "You must deal with this all the time, being a hummingbird. Do you see a lot of people get hurt? From love?"

Once again, Aesara knew the bird wouldn't respond, but it was nice to talk about it aloud. Her emotions ran rampant the more time she spent away from the castle and her father. In Ascen, she was angry and hurting. It wasn't often that she felt much else.

Aesara sighed and sat across from the hummingbird, resting her head on the desk. Now she felt so many things she didn't know what to do.

She heard Vance before she saw him, his steps heavy on the deck. Aesara sat up just as he entered the cabin.

Aesara watched him as he took off his boots and coat, untucked his shirt, and loosened the knots on his trousers. He flopped onto the ground where he had created a makeshift bed.

"We leave tomorrow night," was all he said before he rolled over, turning his back to her.

Aesara placed the hummingbird in its cage with some food and water before crawling into her own makeshift bed by the window. She fell asleep with the hope that tomorrow would hold some answers.

Aesara waited impatiently for the cover of darkness. She paced, her only thoughts on what would await them on the ship. Aesara's appetite was little to nothing all day, and when Vance told her it was time, she nearly fainted. Whether it was from nerves or excitement, Aesara couldn't tell, but she hid the shaking of her hands well, not wanting Vance to abort their mission.

With the bird as their guide, Aesara and Vance rowed their way to the Sodayan ship. Even in the night, Aesara could make out the vibrant blue hues painted on the ship. It matched the flag that waved atop its mast. It had been a long time since Aesara had seen the colors so close, and her heart only raced faster.

If she were to be caught... She shook her head at the thought, taking a deep breath to calm herself. She clasped her hands tightly in her lap and tried not to think at all.

As Vance rowed them closer, a heavy weight blanketed itself across Aesara. Her plan had sounded so much easier when that was all it had been, a plan. Now, as the ship shadowed over her, she prayed all would be okay.

She released a slow breath. "G'iv be with me. Guide me safely and swiftly."

For once, Vance said nothing about her prayers. He did not shush or tell her she was being silly. That told Aesara that even those who didn't believe needed a little faith sometimes.

Silence filtered through the ship. Guards were posted around the railings, armored and armed. Aesara and Vance let the rowboat drift quietly through the water. Once it was close enough, Vance put his arm out to stop it from hitting against the ship. He did it so gracefully, Aesara wondered if this wasn't his first time stealing away on a ship.

"We get in and we get out. We do not engage, understand?" Vance whispered.

Aesara nodded. *As if she'd want to stay longer than necessary.*

Vance locked his hands together, creating a foothold for Aesara to hoist herself up through the cannon hole.

She landed unceremoniously, cringing at the sounds she made. She blinked several times, trying to adjust to the near pitch black of the inside. Aesara crawled forward on her hands and knees, doing her best to ignore the slimy dew on the boards.

She felt around until her hands landed on a pile of rope connecting the cannons together. She smiled in the darkness and made her way back to the hole.

Aesara poked her head out.

Vance stood on the rowboat, trying to keep it close to the ship. "Hurry up, would you?"

Aesara ducked back in and made sure her end of the rope was tied tight to the heavy cannons. As she moved to throw the rope, Aesara froze. She contemplated leaving him there. She could let him row back to his own ship and leave her to stow away here.

But she didn't know where this ship was headed. By G'iv, she didn't even know what direction she faced. And what if she was caught?

With that last thought, she tossed the rope down. Vance tied the rowboat off and climbed.

He *thumped* onto the ship and Aesara flinched instinctively, watching the darkness, but no one came.

"What took you so long?" Vance asked, interrupting her trailing thoughts.

"My hands were wet. The knot kept slipping." The lie fell off her tongue easily enough, and Aesara wondered what G'iv thought of her then.

Vance didn't let her ponder for long. He tugged her along. "Their ship should be built relatively close to mine. Stay by my side and stay quiet," he ordered.

Aesara found herself nodding.

Footsteps sounded overhead and they both froze. Words were exchanged, but they were too soft for Aesara to hear them.

"It's the changing of the guard," Vance whispered.

Once again, Aesara nodded.

With every creaky step, Aesara's heart raced more and more. She was surprised they hadn't been caught based on her thundering heartbeat alone.

Ahead of her, Vance stopped. He pointed to the stairs and then put his finger to his lips.

They inched their way up the steps. Vance poked his head out just enough to see.

Aesara watched the level they were on, though she doubted there was anyone there. When she looked back, Vance had vanished.

She scrambled up the stairs to see him across the deck, hiding in the shadows. It had begun to rain, the cold droplets almost refreshing against Aesara's feverish skin.

Vance held his hand out, telling her not to move. A guard passed in front of Aesara, completely oblivious to her beneath his feet.

As soon as the guard was out of sight, Vance motioned for her to move. Aesara didn't think. She just ran. She collided into Vance, her breathing erratic. He grabbed her shoulders, stabilizing her.

Had she been in a safe environment, she would linger in his arms, make up an excuse to stay near him. But she was not on *The Promisea*, and she was not safe.

Aesara pushed away enough to create space but remain hidden. She avoided his gaze. This was her idea; she shouldn't— couldn't—be scared. They made their way to the back of the ship, slinking in between the shadows and ducking behind crates. At the back, the captain's lights were out.

The window, however, was open.

Vance pulled Aesara close. "I won't fit through there. You have to do it."

Aesara's eyes widened. "O-okay." She tried to think of it like when she snuck into Vance's cabin. *Yes, it was exactly like that and nothing more.*

She swallowed and peeked inside the room. It was set up like Vance's. Hoisting herself up, she slowly inched her way inside. It was a tight fit, but one she could manage.

The room smelled fragrant, like a warm summer day. Aesara crouched low and realized the smell came from the rug rolled across the boards.

Must be a calming oil. It was a smart idea and one that helped Aesara continue forward. But motion to her left had her freezing. The Sodayan captain rolled in his sleep to face her.

Aesara took several deep breaths.

"G'iv be with me," she whispered. She moved slowly, trying to think about anything other than what would happen if they were caught.

Pressing one hand against the drawer and the other against the knob, she pulled the drawer open. It was the slowest she had ever moved, but she didn't dare move faster.

The papers inside were of no interest. It was a shipping manifest listing Sodayan wines. She pulled out another drawer. It was full of knick-knacks and trinkets. She found bottles of lavender and eucalyptus oil and slipped one in either pocket of her trousers. It wasn't much, but if she went through the effort of sneaking on the ship, she wanted something as a trophy.

Aesara wanted to slam her head into the desk. Fragrance oils, what a trophy! There had to be something else.

Thunder boomed, shaking the room. The captain jumped up, startled.

Aesara slid under the desk, tucking herself away in the dark. Vance peeked his head over the windowsill. His eyes darted to where the captain was and then to Aesara before he ducked back out of sight.

The captain grumbled under his breath and light illuminated the room. Aesara put her hand over her mouth to keep herself silent. She could see the green from her power start to glow and counted backwards to try and calm herself down. She listened with dread as his footsteps neared the desk.

Aesara was about to accept her fate when a loud crash sounded outside the door. The captain slammed the lantern onto the desk before leaving.

Aesara didn't waste a moment. She darted for the window and fell out of it. A hand grabbed her arm, pulling her tightly against their chest. She opened her mouth to scream when the hand covered her mouth.

"Shut up," Vance hissed. "It's just me."

Aesara shoved her way out of his arms. "You scared me!"

"Cry about it later; we need to get out of here and we can't go back the way we came." He pulled her toward the railing.

"You can't be serious."

"Very. I distracted them for a little while, but they know someone's here now. You want out of this alive?"

Aesara sighed, knowing he was right. "All right. On three?"

The dark was suddenly illuminated as a Sodayan guard circled the back. They made eye contact briefly before Vance moved. He drew his sword and shoved it through the guard's chest.

Blood bubbled from his mouth and Aesara watched in horror as the life faded from his eyes

This wasn't what she planned.

"Three!" Vance yelled. He pushed Aesara off the ship, jumping after her.

They crashed into the water. Without the sun warming its surface, it felt like falling into ice.

Aesara swam to their boat, the water stinging her lungs. As she hauled herself into their small rowboat, Vance swung his sword into the rope, cutting their connection to the ship. He kicked the ship, sending them away from it.

Aesara coughed, vomiting a mix of stale food and saltwater. If she ever made it land, she was never touching the sea again.

"Please tell me you found something worth all that," Vance said, panting.

Aesara wiped her mouth, shaking her head. "No, everything was...*normal.* It was just a trading ship."

She didn't mention the oils; she figured it would only anger Vance more. Silence fell between the two. Aesara tried to look at him. Blood had splattered on his shirt and face. She stared at the water instead.

"I'm sorry, Vance. I didn't...I thought that..." Aesara sighed. "I thought there would be something, you know?"

"Let's just get back to the ship. It's been a long night for both of us."

"Yeah," she said with a sigh, "okay."

On the ship, Aesara found sleeping hard. The Sodayan guard plagued her mind. Every time she closed her eyes, he was there, mouth agape, blood everywhere. Vance hadn't even given him time to defend himself.

She sat up from her little cot and looked at Vance's sword. It laid on the desk, the silver shining in the moonlight. Aesara walked to it, hovering her hand over its grip.

If everything about it was true, the guard's soul was trapped inside. Aesara shivered. She knew Tecranians and Sodayans worshiped different gods, but surely *this* wasn't the fate they dreamed of.

"You can't help him."

Aesara jumped back. Vance sat in the corner on his makeshift bed. Blankets covered him, but he watched her carefully.

"There must be something I could do. He's—"

"Gone. Aesara, he's gone."

There it was again—her name. It slipped past his lips so easily she wondered if he even thought about it.

Vance tightened the blankets around himself. "Go back to sleep."

"I never fell asleep in the first place."

"I know."

Aesara crawled back in between her blankets, curling into the tightest ball, and when she closed her eyes this time, sleep came.

CHAPTER
Fourteen

WHEN THE MORNING SUN ROSE, AESARA WASN'T SURE HOW TO FEEL. Her body felt refreshed from a long night's sleep, but her mind was still cloudy, filled with blood. *Maybe some food will help.*

Opening the door to the deck, though, she thought maybe she'd be better without.

"What do you mean, 'It's gone?' It can't be!"

The sailor cowered in front of Vance, holding his hands in surrender. "It's jus' as I said, though. No'hing bu' one crate."

Vance rubbed his face in irritation. "Go check again," he growled.

Aesara spoke carefully as she approached him, "What's going on?"

"Apparently, there's only one crate of food left." He threw his hands in the air, exasperated. "How is that possible when I planned for every mouth, every portion?"

"Are there rats?"

He halted, glaring at her.

She took a step back, lowering her head. "It was just a question. I'm just trying to help." The better she feigned her innocence, the less they would suspect her.

"Yes, I'm sorry." Vance sighed. "Rats are a possibility, but there would be evidence of them around the ship. I haven't seen a tail or droppings."

"Who has access to the food? Maybe someone took extra portions, not realizing how much it affected the ship?" Aesara didn't smile, but she was proud of herself. If there was one thing she was good at, it was playing politics.

"Anyone can get to it. I don't know how your food was stored in your castle, but we don't have specialty locks and doors for ours."

Yes, hers did have specialty locks. But her father had made it to keep her *out, not others.*

Aesara smiled at Vance. "Of course. How long will the crate last us?"

"One crate?" he scoffed. "A day, maybe two, if we're lucky."

"Then I suppose we need to sail for land."

Vance paused, looking her up and down. "*You* didn't have anything to do with this, did you?"

Aesara frowned. "How could I have? I don't even know where it is. And you've hardly let me out of your sight."

"Right, yeah." He rubbed his face again.

Aesara almost felt bad for him. *Almost.*

"Byrd," Vance yelled, "set a course for the nearest port. We need provisions only. That means we go into the market and we leave the market. Does everyone understand that?"

The crew nodded, though some grumbled under their breath. Aesara wondered when was the last time they had been off ship for longer than a few minutes, to enjoy the land before being trapped at sea once more.

She smiled to herself, walking to the railing to keep out of the way. She traced her finger along the wood grooves. Letting her mind clear, she felt the magic flow through her veins and down into her palm. It felt like dipping her hand into a stream of water. Right now, the water trickled slowly.

The green light she was all too familiar with flitted from her palm, and where her finger touched the railing, a small flower sprouted. It had vibrant purple petals and a yellow center. Aesara leaned in close and smiled fondly at it. When Sodaya and Tecrane were at peace, Sodaya had sent a bouquet of flowers to her mother.

"I don't think flowers will stop Morana."

Aesara didn't let Vance's words dampen her mood. "No, probably not. But life will certainly do your ship wonders." What she didn't say was that she'd grown it for the guard. Vance didn't need to know. G'iv knew her truth.

"Have you tried anything…bigger?"

Aesara stiffened at Vance's question. "I'm not going to try making a storm again. Not right now."

Vance plucked the flower from the ship and held it in her face. She winced as its fragile petals waved in the breeze.

"This isn't going to do anything, Princess. If you want a chance at stopping her, *actually* stopping her, you need to make something bigger."

"I know," Aesara whispered. She wanted to scream at him to give the flower back, that it wasn't his to take, but she held her tongue.

"Do you?" He handed her the flower and she took it, cradling it gently in her palms.

"I'm not my mother, Vance." Aesara didn't want to cry, not in front of him. She kept her focus on her flower, willing it to survive.

"I'm sorry, Aesara." Vance softened his voice. "I know you're not Siofra. Things just aren't…they're not going to plan, let's just say."

Aesara snorted. "You're telling me."

Vance gave her a small smile. "I am, *Selen Od.*"

Aesara placed the flower back on the railing. In a flash of green light, it was connected to its roots once more.

"Will you ever tell me why you call me that?" she asked.

"Maybe one day," Vance said slyly. "But not today."

Aesara's knowledge of the Silver One was limited. Though she'd studied her religion and its language frequently in the castle, there wasn't much on the Silver One. It was a name given to the chosen child of G'iv, a bringer of war and peace. Aesara didn't want to bring a war, she was trying to *stop* one.

"How soon will we reach land?" she asked, unable to keep the excitement from creeping into her voice.

Vance chuckled. "It doesn't matter. You are staying on the ship."

She whirled her head around. "No!"

"Yes!" Vance mocked her. "I already have to keep my eye on my men, I don't need to babysit you as well."

Aesara crossed her arms, pouting. "I've been stuck on this ship as long as you. The least I could have is a change of clothes."

"You're lucky that those ones are still clean. Stop complaining, Princess. You're not leaving the ship, and that's final."

With that, he left her.

Aesara huffed, twirling on her heel to face the water. *Not leaving the ship. Yeah, right. See if he could stop her.*

She could sneak out. While she didn't think he'd leave her unattended, there were ways around it. There had been at the castle and there would be here, too. Once Aesara had her mind on something, there was no stopping her. All she had to do was wait.

It was night when they arrived at the port. Aesara didn't notice at first. She had a palm full of a small tornado. The same trickling feeling flowed through her veins and into her palm where the wind spun and spun. She'd held up her hand to admire her work when she saw it.

The city's lights.

The lanterns flickered with firelight, and Aesara ran to the railing for a closer look. Unlike Ascen's dock, it was bustling with activity. Some men smoked their pipes as others loaded and unloaded ships. Women flounced about in dresses tumbling with fabric. The corsets pushed their bosoms up and, though Aesara knew exactly what the women represented, she would've done anything to be in a dress again.

As *The Promisea* sailed closer to the dock, Aesara's heart threatened to leap out of her chest with excitement. To feel the cobblestone streets again, to walk without rocking, to stop somewhere and still be in the same place ten minutes later—oh! How desperately she wanted to be back on land.

Aesara looked up at Vance, who was at the wheel. He must've seen the excitement on her face because he shook his head at her firmly.

Aesara hung her head, making a show of herself. He had to be convinced she was distraught about staying on the ship. He approached her moments later as the others readied the ship for loading. Byrd followed closely behind, arms crossed.

"I'm leaving Byrd here to keep an eye on you," he said. "I was going to leave Six, but I don't trust you two together. I told Bryd that he wouldn't have to do much since you'll behave."

Behave? What was she, a child?

Aesara kept her thoughts to herself and nodded. "Of course. Can I ask you to bring me back something? Or is that a no, too?"

Vance thought for a moment. "What is it you're wanting?"

"A fruit tart. Raspberries are my favorite, but I know they can be hard to find." Aesara tilted back and forth on her heels as she said it. Though it was a ruse to keep the captain distracted, raspberry tarts really were her favorite.

Vance shook his head. "I don't have time to look for a tart, I'm sorry. I'd like to get in and out of here as soon as possible."

Aesara deflated. "Oh, all right."

Vance gave her one last look before heading off the ship. As he and the crew departed, Aesara inched away from Byrd.

"Don't even think about it," Byrd said without even looking at her.

Aesara stopped, unsure of what to do. Vance had disappeared into the crowd, his red cloak nowhere to be seen. If she made a run for it, would she be able to get back to the ship before it took off? Would he wait?

She didn't think about it twice. Aesara darted around Byrd, his arms already outstretched to catch her. But she was smaller than him—much smaller. She ducked under his arms, sliding on her knees. She grimaced as her skin burned but was thankful for the pants she wore. She launched herself up from the deck and ran down the plank.

"Aesara!" Byrd yelled after her, but when she looked back, he remained on the ship.

She smiled as she blended in with the crowd. She pushed her way through, finally breaking out into a small alley. Leaning against the stone wall, Aesara panted, trying to catch her breath. The rush of escaping was slowly winding down. When she looked down, she could see a small patch of blood forming on the knees of her pants, the fabric torn.

Well, it looks like she needed new clothes after all.

Aesara poked her head out of the alley. She didn't know what town they had stopped in, but it looked like hers, only much livelier.

That meant they had to still be within her father's kingdom, within Tecrane. Aesara stepped out from the alley and watched the crowd. There was a woman leaning against one of the walls, fanning herself slowly. Her eyes scanned the crowd like a wolf hunting its prey.

Her dress was vibrant against the stone wall, and Aesara wanted nothing more than to be like her, confident and sure.

"Excuse me?" Aesara asked as she approached. She wasn't sure what she would say to the woman. She could ask where to buy a dress, that would be a start.

The woman didn't look at her. "What do you want?"

"I want a dress." It wasn't how she wanted to say it, but Aesara felt like a little girl again, grasping at her mother's hems for attention.

The woman turned and looked at her. Suddenly, Aesara wanted to cover herself. She couldn't imagine how messy she looked at the moment with her ill-fitting clothes and dirty face.

The woman raised an eyebrow. "Why tell me? I'm not exactly the person you go to to get clothes—quite the opposite, really."

Aesara looked at the crowd. She noticed the way both men and women's eyes were drawn to the woman whether they meant to or not.

"Look at them," Aesara said. "They see you as you tuck yourself against the wall, fully clothed. They want more from you than just your body, and you know that." Aesara smiled at the woman. "I imagine you have a high price."

The woman smirked. "The highest here."

Aesara thought for a moment. "It must get lonely, being that expensive."

"It can." The woman shrugged. "I'm used to it, though. I take what I want and I don't give anything back. You wouldn't do so well with it."

Aesara stiffened. "And why not?"

"Don't take me the wrong way. We all have our qualities, and something tells me yours lies in something more promising."

"Oh." Aesara was at a loss for words. She wanted to be offended, but the kindness behind her words had her unsure of what to do or say.

The woman noticed and smiled. "Come with me."

She tugged Aesara with her as she weaved through the crowd. Aesara didn't try to pull away or stop her. Something about the woman made her feel safe, like the world couldn't hurt her when she was around.

They went into a small bed and breakfast. Dim lanterns created a dark atmosphere. A couple patrons sat in the booths, smoking their pipes. They didn't bother looking up as they entered. Aesara tried to look around more, but the woman tugged her up the stairs, sparing her no moments.

Upstairs, it was a single room with the bare necessities. A double poster bed sat in the middle with a single nightstand. The woman lit the candle within the chamberstick and led Aesara to the large trunk along the wall. Aesara wondered why the room was so bare if it cost so much to spend a night with the woman.

She kept her thought to herself, though, knowing it would be rude to ask.

The trunk was the only other furniture in the room. The woman threw it open and pulled out a large dress. It was a dark purple with an iridescent shimmer in its lining. Aesara didn't think she'd seen a more beautiful dress, even living in the castle.

"What do you think?" the woman asked.

"I—well...it..." Aesara struggled to find her words. "It's stunning." The woman beamed at her. "I figured you'd like it. Come, come. Let's get you in it."

Aesara blinked, backing up. "I couldn't! That's too beautiful." Aesara couldn't be in a dress that gorgeous. It belonged on someone with a figure to hold it. Aesara wasn't full enough, and the scars on her back would show. She wasn't ready for that; she didn't know if she ever would be.

The woman waved her hand. "Psh, come here. I haven't fit in since I was a girl, and you'd look so beautiful. Your eyes would match it perfectly."

Aesara put a hand to her bandaged eye. She had almost forgotten.

She backed up even farther. What did the scars on her back matter when she could never hide the one on her face?

The woman sighed. She set the dress on the bed and walked to Aesara slowly, her hands out like a mother reaching for her daughter. She grabbed Aesara's wrists gently.

"May I?" the woman asked.

Aesara didn't know what the woman would do. Would she just touch the bandages, or would she look beneath? Aesara hesitated for a moment before nodding. She closed her eyes, letting out a shaky breath.

The woman pulled Aesara's hand away and carefully unwrapped the bandages. Vance had cleaned and wrapped her eye before, but this felt intimate. There was more to it than two strangers in the night or two people getting to know one another. Aesara felt a tear slip past as she thought of the tender moments with her mother. As the woman unwrapped them, Aesara felt a soft tingle, and from beneath her eyelids, she saw a blue glow.

"Okay," the woman whispered, breaking the silence. "You can open them."

Aesara opened her eyes and the woman smiled sadly at her. She grabbed a handheld mirror and passed it to Aesara.

"It was too far in the healing process to fix it completely, but it shouldn't bother you anymore. You don't need the bandages anymore, at the very least."

Aesara stared at her reflection. There was a long scar from the top of her eyebrow to her jawline. Her once golden eye was pale, its bright color faded to a dull yellow. The world, for the most part, was clear, but there was one corner that blurred.

Aesara's mouth wobbled as tears welled in her eyes.

The woman ran up to her, hugging her. "Oh, no, hun! Don't cry. You still look beautiful."

Aesara shook her head, wishing she could get the words out fast enough, wishing she could explain the truth. "No, no. Thank you. This is better than any dress." She looked at herself in the mirror once more, smiling.

The woman eyed her with confusion and went back to the trunk. She shuffled some things around and pulled out another set of clothes. Instead of a dress, it was a pants and shirt set with a brown leather corset. It had brass buckles on the front to make it easier to put on.

"Here," the woman said. "Take this instead. I think you'll like it better than *that.*" She looked at Aesara's current outfit in disgust.

Aesara laughed and took the clothes. She could agree with the woman. Though she was grateful for the clothes Vance had let her borrow, they hung from her frame sadly and did nothing to make her feel like a woman. "Thank you, uh…" She trailed off. "I never caught your name."

The woman winked and tugged at Aesara's dirty clothes. Aesara could understand her silence when it came to her name; it was the same reason Aesara had never said hers.

After Aesara was changed, she smiled at herself in the small mirror. She couldn't see herself entirely, but she didn't need to. This was the most beautiful she had felt in a long time. Her hair had started to grow out as well, and Aesara's smile widened at the thought of being able to braid it again soon.

She swiveled to face the woman. "How could I ever thank you? I don't have any coin on me, I'm afraid, but there must be something!"

"Don't worry about it."

Aesara thought for a moment before crouching. She let the trickle of water flow through her veins once more and prompted a Fire Lily to grow. Fire Lilies were rare in Tecrane and worth as much as fifty gold coins, if not more. They were often used for dye as their fiery color was hard to find. If the woman knew the town as well as Aesara suspected she did, she would be able to sell it for much more.

The woman gasped. "This…you…but I couldn't!"

Aesara smiled. "Sell it. It should give you more than enough coin for everything you've done for me."

With that, Aesara hugged the woman and ran back to the ship, leaving her with her mouth agape. Aesara had a warm feeling flowing through her; she had never felt so *good*.

She giggled as she ran, jumping up. She ignored the odd looks people gave her and sighed with relief as she saw the crew still loading the ship. She was about to approach when she paused. If her guess was right and she *was* still in Tecrane, why was she going back? She could easily map her way back to Ascen from any town or city.

"Let's go! I don't want to be here all night."

Vance stood at the bottom of the plank, supervising the crew. If she left now, she wouldn't have any allies. She would turn up at the castle and her father would do the same as he had before; nothing would have changed. Running her hands along her new corset, she stood taller and walked up to the ship. Whether she liked it or not, she still needed *The Promisea* and its captain.

"Byrd didn't stop me," she said as she approached. She wanted—no, *needed*—to have the first word.

"Just get on the ship," Vance growled, refusing to look at her.

"Hmm…maybe I will, maybe I won't."

He faced her, mouth open to speak, but no words came out.

"Something wrong?" she asked, tilting her head.

"You look…"

Aesara waited. Vance shook his head. She tried not to be disheartened by his lack of response and kept her head held high.

"Where did you get those?" he asked.

"Don't worry. I paid." She walked onto the ship confidently. For once, her father's shadow didn't cover her. How could it when the only thing they shared was now different? King Ciran could keep his golden eyes and Aesara would keep hers.

As they drifted further and further away from the dock, Aesara wondered if she was making a mistake. That had been her chance to escape, and she didn't take it. Was she a fool?

No, she thought. She knew what she was doing. She needed someone on her side, even if it was the Reaper.

"So," Vance said, walking up to her, "you went off the ship and still came back?"

"Better to run with a plan than without one."

"You didn't know what port we were at, did you?" He smirked at her and Aesara wanted to smack it right off.

"Baydenn." It was Aesara's turn to smirk as Vance's own face dropped with disappointment.

"I studied every city, town, and village within Tecrane. You think I wouldn't know this one?"

"All right, Ms. Know-It-All, if you're so smart, what's your plan?"

Aesara paused. "My plan?"

"Your ship was useless. I agreed to help you so long as you're helping me. So, what's your plan?"

In truth, Aesara hadn't thought that far. When they had gotten back to *The Promisea*, all she could think about was the poor Sodayan guard. When they got to the port, all she could think about was land. She was so focused on the next step she barely thought of the bigger goal.

"If there is going to be a war, there will be more than one letter flying through, I can guarantee that," Aesara said. "We can glean what information we can from them and follow the trail they leave for us."

Vance nodded along. "And when we reach a point of confrontation?"

Aesara looked at her hands, a phantom trickle of magic in them. "I hope I'm ready."

"Well, this might help you." He reached into his back pocket and pulled out a small parcel wrapped in white cloth.

Aesara unwrapped it gently to reveal a tart. She stared at it with wide eyes. "You...you actually got me one?"

"They didn't have raspberries at the stall I found, but they did have blueberries."

Aesara smiled softly, inhaling the buttery sweet scent of the dessert. It had been so long since she'd something so fresh. She took a bite, closing her eyes and moaning at the burst of tart and sweet flavors mixing on her tongue.

It reminded her of when she would sneak into the kitchens as a little girl. Her mother would always sneak her another tart as she distracted the chef for Aesara to get away. They would celebrate their victory together under Aesara's bed, hidden away, snacking on the sweet treat.

Aesara knew now, of course, that the chef knew of their little ruse. There was still good left in the world, even if it was just a pastry chef unknown to many.

"Thank you, Vance," Aesara whispered.

He hummed a response. "Enjoy it. Nothing is going to happen to these rations. We aren't stopping for a while."

"Did you ever figure out what happened to the other ones?" Aesara asked, her mouth full.

Vance shook his head. "No, but if anyone on this ship had anything to do with it..." He trailed off, looking around at the crew. Everyone moved as they should, carrying out their normal tasks.

Aesara said nothing. Vance wouldn't find a traitor amongst his own crew. Though, Aesara wouldn't complain if he did.

She swallowed, the pastry suddenly thick in her throat. How could she think that? She couldn't let them take the fall for her. *But if they were already a traitor, what would it matter?* Aesara's mind flipped back and forth. Would she be guilty of letting it happen?

"Princess? Are you all right?"

Vance's face came into view, worry written across it. Aesara laughed inwardly at herself. She was worrying for nothing. There wasn't another traitor amongst them, only her. But that thought only planted another question in her mind.

"Do you think I'm a traitor?"

Vance looked taken aback. "A traitor? Why would I think that?"

Aesara paused. And then she laughed.

"You must think I'm crazy," she said in between her laughter. She slumped onto the ship's railing before sliding down to sit on the deck. With her legs sprawled out in front of, her body shook silently, her breath taken away.

"Aesara?" Vance crouched to be eye-level with her. "What's going on?"

It took her a moment to regain her composure. She took deep breaths, trying to balance out her breathing. "What do you think my life was like at the castle?" she asked finally.

"Well, I thought you were spoiled, but now that you're asking me, I don't think that's right."

Aesara shook her head. "No, I wasn't spoiled. My father was as cruel to me as he was to everyone else, and I'll be damned if I don't help my kingdom—my people—get away from him. But—" Aesara glared at her hands. She curled her fingers into a fist, her nails digging into her palms. "Then I ended up on this ship, away from the castle, from the *one* place I could make a difference. I try to help, but if I fail, if I can't help, would that make me a traitor?"

Vance smiled softly, taking her fists in his own hands. He slowly uncurled them, one finger at a time. "No," he said, voice low. "I don't think you're a traitor. I think you're trying your best, and sometimes that's all we can do."

He traced small circles on her hand before leaving without another word. Aesara pulled her hand in close, holding it to her chest. The longer she spent on the sea, the more she saw herself in the waves, in the wind coasting the surface. She wondered how much Vance saw of himself in the water.

CHAPTER
Fifteen

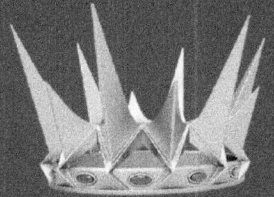

THE NEXT FEW DAYS PASSED BY IN A BLUR. AESARA PRACTICED WITH her magic, but the bigger she tried to make things, the more she lost control. She could grow rows and rows of small plants and flowers, but anything more took too much. The single small flower still sat on the railing, waving in the breeze.

Aesara looked at it then. She took a deep breath and closed her eyes. It felt odd, being able to close both without any pain or discomfort, but she was slowly getting used to it. She would forever be grateful to the nameless woman and hoped that she had used the Fire Lily.

Aesara thought of the elation spreading through her as she'd run from the woman. She held out her hands and let her magic flow outward. A small sapling began to grow. Instead of letting it stop, though, she tried to make it bigger. The trickle of magic grew into a small stream, but as soon as she thought about making it bigger, she could feel it about to crash in a wave. Aesara panicked, opening her eyes, and slammed the floodgates closed.

She panted, beads of sweat on her brow. Shifting her focus, she turned away from the sapling, its small leaves already withering. Aesara found that if she didn't have the energy to sustain the magic or tether it to something, it would die rather quickly.

The small flower she'd created was connected to the wood of the decks. While they were no longer growing things, they hadn't yet rotted. The flower would slowly seep whatever life was left in the wood, but it would take a long time before something that small took all the life from the ship's wood.

Aesara pursed her lips and blew, pushing more force behind her breath. It created a stronger wind and lifted the leaves from the dead tree into the breeze.

Aesara released a sigh. She was learning too slowly for her liking. She had always been a fast learner, so not being able to immediately grasp her magic infuriated her more than anything.

Vance kept his distance while she trained, but he would always find her after, asking how it was going and what she'd accomplished that day. Some days his questions irritated her, but he was getting better at recognizing when it was a good day versus a bad day.

The sky was clear ahead—a few stray clouds here and there, but nothing to cause worry. Aesara watched every day, hoping for a bird. At this point, she didn't even care what the bird was, though a crow would be preferred. She brought her eyes back down and walked toward Vance. He stood at the helm, talking with Six and Byrd.

"Taking a break?" Vance asked as she approached.

Aesara rolled her eyes. "Exhausted, more like. I can't seem to make anything larger than a flower or a light breeze! I try and it starts out okay, but then the magic starts to flow more and then it starts to rush and flood and then…I panic."

"Flood?" Six asked, confused. He and Vance shared the same look.

Aesara waved them off. "Never mind. It's just hard to make anything like the storm." A silence settled awkwardly. "So, what were you three talking about?"

"Fish," Byrd said curtly.

Vance rolled his eyes. "What he meant to say was that we usually try to catch some fish in our nets so we're not using up our rations too quickly, but there haven't been fish for days."

"We are pretty far out at sea. Maybe the nets aren't going down far enough?" Aesara suggested. To be frank, she knew nothing about the waters and fishing. It just seemed like the most logical answer.

Six shook his head. "No. Our nets were enchanted by Mori...a mage, long ago. It's definitely the fish."

Aesara ignored his slip-up, not bothering to tell him she already knew about Morana. "Then what about—"

"We think it's the temperature," Vance interrupted.

"No, Captain, *you* think it's the temperature," Byrd said, crossing his arms. "I think it's the current."

Aesara watched as the three of them began to argue about the different reasons it could be. "What if it's both?" she chimed in.

They paused.

"Both?" Vance frowned. "I hadn't thought of that. If both the currents and the temperatures are somehow different, fishing is going to be even more difficult than we originally thought."

Despite her suggestion, Aesara had a question. "But why would either be messed up?" She was confused frequently on the ship, but that *really* didn't make sense.

Vance eyed her and she resisted the urge to fidget.

"I wonder if it's you."

"Excuse me?" Aesara had heard many odd things in her lifetime, but to accuse *her* of being the reason there were no fish? That was just absurd.

Vance shook his head. "No, no. Think about it. You're a natural mage. Magic has consequences, everyone knows that. What if whatever it is you're doing is causing a shift in the waters?"

Aesara let the thought sink in. "Maybe…but would what I'm doing cause such dramatic shifts? I mean, I haven't tried using my magic with water since the storm. Everything has been either on your ship or on land, however brief it was."

Vance rubbed his face, holding his hand to lips in thought. "This is true, but it's the only explanation I can think of."

Aesara opened her mouth to speak when another crewmember yelled from the crow's nest above them.

"Captain, crow!" He pointed to the sky. In the distance, a black dot flew.

Aesara flung herself forward without a second thought, standing on the edge of the ship. She squinted, trying to see what the crewmember saw.

"Vance! See if you can sail us toward it," she called.

"I know I said I'd help, but sail my very large ship toward a tiny bird? Aesara, you really have lost it!"

It didn't matter; she wasn't listening anymore. The crow was coming into view. Aesara swung herself along the ship, climbing ropes and nets looped to the masts. She looked out again.

Perfect.

She held out a hand and let her magic flow. Connecting with animals was a far different kind of magic, but Aesara could persuade the wind to change and bring the crow toward her.

The floodgates inched their way open and Aesara started to panic. *No!* She couldn't lose this. Not when it meant so much.

She held the gates shut, letting just enough of her magic through to make the wind shift. Her hand shook as the green of her magic swirled around her. In mere moments, she felt the sharp tips of talons resting on her hand.

Aesara opened her eyes, the world tinged in green light, to see the crow peering at her curiously.

"Oh, Silver, it worked. It really worked!" She resisted the urge to jump around, lest she disturb the crow and ruin everything she had just done.

Carefully, she wound her way down from the railing and back to Vance. "We have our next step," she said, beaming.

Vance gave her a small smile, daring to show a little pride behind it. "So we do. Come, let's bring it into my cabin."

Byrd watched them warily as they departed, and Six gave her two thumbs up, his smile matching hers.

Inside the cabin, Aesara let the bird rest in the cage, leaving its door open. She had full confidence that it wouldn't leave until she gave it permission.

The letter attached to its leg bore a familiar seal, though it certainly wasn't her father's. The laurel crown was the symbol of the royal family of Sodaya, the Chavalons.

"Well?" Vance asked, sitting down at the desk. "What does this one say?"

"I haven't opened it yet."

He frowned. "Why not?"

She was scared, though she dared not say that out loud. It was one thing to open a letter from her father, Aesara knew him. Despite her hope that he would choose differently, she knew what he would say. She did not have an inkling of what King Onuphrius would write.

Her hands shook as she handed the letter to Vance. He took it from her slowly, watching her. With a swift swipe of his knife, he lifted the seal from where it had been holding the papers shut. He did not, however, unfold the papers.

"Aren't you going to read them?" Aesara asked.

"Only if you tell me why you didn't open it."

Aesara resisted the urge to grumble. She hated it when he bargained. It was always a barter, give and take.

"I just don't have as steady a hand."

"Liar."

His gaze held hers, his dark eyes seeking answers within her light ones. Aesara sighed. "Fine," she spat. "Since you must know everything. I am fearful of what it might say. If I don't look at it, part of me can pretend it doesn't exist at all."

Vance's eyes softened and he unfolded the letter, handing it to her.

"I might have a steadier hand, but you certainly read better than I do."

Aesara started reading the words before she had even fully grasped the paper. She frowned and reread it. "I don't understand," she said. "They're demanding *we* vacate their shores. Didn't they start all this?"

Vance hummed. "Politics. Always turning things around. They started it but want to blame the other. No one wants to claim they started a war, not unless it serves a purpose."

Aesara slumped in the chair across from Vance. "I've been trained to deal in politics all my life and yet it's still so exhausting. This means that and that means this. Why is nothing clear?"

Vance chuckled. "You're still young. Once you've dealt with royal bastards long enough, you'll start to catch on much quicker."

"Maybe."

Aesara read through the rest of the letter. It was polite—respectful, even—but its overlying theme was the same. *Get out.*

Aesara set the letter down, leaning against the desk. "I thought it would provide more insight, but it only served to confuse me more."

She traced her finger along the desk, following the pattern in the wood. *If this letter was just a dead end, what more would the birds provide?*

Vance stood, but Aesara paid him no mind. She was too stuck in her own thoughts. She didn't know what step to take next. She doubted Vance would let her go back to shore after the stunt she pulled last time.

She jolted as her chair was pulled away from the desk. Vance dragged the seat so that the two of them faced one another on the same side.

"Vance! What are you doing?"

He didn't answer her. He sat back down, leaning forward and grabbing her underneath her thighs. His hands were large, the warmth from them spreading across her body. He moved his hands down her legs, pulling them up and into his lap.

Aesara was stunned at his actions and frozen in her seat. "Vance?"

"You are wound tighter than Byrd, I swear."

He took off her boots one at a time before rubbing the pads of her feet, gently at first and then applying more pressure. Aesara melted. She hadn't realized how sore her feet were until that moment. After wearing ill-fitting boots for weeks on end, it only made sense.

"You need to learn to relax, *Selen Od.* Take control of what you can, but do not let the rest consume you."

Aesara let his words sink in as he rubbed her aching feet. "But if I do not worry, who will?" she asked. She tried to sit up more, but Vance pushed her back down.

"No one. Let the worries go to the wind. For once, Aesara, let go. The crew is planning for a revelry tonight. Join."

A revelry? "Like a ball?"

Vance laughed. "A little—no, *a lot*—less formal than a ball. Like a festival, a party."

Aesara had never been to a festival, much less a party. Her father had never let her attend anything of the sort.

"What do you do at a party? Do you dance?" she asked. She thought of the crewmembers and grimaced. She would rather jump into the sea than be forced to dance with them. She wouldn't mind dancing with Six, but the others not so much. They were kind, sure, but they were filthy beyond belief.

Vance shrugged. "If you want. Bog likes to dance after he's had a couple cups of mead. Fret likes to sing—not very well, but he still does it. Mostly, we just enjoy the night. We don't worry about the ship or the water or even status."

He set her feet back down on the ground, grinning at her when she whined. A flush crept up at her face as she realized what noise she had made. Vance folded the letter back up, sealing it as it had been before and giving it to the crow.

Maybe the next one would have something more useful.

Vance strode back to her, using his thumb and forefinger to tilt her head to face him. He towered over her as most men did, but

Aesara found that she wasn't afraid; instead, she leaned further into his touch.

"Think about it, yeah? You might enjoy it." He tapped her lips with his thumb and left the cabin, leaving Aesara and her thoughts reeling.

Aesara licked her lips, almost wishing there was something left of him there to taste before standing so quickly that the chair was knocked to its side.

"What in the Silver was *that*, Aesara?" she asked herself.

She paced the cabin, her socks catching on some of the splinters in the wood. She couldn't be thinking of Vance like that. He was an ally, a means to an end. That was it. If this revelry was anything like what she thought it would be, she should certainly *not* be going.

But it seemed fun. And it had been so long since Aesara had been able to have real, without consequences, fun. She looked at the cabin door. Where was the harm in one night?

As the sun dipped lower and lower in the sky, Aesara grew anxious. She still tipped back and forth on whether or not she would join the so-called party. On one hand, it might be nice. On the other, she had so much to do and plan for if she was to stop a war. She thought of the crow resting in the cabin. It would wait for her. It would still be there by morning.

She watched as the crewmembers rolled out barrels from the hull. They stacked them atop one another, some creating makeshift seats and others creating a bar with food and mead. Aesara had drank wine before. She was told it had a softer flavor than most other alcohols, that it didn't burn going down. She still wasn't quite sure what they meant by burn.

She backed out of the way of Six, who tipped his hat with a smile. She smiled back, tripping on a loose floorboard.

Strong arms caught her and helped her upright, though they didn't immediately release her.

"Did you decide to join?" Vance asked.

Aesara took a few steps away, widening the gap between them. She didn't need more thoughts like she'd had that afternoon.

Vance smiled at her as if he knew. Aesara fought the blush rising to her cheeks.

"I haven't decided yet. It looks like fun, but—"

"But what?" Vance took a step closer, and she took a step back. He frowned. "Why do you keep stepping away? I'm not going to hurt you."

Aesara's eyes widened, and she waved her hands frantically. "No, no, no! I don't think you are. I just…like my space."

Vance could see through the lie, and she knew it, but what was she supposed to say? *He's making her think things she's never thought before and it absolutely terrifies her, so if he could keep a ten-foot distance, that would be lovely.*

She almost scoffed at herself. As if she could say that.

Vance coughed, breaking her train of thought. "Your eyes. They're, um, glowing."

"What?" Aesara ran to the barrel of water. As Vance had said, her eyes were glowing. They were the same vibrant green as her magic.

Vance's face materialized next to hers, and when she looked at him, a crown of flowers grew from her head.

"Ah! What's happening?" Aesara frantically tried to get rid of them, but for every flower she picked, another grew in its place.

Vance chuckled at her, stilling her hands.

"Calm yourself, Aesara. You're still learning your magic. Be patient with it."

Every time she had been this close to Vance, they were in the midst of life-or-death situations. That was not the case now, and she could see his sun-kissed skin beneath his tunic.

Heat rushed to her face, and she pulled her hands away from Vance to cover it.

"It's nothing to be embarrassed about, Princess. Maybe I can help." He tried to smooth the flowers down but the vines looped across his hands, entangling him in the crown itself.

"Well…that didn't work. I'm sorry, Aesara." He tried again to pull himself free, but the vines did not let go. "Maybe Six will cut them for us."

Her body tensed as if feeling the pain of being cut herself. The vines slowly released him and returned to Aesara. She took a step back and took a deep breath.

She willed the flowers to go away lest they want her to cut them off. Though they had no voice, she could hear their exasperated sighs as they shrunk down. With a *pop*, green sparks floated from her head where the flower crown had sat.

This was something she had never experienced before. She knew her emotions controlled some aspect of her magic, but this was new.

"Has that ever happened before?" Vance asked.

"No," she said. Aesara shook her head, wrapping her arms around herself. "Everything is so new. I think I have control and then something else pops up. I can't seem to get a firm grasp. It's like trying to catch the water and hold it within your hand. It stays for a moment and then slips away."

Vance stood there for a moment, watching her, before he darted off without saying a word.

Aesara wasn't sure how to react. As the anger started to rise at his rudeness, he returned, hands filled with two mugs overflowing with a golden liquid.

"Here. This should help calm your nerves."

Aesara took the mug gingerly, though it didn't stop the liquid from sloshing over her fingers. She licked her hand clean and found the liquid sweet, similar to the fruity wines she had drunk at the castle.

She brought the mug to her lips. She tried to drink it slowly but ended up finishing her cup right away. Aesara had never been the best at handling her alcohol. She usually drank slowly and steadily, drinking with the lords but not enough to lose her head.

She didn't need to think here. There was no reason *not* to let it go to her head.

She handed the empty mug back to Vance. "Can I have more?"

He smirked and took her cup. He returned with a bow *and a full cup.*

Aesara took it eagerly, gulping it down. Vance put his hand against the mug, pulling it away from her lips.

"I suggest you slow down. You haven't had much to eat, and this will go straight to your head."

Aesara kept eye contact as she took another drink. She wouldn't let men tell her what to do, not anymore.

She marched off toward the barrels, Vance laughing behind her.

By the time she had finished her third cup, Aesara was feeling giggly. The music thumped around her, and she swayed with it. Vance still nursed his first drink, watching her carefully.

Aesara laughed as Six danced with another crewmember wildly. She could only assume the other one to be Bog, the man Vance had mentioned to her earlier. She lifted her mug to drink only to find it empty once more.

She frowned at it before hopping off the barrel she had made her seat.

"I didn't realize you were such a drinker," Vance said, coming up behind her as she refilled her mug.

"You like to get under my skin." Aesara stated it so matter-of-factly, Vance didn't have any witty response ready. "You do it and then walk away. Every time. My people are going to war, my father is an idiot, I have a dying kingdom, and I am no closer to helping anyone than I was when I first arrived on your stupid ship." The words spilled from her mouth like vomit. She couldn't stop it. "So, yes, *Captain*, I am drinking. Because what else am I supposed to do when the world seems to be crumbling around me?"

Aesara stared Vance down as she chugged her drink. She glared even harder when he smiled.

"Your Highness, you are something else." He raised his mug and finally finished his first pour.

The rest of the night went by in a blur, and when Aesara awoke in the morning, it felt like someone had taken a hammer to her skull. She could briefly remember dancing with Six, but when she had danced a little too close, Vance stepped in, pushing her away. She remembered liking the attention and continuing to do it just to be close to Vance.

She groaned as she rolled onto her side, the sun painfully bright in her eyes.

"You shouldn't drink so much."

Without looking, Aesara threw a pillow at Vance. He laughed as the soft material whacked him. Aesara peeked at him and wished she hadn't. It looked as if he had just rolled out of bed as well. His pants hung loosely on his hips, and he wore no shirt, his tanned chest on display. His dark hair was pulled up in a messy bun, but a couple loose tendrils framed his face.

She wished she still had the pillow to cover her burning face. "Would you shut up?" Aesara hissed. "I have a headache from hell, and you are certainly not helping."

"I brought you something to eat. I thought you might want to know what you did last night."

Aesara froze. *What she did? Oh, G'iv, what did she do?*

The panic must have been obvious on her face as Vance laughed harder. He handed her the plate, taking a seat next to her. He stretched out like a cat, and the sun reflected off him perfectly. Aesara blushed and looked away, choosing to stare at her food instead.

"Don't worry, *Selen Od*, you didn't do anything too bad. But you sure are fun when you're drunk."

Aesara whipped her head back. "What did I do? Oh, G'iv, I know I danced, but tell me I didn't do anything else."

"Oh, but if I did that, I'd be lying to you. And, my dear Princess, I could never lie to you." He winked.

Aesara groaned. "Did I tell stories?" She knew she had her mother's habit of babbling when she was tired, and if she was anything like that drunk, she could only imagine the things she'd said.

Vance nodded.

"Did I sing?"

He nodded again.

"Oh, no. I have a terrible voice when I'm sober; I can't imagine it when I'm drunk. What else did I do? What could be worse than that?"

Vance tilted his head, giving a look at her disheveled clothes.

Aesara gasped. "No! I wouldn't!"

He raised an eyebrow. "You tried, but I stopped you."

Aesara grabbed at her hair. "Okay, okay. So, no one actually saw anything?"

"I made sure your clothes stayed on."

Aesara started to sigh with relief but stopped when he kept staring at her. "What? What else did I do?"

"You kept complaining about never experiencing anything. About being stuck alone."

Aesara's eyes widened. *No. If she had complained about that, with the thoughts she'd been having lately about Vance...* "I didn't! Oh, no...who?"

Vance smirked, and Aesara shrieked.

"No! *You?* No, no, no! This can't be happening."

Vance leaned forward, grabbing her chin by his thumb and forefinger.

"Don't worry, Princess. For someone who lacks experience, you make up for it with enthusiasm."

Aesara squeaked, shoving him away. She quickly stuffed her mouth with bread. Being only a couple days old, it wasn't nearly as hard yet.

Her mind raced. She couldn't believe she'd *kissed* Vance.

"Princess, I'm flattered that I'm what you think about all day."

Aesara swallowed. "Excuse me?"

"Never heard the saying? I suppose you wouldn't have if that was your first time drunk."

"What saying?" Every word out of his mouth embarrassed her even more. She didn't want to know any more.

"Drunk words are sober thoughts."

"I do *not* think about you all day. I think about Tecrane, about Ascen! About what I'm going to do."

Vance smiled, standing. "I know. That's why I came to get you. There's something you need to see. You just look so cute when you're angry, I couldn't resist teasing you a little bit."

Aesara paused. "You jerk! So, I didn't kiss you?"

"No, Princess. But admit it, you're a little disappointed that you didn't." He winked and walked out of the cabin.

Aesara stood up to follow him, and as she did, she realized with frightening clarity that she *was* disappointed.

She shielded her eyes as she exited the cabin only to halt completely. The deck was lined with fish.

"I don't understand," she said. "I thought the nets weren't working?"

"And now they're working almost *too* well. We've never had this many fish. So, the question remains—what's causing the shift in patterns?"

Aesara rubbed her temples as another round of violent thumping beat against her head. "Vance, maybe now isn't the best time to ask me questions. Can't this wait till I don't have a raging headache?"

"Can the princess not handle her alcohol?" Byrd lingered by Vance. It would seem he never strayed too far from his dear captain.

"If I had a bottle of wine, Byrd, I'd show you just how well I can handle my alcohol, and then I'd shove the bottle right up your—"

"Okay!" Vance stepped between the two of them in an attempt to break the tension. "That's enough from both of you."

Aesara glared at Byrd. She hadn't meant to be so crass with him, but he irritated her. He was like the sibling she had never wanted and suddenly had.

"You"—Vance pointed at Aesara—"go get some food and water. Only water. Byrd just…just shut up."

Aesara grumbled under her breath and stalked away. It had been Vance's idea to have her drink and let loose. If this was anyone's fault, it was his. She grabbed her food from the cabin and walked around the ship, trying to be alone, but there was *someone* around every corner. And she certainly didn't want to be stuck down in the damp and the dark.

She finally plopped down in the small walkway behind the cabin. It was shaded at the moment; the sun hadn't quite reached its peak. She chewed on the food slowly, trying not to think about everything.

As she listened to the waves lap against the side of the ship, she felt her lip quiver.

"No, no. You are not doing this." She sniffled, wishing the tears would go away, but they did not.

Aesara broke. She cried silently, unwilling to let anyone know. If her mother was there, she would wipe away the tears, telling her nothing was worth them. If Carina was there, she would hold her and tell her it would be okay. If Ryn was there, he would stand with her until she was ready, a friend until the end.

But none of them were there. Aesara couldn't even be sure if Carina and Ryn still lived.

She took a deep breath, her tears finally slowing. She swiped them away with her sleeve and bowed her head.

"I don't know what I'm doing. I was prepared to be a princess my whole life, never a queen. Give me strength. Guide me. I need You more than ever. *Tmes visith fi,* blessed be this day."

Someone cleared their throat. Aesara jumped, turning to see Six.

He sat down next to her slowly. "I didn't mean to scare you. I debated not interrupting, but it seemed like maybe you needed a friend."

Aesara swallowed and opened her mouth to speak, but no words came out. Instead, the tears she thought were done spilled once more. Six let her slump against him, uncaring that she cried against his shoulder. Eventually, the tears stopped, leaving her sniffling.

"I'm sorry," she whispered, adjusting her head so her temple rested against him. "I didn't mean to cry on you."

Six laid his head against hers. "Don't worry about it. What are friends for if not to let you cry and snot on their shoulder?"

Aesara let out a small laugh. "I did *not* snot on you."

"No, but I made you laugh, so I'm doing my job somewhat right." There was a moment of silence before Six spoke again. "I heard you speaking a different language earlier. What was it?"

"*Tmes visith fi*. It means blessed be this day. There's a second half to it, but…well…"

"Well, what?" Six prompted.

Aesara took a deep breath and gave a huff for a laugh. "I only ever say the first half of the phrase. My father thinks it silly, but I believe I'll know when the time to say it comes."

"Well, your father is, no offense, an asshole."

Aesara let out a full laugh at the bluntness of his sentence. "You couldn't be more right, Six, not even a little bit."

"I won't ask you to say the phrase, but can you tell me what it means? The second half?"

Aesara lifted her head and smiled wryly. Six shook his head at her. She ate the rest of her food and sipped her water till it was gone. Her headache had lessened, and for that she was thankful.

"I should apologize to Vance. I said some rather unkind words to him this morning."

"I'm sure he's heard worse," Six said dismissively.

Aesara shoved herself to her feet, Six following behind. "I know, but I'm not like that."

As she turned to return to the main deck and apologize to Vance, she saw a dark cloud in the distance. She squinted, trying to understand what it was. It was moving much too fast to be a cloud, and, as far as she knew, she was the only one on the ship who possessed powers. She squinted before backing away with wide eyes.

She took off running toward Vance. It definitely wasn't a cloud. It was a swarm of birds.

Vance stood at the helm, Byrd still at his side. Aesara weaved between the crewmembers trying to put the fish into empty barrels.

"Vance! Your fish!"

He turned and looked at her strangely. Aesara pointed at the birds that had flown even closer in the time it had taken her to run to him.

"Shit! Cover those barrels, men, or everything we just caught is going to turn into bait!"

Aesara was thrown to the side as the men rushed to cover the fish, but it was too late. The birds were good for many things, but if you had food, they would find it.

Aesara scrambled onto the railing, trying to keep her balance.

"I'm not going after you if you fall!" Vance had barely looked at her, and, despite what he said, Aesara was certain he *would* go after her.

"I'm not going to fall!" She had learned her way around her ship well enough after this long. She hadn't been counting the time, but she knew at least a month had passed.

She gripped the ropes tighter as the first few birds started to land on the ship. Owls, sparrows, doves, falcons, and even a swan landed. But they weren't what Aesara wanted.

Amongst the brown and white feathers, Aesara watched for black. There had to be one. That was all she needed. Just one.

There!

Aesara moved quickly. She fell off the railing, scraping her palms. She ignored the stinging and darted for the crow. It pecked at a fish, sharing it with a nightingale. Aesara scooped it up in her hands, escaping the feast and ducking into the cabin. Vance followed quickly, slamming the door shut behind him.

"Not what I had intended for the fish, but I suppose we got something out of it."

Aesara glanced at him as she unrolled the letter from the crow's leg. "We can only hope."

She opened the letter and paused.

"What's wrong? Don't tell me it's something we already know."

She shook her head. "No, it's a different language."

"Sodayan?"

"No, it's neither Tecranian nor Sodayan. This is..." She trailed off, trying to recognize the strange pattern of letters. "I think this is Eshen."

"Please, tell me you can read that."

Aesara blew out a breath. "I can try. It'll take me a little bit. Eshen is... Imagine if you had nine or ten different languages, mashed them all together, and decided that *still* wasn't enough, so you made up new letters and threw those in there, too. *That* is Eshen."

Vance groaned, dragging his hand across his face.

"I can tell you this, though. My father wrote this. It's his handwriting. If he's writing to Eshenia, he must be desperate. For what, I'm not sure, yet."

Vance opened his mouth to speak when something thumped against the door, followed by a string of curses.

"You start working on the letter. I'll deal with the rest of the birds."

Aesara nodded, her head already bowed, eyes scanning the page for words she recognized. She was disappointed in herself when she realized how few she could read. *This was going to be a long day.*

By the time the birds had stopped squawking, Aesara had only deciphered the first three sentences, which were just a perfunctory greeting. She groaned and let her head fall onto the desk.

"It's going well, I take it?"

Aesara lifted her head just enough to see Vance, a plate of food in his hand.

"I figured you'd be hungry by now. How far have you gotten?"

Aesara sat up and cleared her throat dramatically. "Oh, Great Son of Kings, may your frost melt into rivers and your crops be plentiful. I hope I am welcome when I make plans to visit your great kingdom and see its splendor. Though for now, I must witness it from afar."

"That sounds…pathetic."

Aesara ripped into her piece of bread. She loved bread, truly, but not like this—hard and days, maybe weeks, old. She liked fresh bread, warm with a nice crust and soft to the teeth on the inside.

She chewed slowly. "That's because it is. The first sentence is standard in writing to Eshenia, but the rest? My father wants something from them, and he thinks this is how he'll get it."

Vance watched her carefully. "And what do you think?"

"Me? I hope they'll see through his lies."

"But what do you *think?*"

Aesara sighed. "Unfortunately, I think it'll work. King Sol is known to like his…treasures. My father will shine whatever it is he has to offer and dangle it in front of him. There's a reason he remains king." She rubbed the scars on her wrists. "My father is brutal, yes, but his cunning makes him far worse."

Silence settled briefly before Vance stood, pushing Aesara's chair to the side to make room for his own.

"What are you doing?" she asked, raising an eyebrow.

"Helping. Teach me Eshen. Let me help."

Aesara looked at him as if he had grown two heads. "Teach you Eshen? Right now? It took me years to learn it!"

"Better start teaching, then."

Aesara let out an exasperated sigh, throwing her hands in the air. "Fine, fine! See this word?" She pointed to the smallest word she could find. "It means 'to.'"

"Great, so then all the other ones mean the same thing."

"Not quite."

Vance raised an eyebrow. "'Not quite?' What do you mean 'not quite?'"

"This one means 'to.' But when *this* word is in front of it, it means 'from.'"

"That wouldn't even make sense! There's only one word in front of it. There's no way that sentence logically makes sense."

Aesara laughed. "You can't apply sense to Eshen. That was your first mistake."

Vance growled and pointed at another word. "What does this mean?"

Aesara read the sentence. "Cave? I think. Maybe cove. They're very similar."

"And this one?"

Aesara frowned. "Beef? That can't be right." She reread the sentence. "Maybe not beef exactly, but food. Something along those lines."

She pushed the letter back to Vance, tired of looking at the words—if she could even call them that.

"You're telling me this letter mentions caves, or coves, and food within the same paragraph? Does King Ciran also have a secret stash of greenroot?"

"No, Vance." Aesara covered her mouth, trying to contain her laughter. "My father does not. I think we would have seen the symptoms by now if he was using drugs."

"I think it might be better for us if he was, then. What is this letter?"

Aesara took it back, trying to appear unfazed when her fingers brushed against Vance's. She read through a couple more sentences, picking out words instead of trying to decipher the entire thing.

"I think…" she said, "I think he's promising food and land if Eshenia aids him in the war."

"How does that work when Tecrane is, for lack of better terms, suffering?"

"It doesn't. That's why I need to read the rest of this letter. There must be something else that we're not getting. Tecrane doesn't have land—not healthy land, anyway—and we certainly don't have food. We can barely feed the people in Ascen. Sure, some of the port cities get along better, but not well enough as a kingdom." Aesara hunched over the letter, but the rest only held more flowery praise. She threw her hands up in exasperation.

"Maybe we should take a break, Aesara." Vance placed his hand on her shoulder. Warmth flooded her body, and she held her breath.

"Ye-yeah," she stuttered. "That might be a good idea."

They stood at the same time. For once, she was thankful she was shorter than him; he couldn't see the red burning on her cheeks.

CHAPTER
Sixteen

"WHY DON'T WE PRACTICE USING YOUR ATTACKS?"

The thought of using her magic as a weapon hadn't ever occurred to Aesara before. She had seen it done, of course, but her mother was always gentle with her. She didn't even know where to begin.

The crew cleared the deck, leaving just Aesara and Vance. He motioned for her to move forward, to attack.

"Um. . ." Aesara clenched and unclenched her fists.

"Some motivation, then?"

Before she could comprehend what Vance meant, he drew his sword and dashed forward. Aesara yelped and ducked out of the way. The blade embedded itself in the ship, but Vance was quick to yank it out.

While she knew Vance wouldn't harm her, ice flooded her veins as terror seized her. She had been at the end of a blade too many times to not be afraid. Vance stalked toward her, sword gleaming in his hand.

"Come on, Princess! Fight!"

As he raised the sword above his head, Aesara flung her hand out, letting her magic take control. Wide streaks of ice exploded in front her, creating a sharp and deadly wall. Vance stopped in his tracks. He pressed the tip of his sword into the planks, leaning on it with a smirk.

"Now, *that's* magic."

Anger flared inside her. With one swipe of her hand, the ice melted away, a wave crashing along the ship and over the rails. Vance jumped, backing away from the water to avoid being swept along with it.

"I am meant to learn how to control my magic, not depend upon it."

Vance shrugged. "I'd say you're doing just fine."

"No, I am not." Aesara wanted to scream. "I panicked, Vance. I lost control. What I did just then? That wasn't me. I could've hurt you, or worse. My magic follows my emotions; I need control over them first."

"Okay, so we'll try again."

He raised his sword as if asking a question.

Aesara took a deep breath. She didn't think this was a good idea. Still, though, she raised her arms, palms face out in front of her.

Vance circled her like a lion. She knew if she let him move first, she would lose control again. With a yell, she leaped forward, embracing the fear she had and letting it manifest into a weapon she could wield. She crashed into Vance, her ice-sword meeting his steel one. Aesara felt the ice crack as Vance pushed against her.

"What's your next move, Princess?"

Aesara glanced at the widening crack and then back at Vance. She jumped back, pushing Vance as she did. He stumbled, giving her enough time to reinforce the fracture in her sword. She swung at him, but he was too quick. The ice shattered as his blade cut through it.

Aesara shook her hand, ridding it of any leftover frost.

"That was better," Vance praised.

"Not good enough. Again."

The ice came quicker this time, though its form was still choppy. There was nothing smooth about the blade, and Aesara was sure that if she stabbed someone with it, it would tear more than it would cut.

Aesara remembered vividly her mother making it snow in her bedroom. The snow floated in soft, gentle waves. The sword she wielded was hard and fierce. As she clutched the sword tighter, she wondered if her mother would've survived if she hadn't been so soft.

"What are you thinking about?" Vance asked.

Without hesitation, Aesara moved forward, bringing her blade up and then swinging it down. As she did, she let her magic flow into it, making it heavier and letting gravity help her. Vance brought his own blade up just in time to block it.

Sweat dripped down Aesara's forehead as she made eye contact. "What I'm thinking is none of your business."

Vance smirked. He pushed her weight off him easily. With a few rapid strikes, he pushed her until her back hit the main mast. In one last swoop, he shattered her sword once more.

Aesara huffed and tried to move into their starting position when Vance placed his sword at her throat.

He leaned in close, a wicked smile playing across his features, and whispered, "You'll find that *everything* is my business. Especially when it comes to you, *Selen Od.*"

Aesara's heart thumped against her ribs. She looked away only for Vance to tilt her face back up to his. The crackling of magic and ice, however, was enough to draw his attention downward, where she held a dagger at his side.

"And I think you'll find that *I don't care.*"

"Well played." Vance chuckled and backed away. "Shall we go another round?"

Aesara summoned another sword, the ice answering her call quicker each time. "We don't stop until I say."

Vance smirked. "Very well. On your mark, then."

They met each other in a rhythm, but no matter how it started, it always ended the same—with Aesara's blade shattered and Vance victorious.

Aesara had lost count by the seventh or eighth match. She panted, hunched over her knees.

"Aesara, we can stop—"

"We stop," Aesara said in between breaths, "when I say we stop."

She stood straight and created another blade. The ice wobbled as it came forth. Aesara could feel the energy she gave it waning like the energy in herself.

She raised it, pointing it at Vance. "One more. Then we stop."

Vance nodded and adjusted his feet.

The ice dripped from between her fingers. Aesara sighed. Without her full power, she couldn't keep the blade from melting. She could understand why so many people wanted a stone from the Crystal Coves. To have one on her person would mean her magic wouldn't draw energy from her; her magic wouldn't wane like it was now. She'd be invincible against Vance, her power unstoppable.

Power. She stood straight, realization on her face. She let the sword fall from her grip and splash at her feet.

"By all that is Silver, I've got it."

Vance let his guard down. "Got what?"

"The letter!" She ran back into the cabin, Vance right on her heels. Aesara quickly unrolled the letter, careful to keep it in perfect condition.

She pointed to one of the words she had interpreted before.

"I was wrong! My father isn't promising land, he's promising power. There aren't any coves in Tecrane. He's talking about the Crystal Coves in Sodaya."

Vance frowned. "Okay, say you are right. Sodaya would never go to war if it meant there was even a slight chance they would lose. I mean, they hold so much power by controlling the Coves. Why risk it?"

Aesara thought of the crow Sodaya had sent, its strange politeness telling Tecrane to leave. "That was always the question."

She rolled up the letter and tied it back onto the crow. It chirped inquisitively before going back to preening its feathers.

"You're not telling me something, Aesara."

"And you're not telling me something. It's fair." Aesara could tell him what she was thinking. She could tell him that she had suspicions about how the war had really started—about *who* had really started it. But as much as she wanted to, she didn't know if she could trust him completely.

Vance swiped his hand through his hair, frustrated. "If I'm not telling you something, it's for your own good."

"I'll tell you when I believe that." Aesara wanted to trust him. She wanted to believe that he was feeling what she was, but until she was positive, some things had to remain a secret.

She went to grab the crow to release it when Vance placed his hand on her arm.

"You can trust me."

Aesara took a deep breath. "I have only trusted one man in my life, Vance, and it took years for him to gain it. Do not expect to gain it so easily."

She shook free of his grasp and left with the bird in her hands. She was afraid that if she stayed any longer, she would give in and tell the truth. Despite all that she did not know, she did trust him. *What choice did she have? She needed his help.*

As she watched the crow fly away, she knew even that wasn't true. She did have a choice.

Aesara sighed. "What a fine mess you've gotten yourself into."

CHAPTER
Seventeen

OVER THE NEXT THREE WEEKS, AESARA TRIED TO DISTANCE HERSELF from Vance, but as they practiced with her magic, she found herself growing more attracted, more attached. After every session, he would check on her, help her dress any wounds she might've incurred, and stay by her side.

Aesara could control her plants well enough. Vines decorated the ship, and each time Vance said something that made her blush, a small flower would bloom along them. So far, no one had figured it out. She would catch Six glancing at her every now and then, but he never made any mention of it.

Ice and water went hand-in-hand, and Aesara was able to switch between the two with ease. Though her sword was still jagged, it was stronger than when she had first made it. Vance couldn't shatter it as easily anymore.

She didn't use wind very often, but it wasn't as hard to control as Aesara had once thought. Wind was supposed to be unruly. If Aesara thought of it as something to befriend rather than control, it usually worked in her favor.

Aesara had tried to use fire once. It had caused one of the barrels to be tossed out to sea. She'd decided then and there that perhaps it was best not to try when they were on a wooden vessel floating thousands of leagues away from the nearest land. Vance was quick to agree.

Now, Aesara stood in front of Vance, ice-sword in hand, ready to attack. The crew surrounded them. Six stayed close, watching with a careful eye. He didn't like the way they trained, but Aesara was able to convince him that it helped. He'd reluctantly stopped badgering her about it and now hovered like a worried sibling.

She tightened her grip on the sword as Vance adjusted his feet. He moved first, darting forward and then feigning left. Aesara saw it coming and dropped, rolling behind him. She swung her sword out, but Vance was just as fast. His blade caught hers, frost flakes falling between them.

Vance blew them toward her with a smirk.

Aesara put her foot on his knee, pushing away. Vance stumbled but didn't fall. Before he could fully recuperate, though, she struck. Blow after blow, Vance was on the defensive. Aesara left him no room to attack.

Finally, she saw her opening. She dove, letting her blade melt into a small dagger. She poked his hand in between his thumb and forefinger hard enough to draw blood.

Vance cursed and dropped his sword. Aesara was quick to kick it away. She summoned her full blade once more and held it to Vance's throat, extending to her full height to stand above his hunched form.

Vance smiled up at her, pride shining in his eyes.

"If it's you, Princess, I don't think I'd mind kneeling."

"If it's me, you'd be calling me Queen."

She put her foot to his chest and kicked him over. Vance let out a breath as he was knocked over, but his eyes never left hers.

Walking over to the barrels, Aesara watched the skies as she gulped down fresh water.

"We haven't seen a bird, let alone a crow, in weeks, Vance."

Vance took up his spot beside her, getting a cup for himself. "I'm sure correspondences have just been slow."

"No, a week is slow. Two weeks is slow. Three weeks? Nothing was ever sent. We need to go to land."

"And do what, Princess? You expect to ask a stranger about the affairs of royalty?" Vance chuckled. "I don't think you'll like their answer very much."

Aesara scowled. "I don't expect to ask a stranger, you annoying pirate." With that as the best insult she could think of, Aesara slammed her cup down and stormed away.

"Aesara, wait! That's not what I meant."

Aesara paced the cabin, letting her frustration leak out of her through her magic. Wind picked up the loose papers on the desk, creating a tornado of maps and unfinished letters.

"'That's not what I meant.' Oh, yeah? Then what did you mean, Vance?" Aesara mocked him aloud, venting her anger to the wind. "I'm not crazy. Something is different. There hasn't been a single bird. *And* the fish have been scarce again."

The cabin door opened and Aesara turned her back to it, not wanting to see Vance's face and forgive him so easily. She wanted to make him wait and earn her forgiveness, and she knew he would give her a look, whisper sweet words, and she would give in.

"What do you want, Vance?" she asked, crossing her arms across her chest.

"Not the Cap."

Aesara immediately killed her tornado and turned to see Six standing in the doorway, giving her a lopsided grin. She could see Vance behind him. Annoyed, she used the wind to slam the door shut behind Six.

"Sorry, Six. He just...just—ugh!" Aesara threw her hands up in frustration.

"Don't let him get to you too much, eh? He hasn't exactly, uh...dealt? Yeah, dealt with someone like you."

Aesara raised an eyebrow. "Dealt with?"

Six smiled. "Most ladies hear his name and do what he wants. *You* challenge him. You don't give him what he wants. You irk him just as much as he irks you."

Aesara sighed and sat. "So, what? I should just let him?"

Six laughed. "No, no, absolutely not. This is the best time I've had on the ship, watching him squirm under the pressure of liking you."

Aesara's heart stopped. *Liking? Six thought Vance liked her?*

"You think he likes me?" she asked, her voice a whisper.

Six opened his mouth to answer when the door swung open, and Vance strode in. "Aesara! I came to—oh, Six. What are you doing in here?"

"Just talking to Aesara." He looked between the two of them. "I'll be heading back out to the deck now. Come see me later, huh?" With that, he dove back out of the room, shutting the door behind him.

Aesara was still thinking about what Six had said.

Vance cleared his throat, gaining her full attention. "I came to apologize. I should've known you'd have a better idea. I'm sorry I judged so quickly."

Aesara eyed him. "Do you mean it?"

He took a step closer. If he moved again, he would be in her personal space.

"I do. You're smarter than I give you credit for. Now, go on. Tell me your idea."

Despite her better judgment, Aesara let her guard down. Vance took the opportunity to step closer.

The heat emanating from him made her drop her gaze. He never failed to make her feel flustered. She did her best to control her voice and make sure she didn't stutter. "There's always one port that knows everything. I don't know which port, but I would assume you would, being the Reaper."

Vance leaned against the desk, idly picking up one of compasses resting on it. "Let's say I do. What makes you think you can afford the price?"

Aesara crossed her arms, irritation already setting in. "My father may have disowned me, but the kingdom doesn't know that. I've got my title and the gold that comes with it."

Vance shook his head. "They don't deal in gold or silver. They're not...cheap like that."

"*Cheap?* Gold is cheap?"

Vance nodded. "To them it is, Princess. What they deal in is a lot more priceless."

Aesara eyed him warily. "Like what?"

Vance smiled. He set the compass down and took a lock of her hair, twirling it around his finger. The movement made her heart flutter, but she made sure not to show anything on her face.

"Things like memories...thoughts...*desires.*" A shiver went down her spine as Vance whispered the last word, his voice low in her ear. "Tell me, Princess, do you think you could give any of those up? Do you have any that you can think of right now?"

"I have lots of memories and thoughts I'd gladly give up," Aesara whispered.

Vance smiled, leaning closer. "But what about your desires? Do you have any that you'd give up?"

He let go of her hair, letting his hand trail down her arm. He grasped her hand in his, pulling her closer till they were a breath's width away. He held her hand against the desk, keeping her close—as if she even had the strength to pull away.

"That...that's assuming I have desires." She wanted to curse him for making her feel this way—warm and as if she might collapse at any moment—but she couldn't find it within herself to do it.

He chuckled, the sound causing heat to pool in her belly. "Oh, I know you do, Princess. The question is, will you admit them?"

"Well, I..."

He leaned ever closer till their lips almost brushed. Aesara let her eyes drift close as she leaned toward him.

A sharp knock at the door had her springing backwards.

"By all that is Silver, what?" Vance glared at the door. Aesara tried to back away farther, but Vance still held her hand in his, keeping it pinned to the desk.

"Sorry to disturb you, Captain. Byrd said there was something you needed to see."

"Of course he did," Vance grumbled.

Pink tinged Aesara's face as Vance looked back at her. He pinched her chin, forcing her to look at him.

"You're adorable when you blush. I'll have to make it my mission to do it more often."

With that, he left. Aesara stared at the door before her legs gave out and she collapsed into the chair.

She had almost let Vance kiss her. *And she had liked it.*

"Oh, G'iv, what is happening to me?"

Heat ran from the top of her head to her toes. She flexed her fingers, and, to her surprise, a small flame sparked and disappeared just as fast. Aesara's eyes widened, and she quickly stood up, spinning around the room, searching for something she could use should her hands go up in flames.

There was nothing. She would have to leave the cabin if she wanted to put out the fire.

Aesara took a deep breath. She should be fine as long as she didn't think about Vance. And how close he had been…how he had almost kissed her.

Aesara's eyes drifted closed as her imagination began to run wild. Her eyes snapped open when she smelled the smoke coming from her hands.

"Oh—oh, no."

She shook her hands wildly, but it did nothing to stop the heat. She swore and then cursed herself for swearing. Grabbing the door handle, she flung it open and ran outside.

She ran past Vance and Byrd, who eyed her with her concern as she ran to the nearest water barrel. She shoved her hands in, sighing with relief at the cool contact. Steam rose from the barrel. The water would have to be repurified, but it was better than burning the whole ship down.

"Um, Aesara?" Six asked her hesitantly. "Are you all right?"

Aesara nodded. "Much better now. Sorry for ruining the water. I'll help you fix it."

"I told you she would only cause trouble," Bryd said as he and Vance approached.

"Yes, yes, I know. You've only told me a dozen times." Vance rolled his eyes. "Quite the predicament you've got yourself in there, huh, Princess?" He tilted his head playfully.

Aesara realized her hands were still submerged and hastily pulled them out, wiping them dry on her pants.

"And I wonder whose fault that is."

Vance shrugged. "I couldn't possibly imagine."

Aesara resisted the urge to snap back, or better yet, strangle the man. Taking a deep breath, she looked at the sky. Dark clouds rolled overhead.

"A storm is coming."

"Yes, that was what Byrd wanted to show me. We'll need to tighten up the ship."

"Would it not be better to make for land?" Aesara asked, hopeful.

"Considering land is *through* the storm, no, it wouldn't."

Aesara was truly hopeless when it came to navigating the sea. She had tried to study the maps, but they made no sense once she walked out of the cabin. On land there were signs and roads.

The sea had no such forgiveness.

She sighed. "It was worth a shot."

Six clapped her on the back. "*The Promisea* has been through worse than this. I imagine you'll want to stay in the cabin, though. I doubt you've been through something like this."

"You mean you don't think I've been stuck on a rotting ship in the middle of the sea during what looks like to be the biggest storm G'iv has ever sent?" Aesara gave him a deadpan look. "What gave that away?"

"Hey! My ship is not rotting." Vance pointed his finger at her. "You're lucky I like you."

The phrase made Aesara's heart flutter, but she quickly smothered the feeling.

"Or what?" she asked. "You'd have Byrd throw me overboard?"

"That's exactly what I'd do." He winked at her before turning away, discussing the ship's various weak spots with Byrd.

Aesara looked at the clouds once more. The pace they moved at made Aesara uneasy; no cloud should be able to move that quickly. As she returned to the cabin, she said a prayer, asking for strength. Something told Aesara they would need it.

CHAPTER
Eighteen

Aesara had been right. The wind whistled and batted against the ship, pushing it this way and that. The rain pelted the ship like icy daggers, and Aesara feared that it might not survive once the waves came.

Vance entered the cabin, slamming the door shut as the wind washed rainwater in. He was drenched from head to toe, his hair plastered to his skin.

He said nothing as he wiped his face with a dry cloth. Aesara opened her mouth to speak, but Vance beat her to it.

"Don't," he warned. "Don't say a word."

Aesara crossed her arms, pouting. "I wasn't going to say anything."

"You were, and I know that it wasn't going to be remotely helpful. So, unless you have something nice to say, don't say anything at all."

He peeled off his shirt, tossing it into a soaking heap on the floor. Aesara scrunched her nose, silently picking it up and draping it against the desk chair. Just because he was in a grumpy mood didn't mean the cabin needed to smell of mold.

"Can't your magic do anything?" he asked.

Aesara shook her head. "I didn't create this storm, Vance. It'll be much harder to try and calm it." She didn't bother mentioning that she had already tried. The water wouldn't listen to her.

He grumbled under his breath and plopped onto the floor. He grunted as he tore off his boot, dumping out the rain and seawater. Thunder clapped overhead and Vance sighed, leaning his head back against the wall.

"Can I help?" Aesara asked. She hated sitting around while everyone else worked.

"Not unless you can stop the waves. The rain I can deal with, but the waves? They're the worst."

No sooner had he said it, the ship was knocked to one side. Aesara fell forward, landing right in Vance's lap.

"Sorry!" She tried to get off, but once the waves started, they didn't stop till the storm did.

Vance wrapped his arms around her, pulling her to her feet as he stood. "Try not to hurt yourself while I'm gone, Princess."

She stared at him as if he was crazy. "You're going to try and sail in this?"

He shrugged, tugging his boot back on. "Have to. If I don't, the ship is sure to sink."

Aesara glanced down at her hands. There had to be something she could do to help. She followed him, only to immediately regret her decision.

The rain stung as it hit her skin, and her hair whipped wildly around her. Aesara disagreed with Vance; she'd take the waves over the rain. She had to squint to keep it from pelting her eyes, and the wind pushed against her so harshly she was impressed that anyone remained standing.

Aesara nearly slipped but managed to use the wind to her advantage. She guided it behind her and used it to propel herself forward and back onto her feet. *There was no way they would survive this if they couldn't even stand.*

She paused, looking at the fading green light surrounding her hands. *Maybe she didn't need to control the* entire *storm.*

Aesara ran around the bustling crew and to the center of the ship.

"Vance!" she called. He turned his head, surprise written across his face. "Here goes nothing," she said, more to herself than anything.

She flung out her hands, letting her magic loose. She couldn't calm the storm, she wasn't that crazy, but she could slow it. The rain paused midair before slowly falling, as if it were snow on a calm day rather than this hell.

Vance looked around and then back at her. "Are you crazy?" he yelled.

"Probably!" Aesara gritted her teeth as her energy depleted rapidly. She wouldn't be able to keep this up much longer. "Do whatever it is you need to do—and do it fast!"

Her body shook as her vision blurred. She had not counted on the fact that, even though it wasn't the sea, it was still an *entire* rainstorm, not just a pool of water. She took deep breaths and faced away from the dark sky as the ship turned.

"When I say let go, Aesara, let go. The force of the drop should be enough to push us out of the storm!"

Aesara nodded, unable to speak. Her world blacked for a moment, but she shook her head, regaining her vision.

"Now!"

All at once, Aesara reeled in her magic. The rain fell hard, and with the wind now behind them, the ship lurched forward toward the sunlight outside of the clouds. Within minutes, the sunlight reflected off the deck. She slumped onto her knees, her body numb as the magic slowly stopped taking her energy.

Vance ran to her, a smile on his face. "That was amazing! And you said your magic couldn't help."

"I said that I couldn't calm the storm, which I didn't. I do think, though, that I need to rest."

Aesara collapsed onto the deck. Vance's smile dropped as he rushed to catch her. Her ears started to ring as Vance's face faded in and out of view.

"Do we get to go to port now?" was the last thing Aesara said before blacking out.

AESARA WAS GETTING TIRED OF WAKING UP IN PAIN. EACH TIME SEEMED to get worse, and this time was no different. Without opening her eyes, she rubbed her temples, trying to lessen the agonizing headache. She had full movement of her limbs, however, which was a good sign.

"Shhh," she hushed Vance before he spoke. She was in no mood for his antagonizing.

"I didn't say anything." Aesara could hear the smile in his voice.

"I know, continue doing that," she said, draping an arm over her eyes.

"Even if I have food to offer?"

Aesara peeked one eye open—just a crack—to see what he had brought her. In his hands was a steaming bowl of soup. She could smell the broth, its delicious scent making her mouth water.

She sighed, sitting up. Vance had shoved blankets in the windows as best he could to block out the light. Some sunlight still shone through, but not enough to hurt Aesara's eyes.

As she took the soup, she motioned toward them. "Thank you."

Vance nodded. "You're the only reason we made it out of the storm. Trying to make the ship more comfortable was the least I could do."

Aesara wasn't sure what else to say. She'd saved the ship because she needed to survive. But that wasn't quite it. She'd saved it because it would be wrong to let a ship full of innocent lives go down when she could do something to help. But looking at Vance, she wondered if even *that* was the whole truth.

She ate the rest of her soup in silence, trying her best to shut her mind off.

As she neared the end of her bowl, Vance cleared his throat. "When you're done, there's something else."

Aesara frowned. She quickly drank the rest of the bowl and set it down. Vance chuckled and walked to the desk where a blanket covered the birdcage. He lifted it gently to reveal a crow.

Aesara's eyes widened. She jumped to her feet only to sit back down as the room began to spin. She took deep breaths, calming her racing heart. Once her vision was restored, she stood again, slowly.

Vance waited patiently, watching her in case she needed help.

"You caught one?" she asked, opening the cage's door and stroking the crow's feathers. The bird leaned into her touch, letting her pet it.

"I did. I didn't know how long you'd be out for, so I kept looking. Eventually, one showed up."

Aesara paused, her hand freezing along the crow's feathers. *How long she'd be out for?*

"What do you mean? How long have I been asleep?"

Vance looked away, refusing to meet her eye.

"Vance," Aesara demanded, "how long was I out?"

"Two weeks. Almost two and a half."

Aesara blinked. "What?"

"You wouldn't wake up. I tried. Your body responded to nothing—not speaking, or tapping, shaking, nothing."

The crow moved its head underneath Aesara's palm, upset that she had stopped petting it. Aesara jerked before resuming gently stroking the crow. It was smaller than most, she realized. Its body fit against her hand, its tail going just past her fingertips.

"You're a small thing, aren't you?" she asked it, leaning down to look into its beady eyes. She saw her reflection and cringed. Her hair was a tangled mess, and her skin had no color, her days on the ship gone from her pigment. "I wonder if you have a name."

"Aesara?" Vance asked, drawing her attention back to him.

"I'm okay. Let's read the letter. I assume you already took it off him?"

"Yeah, I—him? How do you know it's a him?"

Aesara looked at the crow. It tilted its head, looking at her with curious eyes. "I don't know," she said finally. "It just sounded right."

Vance eyed her but moved on regardless. "The letter's on the desk."

Aesara took the scrap piece of paper off the desk. The edges were torn, and it had a strange smell of something acidic. Only three words were written on it: *The Harbinger comes.*

"I thought you might know what it means more than I do."

Aesara stared at the words. It was not her father's handwriting, and she didn't recognize it from any of the other letters. She shook her head.

"I don't recognize anything about this."

Vance sighed heavily. "All right," he said. "You win."

Aesara resumed petting the crow. "I win?"

"We're going to port." Aesara started to smile. "On *one* condition."

"Anything." The word fell from her mouth before she could think of what Vance might demand.

"We search for Morana after."

Aesara paused. Going after Morana would be much more dangerous than stopping the weather. She would fight back. She would try to kill Aesara with aim and without mercy. Aesara flexed her fingers, the magic in her veins responding to the motion.

She nodded. "Deal."

The crow cawed, taking flight from the cage and springing into the air. It circled before diving. Vance ducked as it flew where his head would've been, watching with wide eyes as it landed on Aesara's shoulder.

Aesara smiled as she leaned her face toward the bird. It tipped its head down, rubbing the top of its head against her cheek. Its feathers were soft, like what Aesara imagined a cloud felt like.

"I think the same thing, Sono, but what can a girl do?"

"Are you...talking to the crow?"

Aesara hummed. "I thought he needed a name. I like Sono, what do you think?"

The crow clicked its beak, and Aesara decided that meant he liked it.

"Aesara," Vance said slowly, "you can't keep the bird. We have to send it back with the letter."

"I know. But maybe he'll come back. You never know."

"It's a messenger bird. It goes back to its master."

Aesara smiled, ignoring his negativity on the matter. "Which port are we going to?"

Vance looked at Sono sitting on her shoulder one more time before walking to the desk where a map was sprawled out. He pointed to a small port north of Ascen.

"Dria," he said. "You want information, they've got it."

"I'm going to take a wild guess and say gold isn't going to work there?"

Vance chuckled darkly. "No, Princess, no coin will work there. Be sure this is what you want. Once we go, there's no turning back."

Aesara clutched her mother's ring. "I'll do anything to save my kingdom."

"Then prepare yourself. We'll be there in a few days' time."

Aesara nodded and lifted her hand, allowing Sono to walk onto it. She rolled up the scrap paper with the strange message and handed it to him.

"Finish your first mission, please." She wanted to tell him to return to her, but he was not hers to keep. Sono tilted his head once more before taking off. Vance threw open one of the windows, allowing him to leave the cabin.

Aesara found herself sad as she watched Sono leave. She had never been allowed a pet in the castle, and after catching and releasing so many crows, part of her longed to keep one, if only to have a companion to take with her everywhere.

She felt Vance as he stepped behind her.

"You should rest," he said.

Aesara scoffed. "I've been resting for two weeks. I think I've had my fill. Help me train." Without letting him answer, she walked onto the deck. If she was going to fight Morana, she would need as much training as she could muster.

CHAPTER
Nineteen

Sweat dripped from her brow as Vance defeated her once again. She took a deep breath before standing as straight as she could, her ice blade already reforming in her hand.

Vance watched with worry as she wore herself down, but he knew better than to suggest stopping. He raised his sword, ready to beat her again. Aesara stared at the sword with disgust. The one time she had touched it had left her scarred, the slimy, inky feeling returning every time she saw the blade.

If she could not defeat Morana, she would not beg for own life, she decided. She would beg to have the blade destroyed and the souls trapped within it freed.

She raised her sword and nodded. Vance leaped forward. In mere seconds, Aesara was knocked down. She landed on her back, letting out a harsh breath as all the air was pushed out from her lungs.

Vance extended his hand to help her up.

"You go too easy on her."

Aesara grumbled under her breath as Byrd approached.

"I think he's just trying *not* to kill me. Can you say the same?" Aesara asked.

Byrd sneered at her. "You are not being challenged. He attacks the same way. You must learn other moves."

"Byrd, I don't think that's a good idea," Vance said, shaking his head.

"Of course it is. Just try. I promise not to hurt the little princess."

Aesara hated the way he called her "princess." When Vance did it, it sounded cute, sometimes as if he was trying to seduce her. When Byrd said it, it was like he was demeaning her. Aesara hated everything about the man.

"Fine, I'll fight you," Aesara agreed without thinking. Byrd was twice as big as Vance and just as good with a blade. He would wipe the deck with her easily.

Byrd nodded. "We begin tomorrow."

"Tomorrow? Why not now?"

"I want to give you a chance," he said, a smile on his face.

Aesara scowled. She well and truly hated the man. As he turned away, she sent a small trail of slick ice under his feet. He fell quickly, landing on his back. Aesara quickly withdrew the ice and turned away, holding her laughter in as others asked if he was okay.

When tomorrow came, Aesara hurt. Her muscles were sore from practicing so long with Vance, but it was too late to back out now. She had to face Byrd.

He waited for her on the deck, a slew of weapons laid out across the barrels.

"What's this?" she asked.

"We pick one that suits you and then you match your ice to it. It is the best way to wield magic blades."

Aesara tried to find where there could be a trick, something to make fun of her with, but Byrd seemed to be genuine and his logic was sound. She was deathly curious where he'd learned how to fight with magic, though she knew better than to ask.

Aesara walked along the numerous blades of various shapes and sizes. She picked one up. It was heavy in her hand, and she nearly crumpled holding it.

"No," Byrd said immediately. "Too big for you."

She bit back a smartass response, keeping her unpleasant thoughts to herself. Aesara set it down and moved to a different one. Byrd didn't turn it down immediately, which Aesara counted as a good thing. It felt light in her hands, the blade a perfect fit to her. She looked to him for approval.

"Decent. Now, match your ice."

Aesara inspected the sword. The blade itself was long and skinny, yet still durable enough for battle. There were small knicks along the edge showing its use. Its hilt was nothing of great interest, simple yet elegant. The lightweight blade would allow her to swing it with ease, while its length would give her greater reach against others. Aesara eyed Byrd's arms that seemed to be as long as her.

Yes, reach would help her significantly.

She held the sword in her left hand and mirrored herself with her right, allowing her focus to go toward creating her own blade. When the sword was done, she raised it, shaking off the chill that using ice magic always left behind.

Her self-made sword still wasn't perfect, sporting cracks and a frosted covering, but it was better than her other attempts. Aesara looked at Byrd.

He stared for a moment before giving the slightest of nods. "It'll do for now," he said. "We'll practice more later."

Despite her hatred for the man, Aesara couldn't help but feel proud at his approval.

"Stop smiling and get into position. Now, we fight."

Aesara did as he said, acutely aware of Vance watching from the helm. She sneaked a glance, only to have to immediately block Byrd's attack.

She slid back, knocking into the mast from the force of his hit. Aesara glared at him, stomping back to her starting position.

"You didn't say you were starting!"

"You think your enemy will? You think they'll give you time to get up? To rest? To make more swords?" With each question, he swung his sword against hers, forcing her back with each blow. Aesara strained against his strength. "They do not care, so I won't either."

He hit her blade one last time, sending her sprawling on the ground. Aesara's heart raced as her anger built.

G'iv be with her.

She sprung to her feet, tightening her grip on her sword and reenforcing the magic coursing through it. With a yell, she brought it down on Byrd.

He blocked it, but Aesara didn't give up. She moved from side to side, trying to find an open spot. Byrd was right, he didn't fight like Vance, but he had helped Aesara create a better sword. She didn't have to spend more than half her energy keeping the blade solid.

She swung harder with each thrust, moving faster than Byrd's large frame could keep up with. With one final hit, Byrd's sword clattered to the ground, Aesara's own at his throat.

She breathed heavily, the rush of adrenaline still coursing through her.

"Yield," she demanded.

Byrd smiled. "I yield."

She let her magic fade, the ice melting down and dripping off the tips of her fingers. She walked to the edge of the ship and sat against the railing in order to catch her breath.

Vance's boots came into her vision.

"You've been holding back on me," he said, sitting next to her.

"I didn't know I could do that."

"You may not like him, but Byrd used to be a captain of the guard. He knows how to train in fighting better than anyone else."

Aesara watched Byrd as he walked to get water. She had not recognized the ink across his torso when she first arrived on the ship, and she still couldn't ascertain where it was from. Wherever he was from, she had not learned about it in her studies.

"You could ask him."

Aesara was wrenched from her thoughts as Vance spoke. She frowned. "Ask him? About what?"

"What's written on him."

Aesara shook her head softly. "I don't think he'd tell me."

"You never know till you try."

"How close are we to Dria?" Aesara was curious about the ink, yes, but she wasn't sure she wanted to know Byrd yet.

Vance chuckled. "We'll arrive by dinner, Princess. Don't worry; when we get there, I'm almost sure you'll wish we weren't."

"Almost?"

"Sometimes I think I know what you'll do, what you're thinking, and then you go and prove me wrong." He looked her up and down, smiling wolfishly. "It keeps me on my toes."

Aesara rolled her eyes. "And you keep annoying me."

She kept her expression neutral to hide the anxiety building in her chest. If what he said was true, they would be on land before she knew it. The one thing she had been hoping for since her father forced her onto *The Promisea* was finally coming true, and Aesara was terrified.

As the sun sank lower in the sky, Aesara's fears did not lessen. In the distance, she could see flickering lights. If she listened closely, she could hear music.

"G'iv be with me," she whispered.

Docking the ship was different this time. There was no telling her to stay on the ship or trying to stop her from leaving. She was free to observe and, once the gangplank was down, free to leave. She hovered at the exit, staring down at the cobblestone walkway. Six was already on the dock, waving her to come down.

Vance nudged her shoulder. "Aren't you coming? You've only been pestering me since we met."

He walked down the gangplank with ease, laughing at Aesara's hesitation.

"Bastard," Aesara muttered, finally mustering the courage to follow him. Baydenn had been full of life and colors. Dria reminded Aesara of The Drain in Ascen. It was a tavern you went to when you wanted to drink your weight in alcohol, when you wanted to forget.

Murky puddles filled the dips in the uneven cobblestones, and Aesara was almost certain that the puddles *weren't* just water and mud. Men and women alike stumbled with dirty glasses in their hands, dark liquid sloshing on the streets and their clothes. As they passed an alley, Aesara lit up red at the uncouth noises coming from the dark.

"Liking Dria so far?" Vance asked.

Aesara stood in between him and Six. She imagined they did it to make her feel more comfortable, and she was all the more grateful for both of them.

"No," she answered honestly. "But if it has what we need, I suggest we get in and out."

"Getting in and out is well known here, or couldn't you tell?" Six asked, stifling a laugh.

It took Aesara a moment to understand the joke. She scrunched her face in disgust. "Ew."

Vance laughed and wrapped an arm around her shoulder. "Just how innocent are you, Princess?"

Aesara turned her nose up at him. "As you just said, I'm a *Princess*. I have standards, unlike you."

Vance mimicked a pained noise. "You cut me deep."

"Not deep enough, apparently." She looked around the unfamiliar street. "Where are we going?"

"You want answers about a war? Kimi is the person to see. She lives for battle; says it's her *calling*. I don't scare easily, but if Kimi was against me, I'd drop to my knees immediately."

An image of a large warrior woman covered in armor and blood entered Aesara's mind.

"And you're sure she's...safe to be around?"

Six laughed. "Not in the slightest. She—" He cleared his throat as Vance glared at him. "She's fine if you don't make her

148

mad, which I'm sure you won't. If anything, Cap will do that for you, so we're safe."

Before Aesara could say anything else—or change her mind—Vance guided them into a small shop. Candles illuminated the cluttered room. Crystals of all shapes and sizes lined the shelved walls. Various bones, herbs, and books were strewn about the room.

A shiver shot down Aesara's spine as a windchime rang softly in the corner as the door shut behind them.

"Kimi," Vance called, "I know you're here. Don't know what you're doing, don't want to know what you're doing, just need your help."

For a moment, nothing happened. Then, "You have a habit of interrupting me, Reaper."

Aesara yelped, pushing herself further into Vance's side as a woman appeared next to them from the dark. She was tall and slender with long black hair and red eyes. She pinpointed Aesara quickly.

"Who's your friend?" She smiled to reveal sharpened teeth. Aesara's heart raced, and she was thankful for Vance as he tightened his grip around her.

"Not for you. I want to know things."

Kimi's smile dropped, annoyance replacing her features before she caught sight of Six. "Reeve! It's been so long since you've come to see me. I've missed you terribly."

Six closed his eyes slowly and shook his head. "Damn, Kimi, you have to use my name?"

Aesara put her hand over her mouth to cover her growing smile. "Reeve?" she asked.

"Don't you dare go telling anyone, got it?" He pointed a finger at her.

"Of course not. I would never…Reeve." Aesara giggled. Oh, she would enjoy this bit of information.

Six gave Kimi a look. "See what you've done?"

Kimi smiled and wrapped herself around him, embracing him as if she were trying to seduce him. "I wouldn't if you'd visit me more."

Aesara had so many questions for Six when their visit was over. Other than her appearance, Kimi didn't seem like the scary woman they made her out to be.

Six unwound her arms from around him. "Unfortunately, you'll have to take that up with my captain."

Kimi swung her head around and glared at Vance. Aesara instinctively took a step back, trying to get out of her line of sight. Vance, thankfully, still held on to her, keeping her upright.

"You don't bring Reeve or the girl for me," Kimi hissed, the annoyance back in her voice. "What do you want, Reaper?"

Vance smiled. "Like I said, to know things."

"Fine," she spat. "What do you want to know?"

"War between Tecrane and Sodaya. Whatever you can tell me."

Her eyes narrowed. "You've never been interested in such things before, why..." She trailed off, sniffing the air, her gaze going straight to Aesara once more. "Ah, a falcon caught your eye?"

His hands tightened on her arms protectively. "I didn't ask about my life, I asked about war. You should be thankful, it's your favorite topic."

She huffed. "Fine, I'll answer. For a price."

"Name it."

Kimi smiled, tilting her head as she stared at Aesara. Aesara's stomach churned at the look. The woman reminded her of a bird with her unblinking eyes and sharp angles.

"The information isn't for you, Reaper. You don't pay, *she* does."

Vance shook his head. "No. I asked, I pay."

Aesara tried to intervene, "Vance, I can—"

"No." He looked at her, and Aesara could've sworn she saw fear and nervousness in his eyes. It made Aesara blush at the intensity.

Kimi jumped onto her counter, crouching so she was still eye level. "I say nothing unless she pays."

That wouldn't do. Aesara needed to know everything she could. If that meant she had to give something up instead of Vance, then so be it.

She looked up at Vance, but he looked straight at Kimi. Aesara placed her hand on his gently, forcing his attention to her.

"I'll be okay, Vance. You warned me what it would cost, and I agreed."

"You don't understand, neither Six nor I can be in here with you. Kimi only relays information to *one* person."

"Oh." Aesara wanted to say never mind, that they could find what they needed somewhere else, but Aesara knew that wasn't true. "Then wait for me outside. You'll be able to hear if anything goes wrong, won't you?"

He nodded slowly.

Aesara smiled through her own fear. "See? It'll be fine. I'll pay."

Vance growled and glared at Kimi. "She stays in the front of the shop, you can't touch her, and absolutely no magic."

Kimi giggled, jumping up and down. She motioned Aesara forward.

Aesara hesitantly walked forward. When she was within arm's length, Kimi shot forward so that she hung above Aesara. She was so close that their noses almost touched.

Kimi stared into her eyes before squealing, "Oh, what joy! What fun we'll have!"

Vance cleared his throat. "You have to hold up your end of the deal."

Kimi shooed him away. "I will, I will. You want your falcon to trust you? You must trust her first."

Vance looked at Aesara. She smiled despite the fear of being left alone.

"It's okay. I'll tell you everything later."

Vance rolled his shoulders, looking back at Kimi. "I'm coming in here if I even *think* she's hurt," he said. With that, he stormed out of the store, Six following close behind. The door slammed shut behind them.

For a moment, silence filled the room. Then, bottles clinked together as Kimi rummaged through the shelves, searching for something.

"Um…" Aesara hesitated. She wanted to ask, but part of her didn't want to know the answer. She let out a breath. "What are you looking for?"

"Secrets."

Aesara paused, taken aback by Kimi's answer. It was like she was speaking to a child. *A very dangerous child.*

"What kind of secrets?" she asked.

Kimi looked back at her, her red eyes almost glowing. "The kind to be found in a different time."

Aesara wanted to scream. Even if Kimi *did* tell her something useful about the war, she wasn't sure she would understand it. The woman spoke in riddles.

"Aha!" Kimi grinned triumphantly. She held a flask full of a liquid so dark it seemed black. She motioned Aesara forward, dumping the liquid on the counter.

It didn't spread like Aesara thought it would. It stayed congealed in a small puddle.

"What is it?" She could see her reflection in its glossy surface. Her hair was braided back and out of her face, and her scar seemed to blend in with the dim lights of the shop.

"Touch it. Go on."

Aesara jerked back. "Are you crazy? I'm not touching it. I don't even know what it is."

"It answers your questions. Touch it."

Aesara looked between Kimi and the dark goo.

"I'm going to kill Vance," she whispered. And then she touched it. Nothing happened.

"Kimi, nothing's hap—"

Kimi was gone. Aesara spun in a circle. The shop was *empty.* No shelves, no wares, and no Kimi. The only thing remaining was the counter; the rest of the room was bare.

"What the…" Her voice echoed off the walls.

She tried the door. Locked. The doorway to the back had disappeared. Aesara was well and truly stuck.

"Kimi, this isn't funny! Let me out!" Out of where, she wasn't sure.

As she paced the room, she heard the clicking of heels matching her walk. Her heart raced in her chest. If she saw Vance again, she would kill him. *Safe with Kimi…*

Aesara scoffed, then banged her fists against the door.

"Let me out! Let me out! Let. Me. Out!"

She sagged against it. Her banging served no purpose other than bruising her hands.

"Why am I here?" she asked aloud.

"You wanted answers," a voice said.

Aesara sprung to her feet to face…herself. But this Aesara was different. She wore a regal gown of gold and white, pearls strung in her long hair. She still had the scar through her eye, but she wasn't skinny. She looked *healthy.*

"Who…who are you?" Aesara asked.

"I'm you."

"How can you be me if I'm me?"

The Other Aesara shrugged. "We could be the same."

Aesara glared, wanting to scream. This Other Aesara spoke in the same riddles as Kimi.

"You said I was here because I wanted answers."

The Other Aesara said nothing.

"If you're not going to answer me, why are you here?"

"You didn't ask a question."

Aesara paused. So, that was the game. "All right," she said. "Why is Sodaya fighting?"

"To defend their kingdom."

"But they started it!"

Once again, the Other Aesara said nothing. Aesara growled. "Didn't they start it?"

"That depends on who you ask. Tecrane will say yes, Sodaya will say no."

"Then who's right?"

"Who, indeed?"

This time, Aesara did scream. "That doesn't help!" She took a deep breath, praying for G'iv's guidance. "Okay, you say it's a matter of perspective. But someone has to be right…right?"

"Uncertainty is a core feature of humanity. Tecrane and Sodaya can both be right at the same time as being wrong. If I said blueberries were the best and you said strawberries were, would either of us be wrong? Wouldn't we both be right?"

"Well, yes, but we're talking about war, not fruit." Aesara thought for a moment, trying to come up with a better question. "How do I stop the war?"

"Are you not already?"

"You're not me," she decided, "because I'm not this annoying."

The Other Aesara smiled.

"I'm *trying* to stop the war. But I don't know what else to do. My father—" She looked at the Other Aesara. "Our father is asking for aid from Eshenia. They have soldiers, yes, but still nothing to compare to Sodaya's strength. If he's trying to rally the western kingdoms, I'm afraid he'll succeed. More than that, I'm afraid of what will happen if he *doesn't*. Tecrane cannot withstand Sodaya alone, which is why I must know why they fight. Will you tell me, please?" Aesara begged.

The Other Aesara's eyes softened, looking at her with sympathy. "Would it matter if I did?" she asked. "You speak the truth. You know what must be done. What does it matter the why?"

"Because I said so!" Tears threatened to fall as she spoke, her voice growing softer. "I don't want to believe he would start a war. I have to—I have to believe there's still some good left. Some of what Mother fell in love with *has* to be there."

She fell to her knees, tears falling freely. She hated her father, but her parents' marriage hadn't been arranged. They had chosen one another of their own free will. Aesara remembered her father doting on her and her mother endlessly in times before. The man must still live beneath the monster somewhere. He had to.

"Will you tell me?" she asked again.

"No," the Other Aesara said. "I will not."

"Then why am I still here?"

"You have more to ask."

"Am I doing it right?" Aesara didn't clarify. Something told her the Other Aesara would understand.

"You are doing what you believe is right."

"Does that mean it's a mistake?"

"Nothing is without mistakes. That does not mean it is the wrong path. Let your heart guide you, *Selen Od.* You will know what's right."

Aesara took a deep breath, calming herself and willing the tears to stop. "I'd like to return home, now. Can you take me?"

The Other Aesara smiled. "You are home."

Aesara's throat tightened and she struggled to breathe. She gasped for air, clawing at her throat. A hand hit her back, dislodging the object in her throat. She vomited onto the wood floor, mostly food and water, but there was something else. Metal glinted in the firelight.

"Aesara! Are you all right?"

She blinked, looking up to see Vance. "What're you doing here? I thought you couldn't be here."

"It's been two hours, Princess. I came back to get you, but you weren't entirely here."

"She had her questions answered," Kimi said, bending down and plucking a ring from the vomit. Aesara suppressed a cringe as Kimi cleaned it off.

"What did you do to her, Kimi? I told you not to touch her!"

The woman bristled at his tone. "And I didn't," she said, glaring at him. "I keep all my promises. Do you?"

The two glared at one another until Aesara spoke, "Could I have some water? Maybe a mint leaf, if you have it." They could argue all they wanted, but her mouth felt disgusting.

"I have everything," Kimi stated matter-of-factly. She went to the back, returning with a glass of water, mint leaves floating atop.

"Thank you," Aesara murmured.

"You shouldn't be thanking her," Vance said. "From the looks of it, she almost killed you. I'm almost tempted to leave without having you pay her."

Kimi bared her sharpened teeth at him.

"She will pay. Which ring she uses to pay will be up to her."

Aesara frowned as Kimi dropped the ring into her hands, the silver shinier without regurgitated food on it. Aesara stared at it in shock. The glass of water slipped from her hand and would've shattered if Vance hadn't caught it.

"What is it, Aesara?" he asked.

"It's…it's my father's ring."

Vance frowned. "It doesn't have the Virral seal, how can it be his? How can you be sure?"

Aesara lifted the chain around her neck, placing her mother's ring next to the other. They were identical in every way except size.

"It's not the seal, Vance. It's my father's wedding ring."

"Now, Kimi gives you a choice. Which ring will you part with?"

Aesara blinked at her. She didn't want to part with either. They both represented the last of her loving parents. They held the memories of happiness and family. How could she part with one?

"Aesara?" Vance asked. "Are you okay?"

No, she was not okay. She'd thought Kimi would just ask for a happy memory or something, not this. More than that, she wanted to know how her father's ring got here in the first place. He always wore it, even after her mother's death.

Aesara closed her eyes and clenched her fists around both rings. She couldn't help the tears that escaped as she dropped her mother's ring into Kimi's open palm.

CHAPTER
Twenty

As the pair left the shop, Aesara was only sure about one thing—she had to continue her path. She couldn't be sure who, or what, the Other Aesara was. If she was her subconscious, why would she call herself *Selen Od?* If she was something else entirely, why take that form?

"Are you all right, Aesara?" Vance asked.

They walked down the street, the nearly burned-out lanterns doing little to light their way.

"I…I don't know," she answered honestly. "I have so many questions. More than I have answers." She clutched her father's ring in her fist as if holding it tighter would give her what she needed.

"Did Kimi tell you anything that we wanted to know?"

"Kimi didn't—she wasn't—it's hard to explain."

"She sent you somewhere, didn't she?"

Aesara stopped walking to look at Vance with wide eyes. She took a step closer to him, invading his space.

"Has she done it to you, too?"

Vance huffed. "More times than I'd like. What did you learn?"

"I'm on the right path, I think. She told me to follow my heart, to let it guide me."

"I hate that advice." Vance groaned. "It's vague, as if they don't know the answer themselves so they let us *think* they do."

Aesara wanted to agree, but something gnawed on her. Something told her the Other Aesara *did* know the answer.

"Well, I—" Up ahead, a flower pot fell, the clay pot shattering on the ground. Aesara yelped, jumping back. "Where did that come from?"

Vance placed a hand in front of her, stopping her from moving forward.

"Wait here." He moved forward, ducking into the alley.

"Vance?" Aesara stood there a moment, waiting for a response. When only silence answered her, she looked around.

The street was eerily quiet; not even the wind moved. She felt foolish standing in the middle of the road. She looked back the way they came. Vance had told her to wait there, but Kimi's shop was at least inside, away from the uncomfortable street.

Aesara started to walk only to have a man emerge from the shadows. He smiled menacingly, a gold tooth glimmering in the moonlight. He twirled a dirty knife in his hand.

Aesara turned back around to find her path blocked again. He had torn clothes, and Aesara swore there was more dirt on him than the ground. He sported no gold teeth, but two were missing.

The men walked forward, closing in on her. Panic rose in Aesara's chest. She could use magic, but there was no guarantee she wouldn't kill them by accident. Her control was still mediocre at best when her heart raced as fast as it was right now.

"G'iv be with me," she whispered.

"You won' find no god 'ere," the one with the gold tooth said, chuckling.

Aesara took a step back toward the alley behind her, her hand clutching her father's ring fiercely.

"My deepest apologies. If you'll excuse me." She tried to move down the sidewalk, away from them, but they moved in front of her, blocking her path once again.

"Now, now, no reason to 'urry. We jus' wanna talk." The gold-toothed man gripped her shoulder tightly, ensuring a bruise. Aesara ducked out of his hold, pressing herself into the wall of the alley. Her hand fumbled, searching for something, anything, she could use against them. She managed to snag a loose brick.

"Look, I don't want any trouble, and I'm sure you don't either. I'm just waiting for my captain to finish his business."

She looked between the two of them, waiting for an opening. One of them leaned to the left. She darted forward, knocking the brick into one of their heads.

He grunted from the blunt force and shifted further to the side. Aesara ran. She watched the shop signs, looking for the familiarity of Kimi's shop. It never came.

She paused. "What? Where did it go?"

She spun in a circle. She couldn't have passed it.

The men hollered, recovering from her attack and running after her. She didn't have time to figure it out now. She kept running.

She turned down an alley. A dead end.

"No, no, no, no, no!"

She tried to call upon her magic to help her jump the wall, but in her panic, it wouldn't answer her. This had never happened. It always answered—sometimes too much, but it *answered*.

The men's voices grew louder. The flapping of wings sounded behind her. Aesara spun, trying to figure out where it had come from.

"Well, looks like someone turned down the wrong alley."

Aesara was slammed into the wall, the brick digging into her back. She gasped and let go of the ring as the air was pushed out of her lungs. One of the ruffians whistled. "Lookie at wha' we 'ave 'ere." He reached for her necklace.

Aesara shoved his grubby hands away. "Back off."

"I don' think I will."

He shoved her against the wall again, causing her head to crack against it. Aesara blinked as her vision blurred. The man tore at her top, trying to get the necklace.

Aesara clawed at him blindly, reaching for anything she could. She felt her nails tear at flesh, and a shiver raked over her body.

The man howled in pain and leaped away from her. "You bitch! You go' my eye!"

Aesara scrambled to her senses and dashed out of the alley, watching behind her. Someone grabbed her arm, pulling her into a small shop. A large hand covered her nose and mouth while their other arm wrapped around her waist, keeping her from moving.

Aesara struggled against them, trying to escape. Her heart raced against her chest, and she tried to scream, but her voice was muffled, too quiet for anyone to hear.

"Stop," a deep and gruff voice whispered above her. "They'll hear us."

He removed his hand from her waist but his other stayed firmly, keeping her in place. He swiped his hand across the shop, a golden glow following.

Another mage.

Bottles rattled and rolled as a shadow formed on the ground. Aesara watched with curious eyes as a shape began to form. It rose from the shadow to create a mirror image of her. She blinked in surprise.

This new Aesara held no emotion or sense of being at all, almost as if it were a puppet.

"Lead them away," the man demanded.

The puppet moved to his command and left the shop. The man leaned toward the window, pulling Aesara with him, and listened.

"'Ey! There she goes!"

The man stayed still until the sound of the ruffians' footfalls disappeared. Only then did he release Aesara.

She gasped for breath, doubling over as she gulped in air.

"Maybe *you* don't need air, but I certainly do," she snapped. She was more than curious about the mysterious man, but her instinct told her to keep herself guarded.

"I had to be sure you wouldn't scream." He moved around her with ease, picking up the broken bottles. He didn't seem bothered by her attitude or her stiff body language, as if it was something he was used to.

Like Kimi's shop, it smelled of herbs, but there was something else there, too. A fiery scent, like there was wood burning.

Aesara took a curious step forward. "Who are you?" she asked.

"No one. You can get out now. They're gone."

The man never looked at her, but she could see he was taller than Vance, who already towered over her. He had dark shoulder-length hair, half of it pulled up and out of his face. It curled at the ends, and Aesara wanted to run her fingers through it. He faced away from her so Aesara couldn't see his face, but she could see the shadow of a beard on his neck.

She cleared her throat. "Yes, thank you. For saving me."

He grunted.

Aesara let a moment of silence spread between them before speaking again. "You performed magic. In front of me. Why?"

"Because I saw your pathetic attempt at using yours."

Aesara winced, still embarrassed that her magic hadn't answered her call. He faced her then. In the dim light of the shop, his eyes were dark, but Aesara could see a golden ring shimmering around the irises. It was the same tone as his magic, brilliant in every way, and it made Aesara wonder if her eyes turned as lively as his.

With the stubble on his face, she couldn't quite tell his age, but he couldn't have been more than five years her elder.

"Are you going to keep staring, or are you going to leave? I don't have time to deal with you."

Aesara blushed. She hadn't realized how long she had been staring. "I'm sorry. I've never seen magic like yours."

He grunted again, as if that meant anything. He bent down to pick up another broken bottle, and Aesara caught a glimpse of white scars poking from underneath his shirt.

"Are you...dangerous?" she asked.

The man stood to his full height and stared at her, face unmoving. "You tell me."

Golden light flooded the room, and the other bottles shook as his power took hold in them. They rolled off the shelves and toward Aesara.

She didn't wait to see what they would form. She ran from the store, risking a glance back at the man. He watched her leave, his magic returning to him, but there was a curious look in his eye.

Aesara didn't have time to think about what it meant. She collided into a figure, their arms catching her by the shoulders. Aesara squirmed, trying to break free. The wind shifted around them as her panic began to rise.

"Let me go!" She pounded her fist into their chest. *Not again.*

"Hey, hey! Stop! It's me."

Aesara looked up with frantic eyes to see Vance. She sighed with relief.

"I have never been happier to see you." She let her forehead fall on his chest, her body relaxing.

"I told you to stay," he said, trying to sound tough, but the worry broke through. "I didn't know where you went."

"I was going to go after you, but these two...thugs? Thieves? Whatever they were, they tried to take my necklace. I had to run."

Vance looked down at her chest, where the ring dangled. He gently lifted the chain and let it fall into her shirt and corset, the cold metal causing Aesara's flesh to prickle.

"I told you to keep it hidden." He pressed his hand against the ring, against her.

Aesara blushed scarlet. "It was! It fell out when they chased me. But then a man saved me."

She swung around to look at the shop, but the lights were out and there was no sign of the man at all. It was as if he had never been there.

"A man, Princess? What man?"

Aesara shook her head. "I...don't know. I never got his name or the chance to thank him properly. He sent me away before I could give him anything."

Vance hummed. "Well, I think that's enough excitement for you tonight. Let's get you to an inn."

CHAPTER

Twenty-One

THE ROOST WAS SMALL BUT COZY. IT HAD THE NECESSITIES AND nothing more, but that was fine with Aesara. What wasn't fine with Aesara was the singular bed sitting in the middle of the room.

She stopped at the foot of the bed. "Where am I sleeping?"

He glanced at her from the chest he dug through and then at the bed. "On the bed."

"Then where are you sleeping?"

He tilted his head at her. "On the bed."

"But there's only one."

"Yes, because they were going to charge me almost triple the price. Be thankful there's a bed. I almost had us stay on the ship for that price."

"But…I—and you…" Aesara fumbled over her words, not sure how to say what she was thinking.

Vance smirked and rose from the chest. He stalked closer to her like a predator stalking its prey.

"Are you shy, Princess?"

"No!" She glared at him. "I've just never, you know, shared my bed."

Vance laughed. "Relax, I won't touch you." He paused, looking at her with dark eyes. "Unless you want me to."

Aesara guffawed and turned away, sitting on the bed with her back to him. "How dare you even suggest that!"

The bed dipped, and Aesara wanted to turn around, to see what he was doing, but then he would win, and she couldn't let that happen. Hands wrapped around her midsection, and she was pulled down onto her back.

She yelped in surprise and tried to get up, but Vance was there, on top of her, pinning her down.

"You should never turn your back on someone," he said. "You never know what they might do."

Aesara scowled. "Oh, forgive me, Captain. And here I thought if you wanted to kill me, you would've done it already."

He had said the words so long ago, but she remembered everything.

"I would've. Maybe I don't want to kill you. Maybe I just want you."

Aesara blinked, his words echoing in her head. "You…what?"

"Is it such a hard thought, Princess? For someone to want you?"

The air grew hotter around her, and Aesara knew what would come next. She hooked her leg around Vance's and used his own weight against him. She flipped them so that she sat on top now.

The memory of her father flooded her head, and ice filled her veins.

She placed a small ice dagger against his throat, glaring at him.

"I will say this once, and only once, Captain Vance. *I* want for things, for others. Others don't want me. That is how this works."

Vance tilted his head once again, his eyes softening. He reached up and stroked her unscarred cheek gently.

"Who told you that?" he asked, his voice a whisper.

"Does it matter?" she asked, following his hand as he pulled it away.

"Very much so. I would have to find them and rip their tongue from their pathetic skull. They clearly don't know how to use it."

"There is much that can be said without words, Captain."

"I liked it better when you called me Vance." He pulled her to him, resting their foreheads against one another. "Allow me the privilege of wanting you, Aesara."

Aesara swallowed, tears threatening to spill. "No one wants me," she whispered. "I am damaged."

Vance chuckled. "Do I look like the kind of man who wants someone perfect?"

Aesara said nothing. What could she say? When she looked in the mirror, she saw flaws, imperfections, someone broken.

"I can't be fixed," she answered.

"Anything can be fixed, Princess. You just have to let me try."

She could not fix herself, that was certain, but no one else had tried to fix her. What if she could be fixed? What if there was still hope for her? She slowly nodded her head.

Vance released a breath. He cupped her face, bringing it closer. So many times, they had been close to this, but now there was nothing to interrupt them.

Panic seized her heart. "Where is Six?" she asked, breaking the moment.

Vance chuckled. "I'm going to kiss you and you ask me about another man? You will be the death of me."

He slowly closed in, their lips barely brushing. Aesara's heart raced as something burned through her. Vance pressed his lips against hers fully and Aesara froze. She didn't know what to do.

Vance moved, sitting up to grasp her and pull her closer. Aesara let him, the soft feel of his lips distracting her from anything else. She grasped his shirt, clutching the material in a tight fist. He licked her bottom lip, and she gasped. He took the opportunity to slip his tongue inside her mouth. He tasted of the sea, and Aesara moaned.

"Make that sound again, Princess," Vance groaned against her lips.

Aesara tried to move closer, but there was nowhere to go. She was already pressed against him as much as she could be. She moved against him, letting him take the lead. Vance tightened his arms against her and pressed upward.

She couldn't breathe. It was too much. His scent surrounded her, fogging her thoughts. There was nothing but *him*. She needed to breathe. She needed air.

Aesara wrenched herself away, gasping for breath. Wrinkles adorned his shirt where she had crumpled it in her hands. He smiled at her, his face holding a red tint.

"Something the matter, Princess?"

"I…I just…" She didn't know how to answer. She didn't want to admit her inexperience. She wanted to kiss him again. She wanted to get lost in him.

Vance pulled her close again and tapped the tip of her nose. "Breathe through your nose. Don't think so hard about it, let your body guide you."

Aesara let her gaze dip from his eyes to his lips. "Okay," she whispered before kissing him again.

She tried to do what he said and not think, but all she could do was think about him. How he felt against her, how her body responded. She pulled back again.

"I'm sorry, I'm sorry." *Why couldn't she even do this right?*

"Don't worry about it, Princess. You'll learn." Vance let her get up, watching her with a lazy smile.

She took a deep breath, regaining her composure. "Where is Six?" she asked again.

"He's running an errand for me."

Aesara clutched a glass of water in her hand as she made her way back to the bed. She curled her legs underneath her, sipping the water. Her body still burned from his touch and the water did nothing to help cool her down.

"What kind of errand?" She needed to keep talking. Anything was better than the silence. The silence gave her time to think—too much time.

Vance waved her off. "Nothing for you to worry your pretty little head about."

Aesara wanted to ask more and push for answers, but she knew it would be futile. When he didn't want to answer questions, he always found a way out of them.

She took a seat on the edge of the bed. "In the vision Kimi gave me, they called me *Selen Od*, like you do. Why?"

"You seem to be more familiar with G'iv than me, shouldn't you know?"

Aesara glared. "I do know more, but I don't know why you keep calling *me* the Silver One."

Vance sighed, adjusting his pants as he sat up. "You really want to talk about this now, huh?"

Aesara nodded. "There's so much I don't know, Vance. You're the only one I can trust right now."

The truth of her statement shocked her. Despite how they came together, he hadn't killed her when he found out she was a woman. He'd helped her with her magic, and he was helping her try to stop the upending war. She knew that he did it for some personal gain, but the deal they made aided them both. He was the only man who had been kind to her.

"I don't imagine there are a lot of trustworthy people for a princess, especially if you decided to trust me."

Aesara shook her head. "There were few others I could trust, and I don't—" She tripped over her next words, her throat tightening. "I don't even know if they're alive."

Vance stayed silent for a moment, inspecting her. Then he spoke, "What do you know of the Silver One?"

"The basics," Aesara admitted. "I know what they represent. The right hand of G'iv. A bringer of war and peace."

"This is true, but do you know where they came from?"

Aesara shook her head.

Vance stole her water and gulped it down. "Story time, then. When Gilan was created, it looked nothing like the maps you see now. There was no division amongst the world; we were one land, one people. But people are greedy. They started wanting more than they needed, more than what G'iv provided them. Fighting broke out, clans formed, and our once-united life was broken."

As he spoke, Aesara listened attentively. She knew the effects of greed and war better than most. She hated the aftermath, the burnt cities and fields, the smell of smoke lingering in the air.

"G'iv gave us a chance to right our wrongs, to purify our sins," Vance continued. "We didn't take it. So, He sent *Selen Od*, born of us but made of Him. To bring peace was to bring war, and war they brought. Nothing we did could stop them—not swords, not arrows, not magic. They were the right hand of G'iv, what could we do? One by one, the clans fell until there was none to oppose." He leaned forward, his eagerness to tell the story matching Aesara's own to hear it. "But G'iv is not one without mercy. *Selen Od* brought us to our knees so that G'iv could help us up. Some accepted His hand, others did not. They sought to covet a higher power of their own, one that would rival even G'iv's. Thus, dark magic was born, so black and vile few dared to attempt it once it was found."

He paused for a moment, his brows furrowed as if the thought of dark magic stirred something he didn't wish to tell. Vance shook his head and continued, "For years, there was peace across Gilan. But peace is a fickle thing; it doesn't last with us. It started as squabbles, then it was fights, and then wars. G'iv watched, sad for us, but there would be no Silver One this time. We could not be saved again; this time it was up to us to reach for help. But He promised that when we needed it most, the Silver One would return to lead us back, to save us once more." Vance gave Aesara a pointed look.

"And you think that's *me?*" she squeaked, her voice rising in pitch. "Vance, I barely know what I'm doing right now. I don't have a big plan. I'm just a princess who can't even get that right."

"There's a scroll, found in Isamund before it was deserted; it shows a woman with golden eyes, standing atop the world."

Aesara paused, letting the words sink in. "And you think it's me?" she asked.

"You're the only woman I know with golden eyes."

Aesara strung her hands through her hair, tugging at the strands. "But what do you care of G'iv and the Silver One? Why does it matter? The only war is between Tecrane and Sodaya—hardly a war worthy of divine intervention!"

"Princess, the world was bowing to you."

She wanted to scream. "I just want to save my kingdom. I don't want to rule the world!"

Vance chuckled, pulling Aesara onto his lap. He played with a strand of her hair, twirling it around his finger. She stiffened, unsure of what to do. She did not want to remove herself, yet she wasn't sure she was ready for such an easy display of affection.

"I don't think that's what it means, Princess," Vance said, unaware of the battle between Aesara's heart and mind. "We have a theory that it means the end of unrest. Gilan has been in a state of turmoil for centuries. We believe the Silver One will guide us out, unite us as one."

"We? Who's we?" she asked, momentarily forgetting her position.

"Everyone. I have committed many wrongs in my time, Aesara, as have many others. If there is a chance to be set free of them, I will take it."

"And you believe this"—she waved her hand—"image is about me?"

Vance nodded. "There are scrolls and legends of the Silver One being born in the winter. It says they will bear the gold as a weight for all to see. For years, scholars tried to figure out its meaning, and then your father rose to power. A king with golden eyes. A weight for all to see."

Aesara frowned. "But he was born in the summer. And you said the image was a woman."

"Yes, that's where most of us lost hope. But then there was the first day of winter and you came."

Aesara took a moment to think. Her head swam with the possibilities of everything. "And what if I'm not?" she asked. "What if I'm not the Silver One like everyone thinks?"

Vance shrugged. "Then we search for another."

He said it so nonchalantly, as if he didn't know what he asked of her. It was too much. Aesara knew the weight of a crown, knew how heavy it laid. But to bear the weight of the world, of Gilan, on her shoulders? She hoped it was someone else.

"I was born late," she said finally. "I was meant to be born several weeks earlier, in autumn. If I am *Selen Od*, if that was my fate, I don't think G'iv would give it such a close chance."

Vance smiled. "Who are we to question the ways of a god?"

"And who are we to decide what it means? I do not question G'iv, but I question humanity." Her voice rose in frustration. *How could he be so calm?!*

Vance shushed her, stroking her back in soothing motions. Her stiff muscles began to loosen despite her best attempts to remain undisturbed by his actions.

"If we don't try to understand it, who will?" he asked softly.

Aesara had no answer. She wanted to understand. There was not a moment that passed that she didn't long for the day she woke up with no uncertainty, no fear, no questions. But that day was not yet near.

"I don't know," she whispered.

Vance shifted so that they were lying next to one another on the bed.

"I think sleep is best right now. Rest, Aesara. We will search for your answers tomorrow."

For once, Aesara did not question him. She rolled onto her side, basking in the warmth Vance provided and the softness of the bed. It wasn't like her bed at the castle, but it was better than the ship, and for that Aesara was grateful.

She closed her eyes, willing her thoughts to calm, and let her dreams take her into the night.

CHAPTER
Twenty-Two

AESARA YAWNED AS VANCE TALKED TO ONE OF THE STREET MERCHANTS. He wore a loose-fitted shirt with a deep V-neck and the sleeves rolled up past his elbows, showing off his amber skin. Aesara blushed as she thought about how it had felt to be held by him.

They had woken that morning tangled in each other's arms, her face pressed against his chest and her legs wrapped around his. She had tried to pry herself from him before he woke, but she was unsuccessful. He had smiled at her and tried to pull her closer, but Acsara had gotten too nervous and pushed herself away so forcefully she had fallen off the bed.

"What are you thinking about so hard?"

Aesara had been so lost in thought she hadn't heard Vance approach. She blushed further as she looked at him. "Nothing," she said, looking away. Vance gave her a knowing smile. "Shut up. What did you buy?"

"A gift." He held up a slender package.

That got Aesara's attention. "A gift? For who? What is it?"

Aesra hadn't received a gift since her mother passed. She didn't mind, she wasn't materialistic, but that didn't mean she didn't like the thought of receiving one. It would mean someone had thought about her enough, cared about her enough, to buy something.

Vance shook his head, a smile on his face. He handed the bundle to her. "Open it."

Aesara let out a small gasp as she did. Inside was a beautifully crafted dagger, polished silver and steel with a black handle. Gold embellished the hilt, glinting in the sun.

"This is beautiful."

"The gold reminded me of your eyes. I don't want you relying on magic here; be sure to keep it on you."

She looked at him with wide eyes. "You bought this for me? This couldn't have been cheap, Vance! You should've let me help."

"I think you're forgetting who I am, Princess. I have more gold than you might think. Now, come. Let's see if we can find more answers."

Vance led her to The Needy Pear, a tavern he told her was known for its hospitality. However, as a man fell through the window, broken shards of glass falling at Aesara's feet, she had a thought that maybe Vance had been toying with her.

Dria didn't seem like a port of hospitality, and The Needy Pear was no different. Mead and beer covered the floor in a sticky coat, and several broken tables were in the corner, out of the way.

Women and men trounced around in little to nothing, allowing the patrons to tug and pull them any which way. They giggled as they fell across their laps, drinking alcohol as the patrons poured it over their mouths.

Lewd noises came from every direction, and Aesara walked closely with Vance, face turning scarlet.

"You are a liar," she hissed. The uncomfortable atmosphere pushed against her. She felt as if she were a delicate bubble that might burst at any moment.

"I said they're known for their hospitality. Everyone seems well taken care of, don't you think?"

Aesara made a face, turning her nose up at him. They stepped over a man face-down on the floor. His trousers were by his ankles, his bare ass to the world. Aesara could see blood pooling by his head, but Vance tugged her along before she could check if he was okay.

"Don't worry, a Pear will check on him," he said.

"A Pear?" Aesara asked, confused.

Vance hummed. "It's what Bliss calls his workers. One of them will check on him."

"He was bleeding."

"He was."

"He could be dead."

"Could be, but I think it was probably too much greenroot." He pushed open a door, guiding Aesara to the back. The moment the door shut behind them, Aesara felt as if she could breathe. She turned on Vance.

"Why bring me here?" she asked. "What could a place like this have for us?"

"Reaper!" A booming voice shouted across the room, shocking Aesara.

She spun on her heels to see a large man, a robe wrapped loosely around him. He laid on a bed with men and women lounging at his sides. They looked blissfully unaware of their surroundings, their eyes tinged red.

The man who spoke placed a small cube of fruit in one of the male Pears' mouths. His eyes rolled back in his head as he moaned. Aesara averted her eyes as his flaccid member became erect.

Oh, G'iv, let her get through this. And not strangle Vance for bringing her here.

"Bliss, my old friend. You're doing well, as always." Vance stepped up to the bed, uncaring of the people in it or their nakedness.

Aesara could not do the same. She stayed close to Vance and out of the way of the people squirming around the bed. She kept her eyes firmly on the large man's face, trying to keep even her peripheral vision from noticing her surroundings. She wanted out.

The man spread his arms wide. "Have you come to join? It's been so long since we last had you here."

Aesara tilted her head at the phrasing, logging it in the back of her mind to ask Vance about later.

Vance shook his head. "No, I'm afraid not. I come with questions I'm hoping you can answer."

The man, Bliss, grabbed the Pear next to him by his member and stroked him, motioning for Vance to continue with his other hand. Aesara hated everything about this place and she hated Vance for bringing her into it.

"As I'm sure you're aware, war is coming and—"

"Bah! War is always coming, coming, coming, and it never does, does it? There's always a truce at the last minute, hmm? They realize they don't want to die for whatever it is they're bickering about and it's all for not."

Vance smiled. "I'd usually agree, but I believe this time to be different. How's your trade?"

Bliss stopped moving, to the objection of the Pear. He removed his hand and sat up, letting the others that were lounging across him fall to the side.

"What do you know, Reaper?"

"I asked you first."

Bliss glared. "You never ask without already knowing an answer. I ask you again, Reaper, what do you know?"

"Your greenroot suppliers are bailing. Your buyers aren't buying. You do well at Dria, but anywhere else? You're dry. You're done. Can't be Bliss if you're not providing, can you?"

Aesara watched the exchange intently. Vance had come prepared. He knew how to make Bliss squirm. She had seen her father do something similar with a traitorous lord, but this was much less violent. It was subtle, it was a play of words—the most powerful thing one could possess.

"What do you want from me?" Bliss asked, still glaring.

"Greenroot never dries. Why is it now?"

"So, the great Reaper doesn't know everything."

Vance shrugged. "Never claimed to."

Bliss watched him carefully before letting his eyes fall to Aesara. "And who's this pretty thing? An offering? A gift?"

Aesara's nostrils flared in anger. "A woman," she spat, "who can speak for herself."

Bliss laughed gleefully. "Oh, I love it when they're strong. They all start out like you, but pretty soon…" He fed a cube of fruit to a woman this time. She screamed in pleasure and moved atop the man next her, riding him.

Fire bubbled in Aesara as she realized the fruit was laced with greenroot. It was an easy drug to get addicted to and a hard drug to stop.

Aesara snarled, flames threatening to spill from her hands.

Vance pushed her behind him, shielding her from Bliss.

"She is mine, Bliss. Touch her and you won't have a fucking thing left. I will destroy every greenroot production. I will make sure it dries and it stays that way. Your Pears will wither, your customers will wither, and then you will come begging to me to fix it."

Vance held his hand against his sword, the stone in its pommel glowing with anticipation.

Bliss nodded slowly, tearing his eyes away from Aesara.

"Good, now you're going to answer my question. Why is the greenroot drying up?"

"Some rich twat is buying it all. Doesn't seem to be using it, but he's buying it—for way more than it's worth, too." Bliss scowled, slamming his fist into the bowl of fruit. It spilled onto the floor, and the Pears were quick to eat it. "Don't know his name, but I can tell you where he's bought from."

Vance smiled. "That will do nicely. Now, was that so hard?"

Bliss looked none too happy as he sat up in his bed. He swung his large legs around the side, the bedframe shaking as he stomped on the ground. "This way."

Vance urged Aesara forward as Bliss walked through another door she hadn't realized was there. With a large desk and maps covering the walls, Aesara could only assume this was his office.

Bliss sat in the chair with a heavy grunt and motioned them forward. He pointed to several red Xs on the map laid in front of him.

"Every one of these is a supplier who's been bought out."

"Can't they grow more Tack? I mean, they're plants, right?" Aesara asked.

"They could, yes, but Tack is a hard thing to grow under the right conditions. This fellow who's buying it all? He's burning their lands after he's bought it."

Aesara frowned. "If the suppliers know he's doing this, why let him buy from them?"

Bliss laughed. "Tell me, girl, do you value a plant over your life? They'll rebuild eventually. Besides, he's giving them enough money for it, much more than it is worth."

"Why?" Vance asked. "Why do that if you're not trying to start a greenroot trade for yourself?"

Bliss looked between the two of them. "Do either of you know what greenroot does? Truly?"

Vance shrugged, motioning to the room next them, where the Pears could still be heard through the wall. "I think I can imagine, Bliss."

"That's only one side to it. Sure, greenroot can give immense pleasure, but what's pleasure without pain? Greenroot draws out our inner desires. For most people, we just want the simple things—to love, to be happy, to be pleasured. For others, not so much. Greenroot triggers their violent nature, their bloodlust."

"No." Aesara shook her head, refusing to believe what Bliss was insinuating.

Bliss smiled. "The girl's got it. Do you, Reaper?"

Vance looked between the two of them, expectant.

Bliss sighed, standing up. He motioned for them to follow him once more.

They followed Bliss through another door adjacent to the desk. It led to a larger room with counters lining the walls and a large table in the center. Glass tubes and jars lay about the counters, filled with Tack Leaves in various stages of decomposition. A small number of men moved about the room carefully, protective wear around their face and hands.

Someone heated the tube gently to burn the leaves of their outer shell, exposing the spores inside—the greenroot. Aesara held her breath as they carefully shook the green powder from the tube into a small dish. They passed it to another man, who separated the burnt shell from the greenroot.

It seemed like a painstaking process, but Aesara had seen its effects. Greenroot was coveted even in the furthest reaches of Gilan, not just Tecrane.

"Greenroot must be treated delicately," Bliss said. "If not—if one little wisp gets away—something terrible could happen."

"Why?" Vance asked. "Someone gets in a fight. Who cares? People have been murdered for less."

"They don't just fight, Vance," Aesara murmured. "A war is coming, and greenroot has the ability to make even the gentlest of men monsters. They wouldn't be in their right minds. Think about it. If every soldier was given a dose of greenroot and sent to fight, what do you think would happen?"

"They'd struggle to get their armor off fast enough to find something to get off on." Vance smirked at his joke.

Aesara glared, grinding her teeth. "No, you idiot. They'd massacre anything in their path. They're scared. They are going to fight—to defend their homes, their families, their land. The only thing on their minds is making it through alive. Give them a drug that amplifies it? It'll be a bloodbath, Vance."

She ran back to the desk, inspecting the Xs. She traced her finger along the map, her body growing heavier with every movement.

"Aesara? What is it?" Vance stepped behind her. He grabbed her elbow, stopping her hand from moving.

"They're all in Tecrane, all the sold-out suppliers. They're *only* in Tecrane."

Vance frowned, leaning over Aesara to peer at the map himself. He traced the same path Aesara had made with her finger, stopping when his hand covered hers.

"What do you think it means?"

Aesara didn't want to answer. She was afraid to—afraid of what it meant.

Bliss squeezed back through the door frame. "I'll tell you what it means. It means that the bastard of a king is planning something, and it ain't something good."

"What do you know of King Ciran?" Aesara asked.

"Enough to know he's giving his daughter to King Sol, and that just isn't right. Can't even get a good night in bed with Sol, the poor geezer."

Aesara swiveled her head to look at Bliss. "What did you just say?"

"Yeah, there was a whole announcement throughout the kingdom." He scratched his neck, thinking. "You could probably find a paper still posted in the town center if you wanted to read about it. Not really worth it, if you ask me. It's not like the princess could've done much else for us, anyway."

Aesara and Vance glanced at once another. If she was here, who was being given to King Sol?

"Thank you for your help, Bliss," Vance said, pulling Aesara with him toward the door. "We'll be on our way now."

They moved toward the door only for it to be blocked by several men dressed in black, blood-stained weapons in their hands. Red tinged their eyes as they glared at Aesara and Vance.

Aesara took a step back and hit her hip against the chair.

"Now, I know it's none of my business, Reaper, but Aesara isn't a common name. And one doesn't see golden eyes every day. You may have power, but so do I."

Bliss grabbed Aesara, hauling her to his side. Aesara squirmed in his hands, trying to free herself. For such a large man, he moved fast. Vance started to move but froze when Bliss pressed a dagger against her throat. A shiver wracked through her as the cold metal touched her skin. Her father flashed in her mind, his hand raised against her.

"I don't know why you have the princess, but it won't really matter when you're dead, will it?" Bliss chuckled, the sound bringing Aesara out of her head and making her cringe. "I'm sure King Ciran will pay a hefty price to have her back."

"You idiot," Vance hissed. "He sold her to me. He wanted to be rid of her. Why would he want her back?"

Despite the truth of the words, they still stung Aesara.

"You expect me to believe that?" Bliss tightened his grip on her. "Why would he declare her betrothal to King Sol if she was already your property?"

"I don't know, Bliss, but just release her, and we can talk about it. We can figure it out." Vance raised his hands to placate Bliss.

"No, you know what I think? I think you *stole* her. Get him!"

The three men in the doorway rushed Vance, brandishing their weapons. Vance cursed, dodging their swings. There wasn't enough space to draw his own sword, so he had to make do with the small dagger he kept on his belt.

Bliss laughed as one of the men's blades nicked Vance, drawing blood. Aesara struggled in his grip, trying to break free, but to no avail. Bliss was too big. Despite her training, she still felt so helpless.

She watched as the men attacked, feral in their motions. They didn't care about themselves, only about hurting Vance. Aesara's heart clenched as one of them sunk their daggers into Vance's side.

"No!" she screamed.

The wind picked up, swirling her hair in front of her face.

"What the hell?" Bliss's grip loosened as the wind howled and the familiar green light of Aesara's magic began to glow.

Aesara made eye contact with Vance, and he nodded. She let loose a torrent of ice and wind. Pointed ice crystals flung into the wall in a dangerous arc. Vance watched the movement and ducked before the ice could strike him. The other men were not so lucky.

Slumped against the wall, ice pierced their skin, already melting against their bodies' temperatures. Blood seeped from the wounds, pooling on the ground in a red puddle.

Aesara stood frozen as her magic died down. Bliss no longer held her. Instead, he hung limply on the wall, his heavy body impaled with several large icicles. Aesara watched as the blood dripped from the ice, mingling with the draining water.

The dagger Vance had gifted her hung on her belt, untouched.

Vance tugged on her arm.

"Come on, Princess. We have to go."

Aesara let him guide her out, her mind still reeling. Once they were away from The Needy Pear, they ducked down an alleyway, away from the crowd. People passed by, but Aesara didn't notice. Vance leaned down to be eye level, pressing her into the brick wall of the alley.

He searched her eyes, concern written across his face. "You okay?" he asked. "You're in control?"

Aesara nodded weakly. "My magic isn't the problem."

She clenched her hands into fists, but it did nothing to conceal the way they shook. Vance took her hands in his own, clutching them tightly, smearing his own blood across them.

"You did what you had to do, Aesara. You gave them a swift death, which is kinder than they deserved."

"But I killed them," she whispered, staring at the blood staining her hands.

"In defense."

"You can say whatever cause you want, Vance, they're still dead because of me!"

A group passing by turned to look at them, curious as to who was shouting. Vance glared at them, walking to Aesara's side to shield her from prying eyes.

He tilted her chin up, their gazes meeting. "The reason doesn't matter. If you hadn't, we'd both be dead, Aesara."

"Don't call me that."

Vance frowned. "What?"

"The people know my name. Bliss was right, Aesara isn't a common name. Add my eyes in and they'll know who I am. We can't have a repeat of what just happened. Whether you think they deserve it or not, I have no right to be someone's executioner."

Vance brushed his finger along her cheek.

"All right," he whispered. "To everyone else, you'll be someone else. But not to me. To me, you are always Aesara."

He pulled her in close, kissing the top of her head.

CHAPTER
Twenty-Three

AFTER CALMING DOWN, VANCE PAID FOR THEM TO EAT. AESARA demanded he see a healer, but he insisted she needed food first. Even as he said it, he clutched his side, wincing as they sat down in a small tavern on the edge of town. Blood stained his shirt from the dagger wound.

"We need to find you a healer," Aesara said quietly, eyeing the few other patrons.

Vance waved her off. "I'll wrap it up later. It'll be fine."

He grimaced again as he adjusted in his seat.

"Yeah, right. We're finding you something now." She started to rise, but Vance quickly tugged her down.

"Not here. There aren't any healers in Dria, and if there are, their services aren't cheap."

Their food was placed in front of them, steaming portions of meat and potatoes. Aesara smiled and thanked the man serving them, shifting to cover Vance's bleeding side. The moment he was out of earshot, she turned back to Vance.

"You're the Reaper. What good is the title if it can't get you healed? It earned you respect at the greenroot-house well enough." She slipped the jab in there, still unsure of how she felt about Vance being well known at The Needy Pear.

Vance choked on the bite of roast, pounding his fist against his chest as he coughed. When he finally managed to dislodge the piece of meat and swallow correctly, he looked at Aesara with shock.

"By all that is Silver, *what* are you talking about?"

Aesara crossed her arms and huffed, refusing to look at him. "Nothing," she said. "All I'm saying is that we need to find you a healer."

Vance stuck a piece of meat on his fork and held it for Aesara to eat.

"And I said I'll fix myself later. Now, eat."

Aesara grumbled under her breath but took the fork, nonetheless. As she ate, she watched Vance from the corner of her eye. He ate slowly and winced as if each bite hurt him.

Aesara stood, walking to the bar.

"Where are you going?" Vance asked. "Aes—Adequin? What are you doing?"

She still hated the other name, but she knew it was for a good reason. Aesara leaned against the counter, smiling at the barman.

"Hello," she said. "Where's the nearest healer?"

The barman eyed her and then Vance, who still sat behind her. "Who's hurt?"

Aesara waved her hands. "Oh, no one. Just my sister. That time, you know? I was hoping there was a healer nearby that could help. Maybe give some tips?"

The man hummed. "Closest healer is in Layshin. It's not too far north from here, 'bout a couple days' ride."

Aesara straightened her back.

"Layshin?" she asked. "You don't have one in Dria?"

The man motioned her forward with a crooked finger. Aesara leaned in close.

"The people of Dria thrive off the dead and the dying. The last healer lasted two days before they killed him. Can't get profits if everyone's being healed," the man whispered in her ear. He leaned back and picked up a dirty glass, cleaning it with an equally dirty rag. "If you want my advice, you'll take your friend and get out of Dria before whoever hurt him finishes what they started."

Aesara thought of the watered-down blood dripping from the icicles. "Thank you for your help," she said and returned to the table.

"What did you talk to him about?" Vance asked as soon as she sat down.

"I asked where I could find a healer."

"You did what?" He gripped her wrist, pulling her so close that she could feel his hot breath fanning across her face. "Aesara, Princess, listen to me. This is not the place. Let me handle it."

She pried his fingers from her arm. "I know. The barman was kind enough to already warn me. Are you done with your food? We should probably leave."

Aesara hadn't been blind during her conversation with the barman. She had noticed the three other patrons listening closely. If all the warnings she had been given were true, they were likely to be attacked.

Vance glanced around the tavern and nodded. "I agree. I am full. Let's head back to The Dragon's Egg Inn." He spoke the name of the inn louder, making sure the attackers heard.

Together, they left the tavern. However, instead of taking the main road back, they dived off into a half-dead field of wheat and settled in to watch the door. The three patrons left shortly after, chattering amongst themselves about what kind of reward they'd receive for the Reaper.

Vance scoffed. "As if they'd get close enough before I cut their bloody heads off." He stood only to take a clumsy step back.

"Vance?" Aesara asked, worry lacing her voice. She knew they should've wrapped his wound first. She should know by now not to listen to him.

Vance reached out to grab something for support only to find wilted wheat stalks. He tumbled through them, falling onto his back.

Aesara yelped, rushing forward. Blood flowed heavily from the stab wound, dark and thick.

Vance coughed. "Shit. Thought I had more time."

Aesara pressed her hands against the wound, trying to stop the bleeding. "What do you mean by that?" she shrieked.

Blood seeped between her fingers, her hands a feeble attempt at help.

"Oh, G'iv. G'iv, G'iv, G'iv. What do I do? Vance, what do I do?"

"It's all right. Just help me up."

"But the man said the closest healer is in Layshin! We don't have time to—"

Vance grabbed the sides of Aesara's face, forcing her to look at him. He smiled despite the pain.

"Princess, you really think I wouldn't know how to fix myself? Just get me back to the room."

Aesara tried to breathe calmly in through her mouth and out through her nose, but it didn't help much. She heard a chirp and looked to see a small crow. Aesara frowned. It looked strangely familiar to her, but she could quite place it. The crow chirped again and hopped toward Vance.

Despite it being a crow, she knew what it wanted. Why the crow wanted Vance saved, she didn't understand, but she wasn't going to question it now. She hoisted Vance up, wrapping his arm around her shoulder and supporting his weight as best she could. When she looked back, the crow was gone.

"Okay, let's get you to the room. But you better not die on me. Not you."

Vance laughed and then coughed.

Dria was a filthy town, but thankfully it wasn't large. Despite the small size of the town, Aesara was panting under Vance's added weight by the time they reached the main strip of inns. She spotted the three that had been at the tavern with them going into the inn across the street, weapons ready.

Aesara hurried as best she could to The Roost. It was surprisingly easy to throw the thugs off their trail. Vance groaned as she took the first step up the stairs, jostling his body in a new motion.

"I'm sorry," she whispered. "We're almost there, I promise."

Standing outside the door, she fumbled in Vance's pocket, searching for the key.

"If you wanted in my trousers so bad, you could've just asked."

If Vance wasn't already on the verge of collapsing, Aesara would've smacked him. Instead, she told him to shut up and unlocked the door.

They fell into the room in a heap. Aesara kicked the door shut and dragged Vance so he was sitting against the bedpost.

"Okay, we're in the room. What do you need? What do you need to fix yourself?" Fear found its way into her voice, into her heart.

Vance motioned downward. "Sword."

"Your sword? But why—you know what? I'll ask later." She untied the sword from his hip, avoiding touching it fully. The uncomfortable, heavy feeling when she neared it returned, but Aesara didn't have time to think about it now.

She shoved the hilt into Vance's hand, wrapping his fingers around it.

"Okay, okay. The sword. You have it. It's in your hand."

Vance nodded. "Unsheathe it."

Aesara did so blindly, flinging the scabbard away. The blade sparkled, almost too pretty to be a weapon of such destruction.

"Vance, what does the sword—"

Before she could finish her sentence, Vance's grip tightened and he swung the sword up, bringing it down upon himself. It impaled him, making a sick crunching sound as it broke through his chest.

Aesara screamed, falling back on her hands. She scurried away, pushing herself into the wall as far as she could.

Inky smoke flooded the ceiling, coming to a point as if it were coming from inside Vance. The cloud moved like a viscous liquid, bubbling like something was trying to escape.

Vance pulled the sword from his chest with a sickening squelch. As he did, the black smoke disappeared, sinking into the new wound. When the smoke dissipated, Vance laid there, chest rising and falling slowly.

Aesara inched her way forward. "Vance?" she asked hesitantly.

Vance gasped, eyes flinging open as he sat up, clutching his chest. The wound on his chest was gone, and the one on his side had healed as well.

He groaned. "Doing that always makes me light-headed afterwards."

Aesara stared in shock. Vance looked at her, tilting his head quizzically. "What's wrong, Princess?"

"You…the sword…what did you do?"

Vance rose to his feet, wiping his hands on his pant leg. He extended a hand to Aesara, smiling.

Aesara looked at it, eyebrows furrowed.

"Come on. You still trust me, don't you?"

Aesara laid her hand in his, allowing him to pull her to her feet. "Unfortunately, I think so, Captain. Now, explain what the hell that was."

Vance sat them on the bed, unstrapping the replica sword and attaching the real one. "I suppose you mean the magic and not why I waited so long?"

Aesara gave him a deadpan look. "What do you think?"

Vance chuckled. "As the princess demands. When you told your version of the legend of the Reaper, you were right up until the end. He was fatally wounded, so he brought the sword upon himself, hoping to preserve his soul in the mortal world. What he didn't expect to happen was to be revived. Instead of taking his soul, the sword *gave* him one. Decidedly, this could never be shared, otherwise people would try to find and kill him for more reason than they already had. So, he killed everyone present."

Aesara listened intently, absorbing every word Vance said.

"But if he killed everyone there, who started the legend?" she asked. "And that still doesn't answer why you waited so long."

Vance smiled. "The Reaper himself. It's better to have a reputation to strike fear into people's hearts; it makes them leave you alone. As for me waiting, I really just thought I had more time."

Aesara rolled her eyes. "You are a pirate after all. I still don't understand, though. If the Reaper started the rumor, then how did *you* come to possess it?"

"Morana gives her gifts for a price. He couldn't pay. She took back her gift. Eventually, it found its way to me as a curse." He flexed his fingers, glaring at them. "Now, I either pay her price or kill her."

"What's her price?" Aesara asked.

"Significantly harder than killing her, Princess, I assure you."

"But how do you know? Maybe I know a way to get whatever it is. We could work together—"

"No!" Vance yelled, startling Aesara.

She pulled her hands to her chest, blinking. He had never raised his voice at her like that.

"Okay," she whispered. "Okay, we'll kill her, if you think it's best."

Vance sighed, pinching the bridge of his nose. "I'm sorry. I didn't mean to yell. Her price is…it's just not something I want you dealing with. We focus on killing her and then we'll both be free of her, yeah?"

Aesara nodded. "A deal for a deal. I'll kill Morana. You help me with the war."

Vance agreed. "Yes, *Selen Od.* You help me and I help you." He trailed a finger down her face with a feather-light touch, just enough pressure to make it tickle. Aesara's heart fluttered, and she glanced at his lips. Before she could move, Vance stood.

"The day is still young; let's go see what else we can dig up. I'm going to secure us some horses to ride out to some of the further houses. Wait here."

Aesara watched him leave, her heart clenching in her chest. She wasn't sure how to feel. She wanted his affection, yet with every person he murdered, every soul he stole, he used it for his own gain, his own immortality. It went against everything she believed in.

She sighed, unsure of what to do. "*Tmes visith fi.*"

CHAPTER
Twenty-Four

A SLIGHT ODOR OF FARM ANIMALS WAFTED THROUGH THE AIR AS THEY traveled along the edges of Dria. Wood planks rotted off some of the houses. The roofs were patched with various materials—hay, wood, and even fabric. Several houses had collapsed in on themselves. If anyone lived out here, they certainly weren't living a life of luxury.

Above, a bird cawed. Aesara squinted, trying to get a better view of it, but all she could see was a black blur against the sun.

The horse Aesara rode snorted, ruffling its black mane. She reached forward, patting its neck. She liked riding horses. It was one of the more calming things she was allowed to do at the castle, and it always brought fond memories to the surface.

"It's all right, boy," she whispered. She looked ahead at Vance, his mare taking the lead. Aesara guided her horse closer to Vance's.

"I didn't realize Dria had farmlands. I was always taught that it was just a port."

Vance nodded, keeping his eyes on the road and the surrounding land. "That doesn't surprise me. Dria's not supposed to have any farmland. The soil is too soft and too salty for most grain to take root."

Aesara frowned at the crumbling farmhouses. "Then why all these houses? This land?"

"How far back do your history books go?"

Aesara opened her mouth to answer and then paused. "They go far, especially for my education. But I think a better question is, what are they leaving out?"

It wouldn't surprise Aesara that her history books didn't tell the whole truth. Even as she was being taught, there were certain things that hadn't made sense to her.

Vance smiled. "Now, you're thinking. Well, before your family took the throne, the Nattores held the throne for hundreds of years, then there was the war, yadda, yadda. I'm sure you know all that, but at one point there was land connecting Tecrane and Sodaya. The soil was fresh; it was good. But there were wars and floods, and now the Silver Sea divides us in land and hearts. They don't like that part of it. It shows how they failed."

Aesara couldn't wrap her head around it. He spoke with such confidence that it was hard not to take his word. "How do you know so much?"

"Not as young as I look, remember?" Vance winked. He urged his horse to go faster, Aesara tagging along behind. It was easy to forget he was older than her by several years, but what he suggested now would mean he was *hundreds* of years older.

Aesara shook her head. That was a conversation for another time. The wind picked up, tossing her hair wildly. It was long enough now that it whipped across her face, obstructing her vision.

"Where are we going?" Aesara yelled, hoping her voice carried over the wind.

"The Twins. They live on the outskirts of Dria in one of the farmhouses."

Up ahead, Aesara spotted one of the few standing houses. It had to be the one Vance spoke of—it was the only one in decent condition. The shutters banged against the house, the paint was faded and peeling in the sun. The roof was completely intact, but discolored patches covered certain parts.

Vance slowed the horse to a stop a good distance from the house. He slid off the back and walked to Aesara, holding his mare by its reins.

"It's best if we go on foot from here. The Twins can be interesting enough without taking them by surprise. I don't want them killing our ride back on accident."

Aesara slid off her stallion, landing unevenly. "They would do that?" she asked, looking at the broken-down house. It was hard to imagine anyone living in it.

Vance shrugged. "Best not to find out."

They led the horses to a rotting post and tied them. If either horse really wanted to, they could break the post easily and run.

Vance stepped up to the door and knocked. The door creaked open from the force of his knock. The house was eerily silent. Aesara thought of how strange Kimi had been and wondered if the Twins would be just as strange or if they'd be worse.

Vance pushed into the house, stepping carefully as he went. Aesara followed his footsteps, wrinkling her nose at the foul stench.

"*What* is that smell?"

Vance said nothing. He continued into a secondary room, stopping in the doorway.

"You've had your fair share of wounds, haven't you, Princess?"

Aesara frowned. "As much as anyone, I suppose," she lied.

"Well, now you know what it smells like when you don't have someone to treat them."

He stepped aside, allowing her to go into the room. She gagged, ducking to the side to throw up her lunch.

Two bodies sat against the wall, holding one another. Their skin hung from their bones, the muscle beneath as rotted as the wood of the house they sat in. Their ragged clothes stuck to their bodies, mold and mildew saturating the cloth. Remnants of open wounds littered their bodies, dried pus and blood staining their skin.

However, it was their faces that horrified Aesara more than anything. She had seen the effects of illnesses and diseases, but this? Their eyes were empty sockets, charred as if they had burned from the inside out. Their jaws were unhinged, tendrils of black smoke still wisping out.

The smell assaulted Aesara, making her vomit again. She backed away from the room, trying to gain as much distance as she could.

Vance walked with her, lost in his thoughts.

"I'm guessing that's not how you remember them?" Aesara asked, wiping her mouth with her sleeve. She would need to change once they returned to the inn.

"Definitely not. I saw them only a few months ago. From the state they were in, this…" He trailed off, clenching his hand into a fist. "Shit!" He punched the wall nearest to him.

Aesara stepped back. She didn't want to be stuck in the crossfire of his anger. "Vance, what's going on? I don't understand."

"If the Twins are dead, it means someone knew what they could do, that they had power." Vance cursed again.

Aesara had a sinking feeling that she knew, but she still found herself asking, "What do you mean? What could they do?"

Vance looked at her then, and for the first time, Aesara saw fear in his eyes. Not fear for her safety or the ship, but fear for himself.

"Dark magic, Aesara. They possessed dark magic."

CHAPTER
Twenty-Five

As they returned to the inn, Aesara thought about what she might say. She didn't know how to bring up anything she wanted to know. How old was he really? Why did he know people who practiced dark magic? Who would possess the power to kill them and leave them in such a state?

Not unlike every other day of her life, Aesara had more questions than answers.

"Ask," Vance said, breaking the silence.

Aesara snapped her head up, her train of thought breaking. "What?"

"Whatever's on your mind, just ask. I don't like the silence; it leaves me in my own head too much. I think you have the same problem."

"How old are you?"

Vance paused, a confused smile breaking across his face. "Out of everything, *that's* your first question?"

Aesara shrugged. "I figured I'd start with the easiest."

"I stopped counting a long time ago, Princess. But to give you a rough estimate, I was a little boy when Leken Resein took the throne."

Aesara blinked. "Resein? But they were…" She paused, trying to calculate the time. "The Reseins were before the Nattores, and Leken was—oh, was he the last of them? No, he was the second to last." Aesara nearly collapsed. "But that makes you more than a thousand years old!"

Vance stared at her, raising an eyebrow. "Probably closer to two thousand at this point."

"That can't be possible! You barely look twenty," Aesara spluttered, unbelieving.

"Magic is an interesting thing, isn't it?" He plucked an imaginary hair from his shirt.

Aesara glared. "Fine," she spat. "If the Twins had dark magic, like you say, who could possibly have more power? And why would they want to kill them?"

Vance nodded slowly. "That is exactly what I've been wondering. Whoever killed them took something from them. And they didn't just kill them, they *destroyed* them—left them withering and burning. There wasn't a trace of magic left in them."

He stood, pacing the room. Aesara sat further on the bed, hugging a pillow to her chest for comfort.

"What do you mean 'they took something?' It didn't look like there was much in that house to take."

Vance shook his head. "I don't mean something physical. Did you notice their eyes?"

"It was hard not to." Aesara shuddered.

"Someone went into their minds, into their magic. They took something like a memory, a spell, maybe. But they didn't do it carefully."

Aesara thought of the few people she held dear and imagined seeing them in such a state.

"I'm sorry, Vance," Aesara said, her heart hurting for him.

"For what?" he asked, frowning.

"I imagine it was hard to see friends like that."

Vance waved her off. "They weren't friends. To be honest, I can't imagine a more fitting fate. No, what worries me is not knowing who did it. Keep your friends close and your enemies closer."

His brutal honesty took her by surprise. It was one thing to say their deaths didn't affect him in that way, another entirely to say they deserved it.

At the castle, Aesara knew what to think. Her father was a tyrant, known for his cruelty. She knew that one misstep, one wrong word, could result in being whipped, beaten, or worse. She knew the boundaries. Here, looking at Vance, watching him pace, she wasn't sure where one boundary started and another ended.

He claimed the Twins weren't friends, and yet, he was going to ask them for help. Would he say the same of Kimi? Of Byrd? Would he say the same of her?

Something gripped her heart, something unfamiliar and dark. Aesara shuddered under its weight.

"I know where to go." Vance snapped his fingers, and his demeanor suddenly shifted. "Come on, Princess. We've got a mage to see."

He threw on his jacket loosely. Aesara stayed seated for a moment. Vance paused at the door, looking back at her.

"Princess? Aren't you coming?"

She snapped out of her stupor. "What? Oh, yes. I'm coming."

Her mind raced with unrelenting thoughts and questions. Though when he looked at her, calling her "princess," she felt the thoughts break away for a different feeling entirely. She was a princess to many, but this was different. This was personal.

Vance opened the door only to shut it just as fast. Two large men had stood outside it, their bulky figures filling the hallway.

"New plan," Vance said. "We're going that way."

He ran to the window as the door shook.

"No point in running, Reaper!" one of them yelled through the door.

Vance pried the window open and poked his head out. An arrow shot up, narrowly missing his head. He ducked back inside, slamming the window shut.

Vance let out a continuous stream of curses as he pulled Aesara to the attached washroom. There was a single small window, too small for even Aesara to fit through.

"What's your plan?" Aesara asked. Adrenaline rushed through her body, but she was far from panicking. She was getting used to Dria.

Vance looked around the room before settling his hand on his sword. "You're not going to like it."

Aesara shook her head. "No. There's been enough killing with that damn sword."

She stomped to the window, glancing downward. No one was waiting for them. She flung it open and stuck her hands out.

"By all that is Silver, *work!*" Her magic bubbled through her veins, responding to her command. Green exploded from her hands, a tree sprouting from the dirt alley with incredible speed and magnitude. Branches broke through the washroom wall, creating an escape.

Aesara panted as she let the magic falter, coming to a stop.

"Let's go," she whispered.

As they started to climb, the two men burst into the room, swords raised.

Aesara yelped and climbed as fast as she could. She stumbled a couple times, clumsily reaching for a branch to cling to as she wound her way down. At the castle, there was no need to climb, nor were there very many trees to do so even if she had wanted to.

She cringed as she watched one of the men hack at the branches, making a larger way onto the tree. While it didn't hurt her physically, the act of harming the nature around her made her heart ache in a familiar way.

"C'mon, Princess. Jump. I'll catch you."

Vance stood at the bottom of the tree with his arms outstretched, more adept and agile than her. She didn't have much farther, but the men were gaining on her quickly.

She pushed against the tree, flinging herself backward. She braced herself, her muscles tightening as she fell.

As he'd said, Vance caught her with ease. She didn't have time to thank him before he grabbed her hand and they took off running.

Aesara dared a glance behind her. The two men were just jumping to the ground when Aesara and Vance rounded a corner. The alley was a dead end, a tall brick wall stopping them. Vance swung Aesara around to face him.

"Can you get us over without them being able to follow?"

Aesara blinked. "Without them..." That would mean she wouldn't be able to grow anything. She flexed her fingers, trying to act quickly. She needed more time. Without thinking, she flung her hand out toward the alley's opening. In a flash of green light, a large bush of thorns grew.

"Aesara? I don't mean to rush—"

She snarled, holding herself back from smacking him. "I know! I'm thinking. I don't see you coming up with any ideas!"

Vance shut his mouth. Aesara took a deep breath, trying to relieve the building pressure in her chest. The cool breeze blew by, brushing against her cheek like the caress of a mother.

"I've got it," she said, backing up to the edge of the thornbush. She motioned for Vance to come with her. "Follow me. Make *every* step I make."

He nodded.

Aesara let out a breath. She grabbed his hand and took off running straight toward the wall. She let the breeze surround her, following her every step. Aesara felt the magic underneath her feet. She thought about using the wind like a staircase, but she didn't know if she could lock onto her magic with such precision, let alone with another person.

"What's the plan, Aesara?" Vance yelled. His hand started to tug at hers. He was slowing down.

"Just trust me. Jump!"

Aesara sent a rush of air underneath them, launching them over the wall unceremoniously. They landed with a thump. Aesara groaned as she sat up. She hadn't thought about how they would get down.

"A little unorthodox, but well done, Princess." Vance huffed, a smile on his face. He laid on his back, chest rising and falling quickly.

Aesara observed him with his tousled clothes and hair. His scruff had grown since they arrived on Dria. She noticed he had a scar, just above his lip.

She bit her own, thinking of their kiss that felt so long ago now. She wanted it again, but at the very same time, she did not. There was so much new information, so much for her to think about, she couldn't let him fog her mind with romantics.

"I know that look," he said, sitting up on his elbows. "Is it the danger that does it for you?"

Aesara glared at him. She shoved herself to her feet. "Let's go find your mage."

Vance laughed. "I'm only teasing you. Lighten up, we're alive!"

Aesara spun on her heels, facing him with red-hot anger. "Because of me! We're alive—*they're* alive—because of me! See how well you do when I'm not there."

She turned to storm off, but Vance grabbed her, shoving her into the wall and caging her in. He held one arm to her throat, lifting her off the ground slightly. The fury in his eyes now matched her own.

"I could've handled myself just fine without you, *Princess*. I would've had their heads in seconds, but I chose to humor you, to allow you to save them. Don't think for one second that I need you to survive."

"But you do, don't you? You said it yourself that you can't kill Morana. Either use me or don't, Captain, but I will not stand going back and forth."

Vance growled low in his throat. "I don't want to use you, Aesara! Make your own choices, dammit. Stop letting everyone make them for you."

Aesara stared, watching as her next words sank in. "It's hard to make your own choices when you never had them to begin with."

Vance took a step back, releasing her. She fell forward, still glaring at him despite the shock and hurt in his eyes. Aesara straightened her back and walked past him.

"Let's go find your mage."

"All right," Vance whispered. "She's this way."

CHAPTER
Twenty-Six

They were silent as they walked. Aesara's anger did not dissipate, but neither did her curiosity. She found herself staring at Vance as he led them further into the town.

He was smug, brutally honest, and an ass more often than not. But he also made her heart beat faster than it should. He made her skin heat and her mind race.

Aesara scowled. *Bastard.* It was easier when she knew what her place was, what she was supposed to say, supposed to do.

She looked down at her feet, kicking a small rock. As they walked farther, the mud started to dry, making it easier for her to keep herself steady. Unknown to her, Vance had stopped walking. Aesara walked right into him, smashing her nose into the corded muscles of his back.

"A little warning next time?" she snapped, rubbing her throbbing nose.

"I thought you were paying attention." There was no venom in his voice, nor was there the softness she had started to recognize when he spoke to her.

For some reason she couldn't quite place, this made her heart ache.

"Well, I wasn't," she said, taking some of the bite out of her voice. She stepped next to him, trying to ignore the heat radiating off him. "Where are we?"

He motioned to a little shop; it looked a little worse for wear, but not nearly as bad as some of the surroundings shops. A small light flickered within, signaling the presence of someone.

"Do I need to be wary of them as well?" Aesara asked. Her body felt heavy. All her time on *The Promisea* she'd wanted to be on land, but since they had landed, she had been tense. It seemed someone or something waited to harm them around every corner.

In Ascen, her demons did not hide in the shadows. It was easier to spot them.

Vance shook his head. "No, Finella is powerful, but she's kind. One of the few left in this town."

He marched forward, leaving Aesara to trail after him.

A small bell rang as they entered the shop. At the counter, a short woman with red hair and freckles hunched over, a magnifying eyepiece over one eye. She mumbled under her breath, poking at whatever was on the counter.

Aesara tried to get a better look, but Vance held his arm in front of her, stopping her from moving closer. She frowned but didn't move further. He had said she wasn't dangerous, but Aesara wasn't risking anything. He cleared his throat, gaining Finella's attention.

"No," she said without a moment's hesitation. "Nope, no."

"But I haven't even said anything," Vance said, hands held up in surrender.

Finella scowled at him. "And that's the way I want it. Every time you come into my shop, something goes wrong, or breaks, or someone dies—the list goes on—and I won't have it. Not this time." She moved around the counter, shooing him away. "I won't be paying for any damages or funerals today. No, thank you."

Vance grabbed her by the wrists and leaned down, a smile on his face. "I always did enjoy our talks, Fin. Now, I have a guest with me this time, so will you at least hear me out?"

For the first time since entering, Finella noticed Aesara standing there. She squinted, wrenching her arms from Vance's hold and walking closer to Aesara.

Finella was shorter than her, her head only reaching Aesara's chest. Aesara leaned back under her scrutiny, uncomfortable being stared at.

"Umm, hi?" she said, unsure of what to say to the woman.

Finella hummed, still studying her. "I suppose you want to know something."

Aeesara blinked. "I do. I suppose *you* want payment for what I want to know."

"I like this one," Finella said to Vance, leaning back with a smile on her face. "Where'd you find her?"

Vance looked at Aesara then, his brown eyes meeting her golden ones. For a moment, Aesara's mind went blank, her anger for him disappearing.

"She found me, actually," he said, never breaking eye contact.

Against her better judgment, Aesara's heart fluttered.

Finella made a face. "Blech. Just tell me what you want to know already so I can get paid and you two can get out of my shop." She sighed. "Because it doesn't look like either one of you will take no for an answer."

Vance opened his mouth to speak, but Aesara beat him to it. "How do I stop the war?"

Finella's eyes widened in shock at the bluntness of her question. "Well, you're wasting no time, huh? Who says I know anything about this war?"

Aesara motioned to Vance, whose face held just as much shock. "If you are what he says, you know exactly what I'm talking about."

Vance stepped forward, almost as if to get between the two women. "I'm so sorry, Fin. She's not usually so…open."

Aesara glared at him. "What do you know about me? You just think I'm a spoiled princess."

"Are we really discussing this now?" Vance asked, exasperation lacing in his voice. "I understand you're angry with me, but be angry with me on our time."

Finella watched the exchange with interest, inching closer to the pair.

"If you understood, you would've apologized," Aesara seethed. She took a step closer to Vance, their chests nearly touching.

"You want me to apologize? For what? For telling you to think about yourself?" He laughed, the sound dry and humorless. "I don't think so, Princess."

Aesara wanted to scream. "No, I want you to apologize for not thinking of anyone but yourself. For assuming you knew my life, what I wanted, what I needed. You think you hold power over everyone, but you do not hold power over me. There is but one man who does, and He is a *god*."

Silence filtered through the room. Vance stared at her, his expression filled with sorrow rather than anger.

"You're right," he said, his voice just above a whisper. "I shouldn't have assumed anything, and for that, I am sorry. But I will not apologize for trying to figure out what you wanted." He lifted his hand, stroking her cheek so lightly she could barely feel it. "You have given me hope, Aesara, and I will see that it is given back."

Aesara leaned into his touch. She had wanted an apology, but what he had given her was something she didn't know what to do with. It was more than she had bargained for, and it made her heart flutter.

"Well"—Finella clapped her hands together, shattering the tender moment—"I'd say you forgive him, yeah?" She spun Aesara to face her. "So, you're Aesara, heir to the Virral throne, princess to Tecrane, all that, huh? I don't know why, but I think I was expecting someone more…annoying. Follow me."

Finella marched behind the counter, brushing aside a curtain and walking into the back of the shop. Aesara looked at Vance for confirmation. When he nodded, they followed her.

The back was a single room with bookshelves lining every wall except for one that had a bench for working. A small table stood in the center of the room. Stairs on the wall lead to what Aesara could only assume was Finella's apartment above her shop.

The counters were littered with glass vials and dishes filled with various substances Aesara couldn't name. Some bubbled and steamed, while others did nothing but sit there. One caught Aesara's eye as it shimmered in its little tube with a brilliant purple hue. As she inspected it further, it began to shift shades from purple to pink and then red. Through the rainbow of colors it went, a breathtaking sight to behold.

"What is all this?" Aesara asked, unable to keep the awe from her voice.

"Experiments. I'm trying to find a way to ease the mind of nightmares with that one you're looking at there. The bubbly green one? It's a way to possibly capture dreams so we can revisit them when we're awake." Finella fumbled away on the table, clearing a space.

Aesara gasped, swiveling so she could see Finella clearly. "You're a seer!"

"You say that like it's a good thing."

"You can make prophecies, understand dreams, even see the future." Aesara stepped up to her, invading her personal space. "Your powers are incredible, Finella."

Finella pulled her hands from Aesara, who hadn't even realized she had grasped them. "Right, well, it's a pain in the ass, too. I can't always control it. So, when someone comes asking for help"—she gave Aesara a pointed look—"it doesn't always go to plan."

Aesara sat at the table, eager to see Finella's powers in action. "Anything you can do would help."

Finella sighed, taking a seat across from Aesara. "So, you want to know how to stop the war? Let's see if my magic is in a giving mood."

She stretched out her hands, motioning for Aesara to take hold. Without hesitating, Aesara placed her hands in her palms. Finella took deep breaths, each one slower than the last. They grew so slow that Aesara worried she might pass out. Finella's eyes snapped open. They had no color, no iris; they were just a pure, blinding white.

"Finella?" Aesara asked. "Are you still there?"

"With magic and emotion as a guide, the serpent's tongue will have lied. The harbinger comes down to fight the demon with a golden crown. Once full and now an empty nest, it is our duty to let the dead rest." Her voice was raspy, as if she hadn't drunk any water for days.

Aesara took a step back, shock traveling through her body. *What in the Silver did that mean?*

Finella coughed violently, falling against the table. Aesara shook her head and stood, reaching forward to help Finella steady herself.

"I hope that was helpful because that's all I've got in me," Finella said, her voice still teetering on a raspy edge.

"It was…something," Aesara said. She didn't want to offend the seer, but she wasn't sure what any of the riddle meant.

Finella chuckled before going into another coughing fit. "Yeah, that's usually how it goes. Reaper"—she turned to face him—"go get parchment and ink. You'll want to write it down while it's still fresh in your mind."

Vance blinked as if he had been in a trance. He nodded without question and left the room.

Aesara frowned at his actions. He had never listened to orders from someone else, not without questioning them first.

Finella shot out a hand, grabbing Aesara's wrist in an iron grip. Aesara yelped and tried to pull away from the burning pain, but Finella only pulled her closer.

"He is not who you think."

Aesara's heart raced at how fervently Finella spoke.

"What do you mean?" Aesara asked, her voice dropping to a whisper. Vance clinked around in the shop, still searching for what Finella had asked for. "Who isn't? Vance?"

"You call him as a friend would, but he is not your friend. The truth has been hidden from you by the very one you trust."

"Well, I, uh…" Aesara stuttered an answer. Her mind reeled at what Finella suggested. "If he is hiding something, he will tell me when he's ready." *Wouldn't he?*

Finella reared back, releasing Aesara. "When he tells you, it will be too late. Don't be foolish. Find me later, without him."

Aesara opened her mouth to speak, but snapped it shut when Vance entered the room, paper and ink in his hand.

He looked between the two women, feeling the tense air. "What did you two talk about?"

"Nothing," Aesara answered quickly. She mentally slapped herself. Her voice had risen in pitch and she'd answered too quickly; he would know something had happened. Thankfully, he only looked at her quizzically before moving on.

"All right. Here are the things you asked for." He tried to hand them to Finella, but she kept staring at Aesara.

"Um, here, I'll write it." Aesara took the paper and inkwell, their hands brushing against one another. Aesara suppressed a shudder. Despite their argument and her warring thoughts, she still fought to control her attraction for him.

She blushed furiously and dropped her head, scribbling the riddle onto the parchment. It had been a few months since she had last written and her handwriting was sloppier than usual, but she still smiled as the ink stained the paper in a flourish. She liked writing. When she was younger, she would spin wild stories for her mother in a makeshift book. She had attempted to illustrate one of her stories once, but she found her ability in describing the picture rather than drawing the picture itself.

She placed the quill back in the inkwell and let the paper dry for a moment before picking it up. She reread the words, trying to understand their meaning. Vance stepped behind her, the warmth of his skin radiating on her back. She wanted to lean into it, but one glance over the top of the parchment at Finella's cold stare had her sitting up straight.

Aesara lifted the paper, allowing Vance to take it. "Any ideas?" she asked.

"I'd imagine it's about a mage. It says 'magic and emotion as a guide.' Sounds a lot like you when you first discovered your power."

"But I'm getting better," Aesara protested, looking up at him.

Vance chuckled and playfully tugged on a strand of her hair. "Yes, I'd say you are."

Aesara couldn't help the swell of pride at the praise. She liked it when he complimented her.

Finella cleared her throat. "If you two are done, the riddle would like more attention. It's not a fun state to be in to get that information, and I'd prefer you'd focus on that rather than each other."

Aesara's cheeks burned with embarrassment at being called out. "Right, of course. Sorry." She peered at the words again, her eyes snagging on one of the lower lines. "'Demon with golden crown?' I can think of someone I'd call a demon that wears a crown, if it's speaking literally...is it speaking literally?" She pointed the question toward Finella.

"It was meant for you to understand. You tell me."

Aesara held in a growl of annoyance. "How cryptic and not very helpful of you."

"Well, I can burn this and let you forget if you'd like." Finella reached for the parchment.

Aesara snatched it out of her hands and held it close, protective of the riddle. "No, thank you."

Finella smiled. "As I thought."

Vance took the parchment from Aesara's hands gently, reading the riddle aloud once more. "Empty nest and the dead. What an odd combination." He hummed.

Aesara frowned, searching her memory for anything that would relate but drawing up empty. "I don't understand," she said.

"Does it mean we should search for a bird, like we did with the crows?"

Vance shook his head. "I don't think so. I think it means a parent. You know, like an empty household?"

Aesara stared at him, waiting for a deeper explanation.

He stared at her in shock. "Don't tell me you've never heard of the phrase."

Aesara still stared.

"Well, when you have children, they say you have a full nest. When they leave to go on their own, you then have an empty nest—like birds."

The phrase made her think about the families in Tecrane. Most couldn't afford to leave home, and those that did never lasted long outside the cities. If they did leave home, it was typically an arranged marriage between a lowborn daughter and a son of higher rank; parents wanted the best outcome for their children even if it wasn't ideal.

Aesara was considered lucky to be born in her status. She should never want for anything. She chuckled dryly at the thought of never wanting. There were many things she wanted—her father to recognize her as he once did, love, friends, her mother back...

She paused. King Ciran used to treat her like a father should treat a daughter, but that was before her mother died. Aesara missed her mother, but she could only imagine how much her father would be willing to give to have Queen Siofra back.

She took the riddle from Vance's hands and reread it several times over, pacing the room.

"Aesara?" Vance asked. "Have you got something?"

She looked up, excitement running through her. "I think I know what it means." She took a step forward. "You remember those letters that weren't adding up? How it seemed like Sodaya was telling my father to stop? It's because they were. Sodaya had nothing to do with this. It's my father—it was always my father." The excitement at the discovery faded into something darker. "He's behind everything. Bliss said I'm betrothed to King Sol.

What if the meeting between him and Sol didn't happen like we think?"

Vance matched her forward step, closing the distance between them. "If this is about your father, it would mean he's using magic. As far as the world knows, King Ciran is a Common. Your mother was the mage."

A shudder ran through Aesara as she thought of the Twins and their mutilated bodies.

"Some magic isn't inherited, though. There is one kind that can be learned." She met his eyes, fear spreading through her. "What if he's using dark magic, Vance?"

Vance didn't answer immediately, the silence deafening. "If he is," he finally answered, "we have a much bigger problem on our hands."

CHAPTER
Twenty-Seven

THE WALK BACK THROUGH TOWN WAS QUIET, BOTH THEIR MINDS racing with the implications of what they'd learned. Siofra had always been fearful of dark magic, and with good reason. It corrupted the soul, took what you loved about yourself and life and twisted it into something vile. It made Aesara wonder just how long her father had been dipping his hand into it.

The rain fell softly, covering her tears as they fell. The summer air was sticky with heat and humidity, and Aesara's black dress stuck to her in patches. The veil covering her face did nothing to hide the coffin as it was lowered into the ground.

Her tears were silent amongst the anguish around her. The villagers took turns tossing flowers over the coffin, a multitude of colors—reds, whites, and yellows. Blue, *Aesara thought.* There needed to be blue. It was her mother's favorite color. She should wear it in death as she did in life.

Slowly, the crowd dispersed, leaving just Aesara. She stepped closer, looking down at the wooden coffin. The silver ring around her neck burned against her skin, the last gift she had received from her mother. Her tears had stopped, but her eyes still watered as if she had more to give.

Aesara stiffened at the footsteps sounding behind her. A hand fell on her shoulder.

"I don't want her to be gone," Aesara whispered.

King Ciran released a heavy sigh. "I don't either, but she is."

"I wish there was something I could do." Aesara's voice wavered, more tears spilling down her cheeks.

"Oh, little one, you already did." Her father leaned down so he could whisper in her ear. "You killed her."

The memory assaulted her, making her stumble against the cobblestone. Aesara hadn't thought of her mother's funeral in years, but thinking back now, King Ciran must've started then. His only motivation in life was Siofra, it would only make sense that he would blame Aesara and seek a way to bring Siofra back.

Aesara caught up with Vance, matching his footsteps. "Vance!" she called, grabbing onto his arm. "I think it'd be wise if we left this town."

Vance searched her eyes before nodding. "I think you're right. There isn't anything left for us here."

He continued forward and Aesara let her hand fall off his arm. She watched him walk away before speaking. "Finella warned me against you," she said quietly. "She said you weren't who claimed to be."

Vance stopped, his shoulders tensing. "Oh? And what else did she say about me?"

"I don't know." Aesara stepped up next to him, bumping her shoulder into his. "I told her if you had something to tell me, you would. I think between saving each other's lives, I can trust you to do that." She smiled, hoping he felt the same.

Vance took a step closer, stopping her from walking forward. "But what about our argument? What about the way I do things? I thought you didn't agree."

Aesara shrugged. "I don't, but you apologized. What is the point of having forgiveness if you never give it?" She tried to move past him, but he stopped her with one muscular arm.

She frowned. "Vance, what are you—"

He didn't let her finish. He dove down, crashing his lips to hers. Aesara squeaked, surprised, but quickly fell limp as he wrapped his arms around her.

She tried to deepen the kiss, but he moved back, peppering her face with kisses. Aesara giggled at the tickling sensation and tried to block him, but he was stronger than she was. Eventually, he pulled back, leaning his forehead against hers.

"I do not deserve you, Princess. Not one bit."

Aesara smiled. "Why's that, Captain?"

He trailed a finger across her bottom lip. "You are so pure against the blackness that is me. I've never met someone so full of hope. You have a fire inside you and, by all that is Silver, I want to burn with you."

Aesara's heart threatened to stop inside her chest. "No one's ever spoken to me like that."

Vance finally stepped back, allowing the night air to cool her skin. "You deserve so much more in this life, Aesara—certainly, more than me. Now, come on. I fear if we linger too long, something will find us."

He tugged her by the hand, and he didn't release it all the way back to the ship, leaving Aesara's heart fluttering.

The ship was as they had left it, no one daring to touch the Reaper's possessions in fear for themselves. Six met them as they walked aboard, raising an eyebrow at their connected hands but saying nothing except that he had found the map Vance had requested.

Aesara blushed and tried to pull her hand away, but Vance only held tighter. A bird's shadow flew over the ship, and when

Aesara looked up, she saw the same crow that had insisted she keep Vance alive.

It was following her. She squinted, trying to get a closer look, and spotted a familiar canister in its talons. It was Sono, the last messenger crow Aesara and Vance had caught and released.

He cawed before diving, entering the cabin as Aesara was pulled inside. Sono dropped the canister on the desk and landed on her shoulder, chirping happily.

Vance blinked as he turned around. "What is that doing here?"

Aesara smiled, stroking his feathers. "It's Sono. I think he remembered me."

Sono cawed as if agreeing with her.

Vance shook his head. "I don't care who the bird is, he's leaving." He flung the door open again, but Sono remained on Aesara's shoulder.

"I don't think he is," Aesara said, chuckling. She tilted her head toward him, allowing him to press his cold beak against her cheek.

Vance growled and opened his mouth as if he wanted to say more, but Sono interrupted him, gliding from Aesara's shoulder to the desk. He jumped on the canister, chirping wildly.

"I think the stupid bird wants you to open it," Vance mumbled, crossing his arms.

Aesara narrowed her eyes at him. "Don't be mean just because he's getting my attention and you're not."

Vance's face flushed a pretty shade of pink Aesara had never seen before. She had to stifle her laughter as he stuttered a response.

"That's not—I'm not—that is—" He huffed, looking at the ceiling instead of her. "I'm not jealous of the dumb bird."

"I'm sure you're not," Aesara chuckled, picking up the canister from beneath Sono. Her fair mood quickly fell sour when she realized it wasn't meant to be sent.

The straps and buckle were broken, one side torn from the other. Deep scratches marred the metal as if it had been fought over. Aesara eyed the crow, who had his head tucked under his wing, preening. She had no reason to be suspicious of him. So far, Sono had done nothing but help her.

Aesara twisted the head off the canister and let the letter within fall out. The letter was old, the parchment yellowed and crinkly as Aesara handled it. She unrolled it carefully, minding where the softest parts of the paper were.

Aesara blinked at the writing, a wave of grief washing over her. It was her mother's writing, a letter written to King Ciran before he was king. Aesara tumbled through her emotions as she read it.

Dearest Ciran,

I fear I won't make it to Ascen to see you again. My powers only grow stronger, and it is something that is coveted here, something nurtured. My father believes it is better for me to stay, to go to the Coves. He won't listen to reason——to his heart.

I'm going to try and make him see my side, see what it is I love and want. If he won't see that, he won't see me at all. My heart knows what it wants, and it wants you, Ciran, my love. Give me two weeks. If I cannot get my father to come to an agreement of our marriage, I will meet you outside the Black Rocks. The Silver Sea is free to navigate; my father will have no say in your ship there, and I know the secrets of the Cove and the Rocks.

Two weeks is all I ask. We have waited this long; we can wait a little longer. I pray this letter finds you swiftly. Be ready for anything and I shall be ready for you.

All my love forever,
Siofra

Aesara's eyes held on to her mother's name. It had been so long since she had seen it. Aesara's heart clenched as her legs gave out beneath her. She fell into Vance, who immediately wrapped his arms around her, gently guiding her to the floor.

"What is it?" he asked. "What does the letter say?"

Aesara blinked away tears. "It's a letter from my mother to my father, before either of them ruled Tecrane. She's asking him to wait for her."

"Ah, well, it seems like he did. Who knew he was capable?"

Aesara huffed a laugh before frowning. She sat up, rereading the letter. "Wait, she's telling him to wait outside the Black Rocks. She says her father has no control over the Silver Sea." Aesara turned in Vance's arms to look at him. "That's not Tecrane."

Vance leaned forward, reading the letter for himself. With his neck and chest directly in front of her, his oceanic and smoky rum scent assaulted her, making her blush.

"No," Vance agreed, completely unaware of what he was doing to her. "It isn't Tecrane. Your mother speaks as if she's from Sodaya or Isamund."

He pulled back and looked down at Aesara, who, instead of facing him with a face as red as a tomato, squeaked and hid her face in his chest. Somehow, Aesara thought it less embarrassing.

"Aesara, are you all right?" he asked, trying to force her to look at him.

Aesara nodded quickly. "I'm fine!" She cringed at how much her voice rose in pitch. Clearing her throat, she tried again, "I'm fine. You think my mother might've been from one of the kingdoms closer to the Coves?"

Vance hummed in agreement, the sound rumbling against Aesara. "She says she knows the secrets of the Rocks and the Coves. There are very few who know that information. If what she claims in this is true, your mother couldn't have been born in Tecrane."

Aesara took a deep breath and finally pulled away from Vance. "I never knew my grandfather on my mother's side. She told me he had passed away before I was born, but what if that's not true?"

So many thoughts whirled in Aesara's mind. *Why would her mother feel the need to lie? Why was her heritage a secret?*

Aesara groaned, letting her head fall forward so her forehead was resting against Vance's chest. "I wish I had a normal family."

Vance chuckled, winding his arms around her tighter. "Nothing about either one of us is normal, Princess."

A soft thud landed next to them, and Sono brushed his beak against Aesara's hand. Aesara stroked him gently, focusing on the softness of his feathers and the way he almost seemed to purr.

"Every time I think I know something for certain, I'm presented with new information. I just wish I could say I knew something that would never change," Aesara said with a sigh.

Vance stroked her hair, twirling the ends between his fingertips. "Change is something that is inevitable. We must learn to accept it when it comes and the challenges it brings with it." He shifted so that Aesara sat in front of him. "I think you've done well for everything that's happened to you. You've been through so much, and even if you can't say you're proud of yourself, I can."

Aesara stared at him, unsure of how to react. Since her mother had passed, Aesara had never felt the same. There was no more praise, no more laughter, smiles, or anything to make Aesara feel the swell of emotion she felt now.

She leaned forward before she could lose her nerve and placed her lips upon his, shuffling so she was in his lap. Vance answered her by pressing further into her. His arms tightened around her, creating a cage of warmth. He licked the seam of her lips, making her gasp. He took the opportunity to invade her mouth, their tongues battling for dominance.

Aesara moaned, her body moving involuntarily against him. Vance groaned against her mouth, the vibration of it sending her mind into a blur. His hands ran down the length of her body, stopping on her hips. He gripped her there, his hands swallowing her.

Aesara was lost to the motions. She didn't want this to end. It felt good and it made her forget the world around her.

She dove her fingers into his hair, feeling the knots and twists here and there. She gave a small tug and Vance answered with a growl. He leaned forward, forcing her to lie on her back. Aesara let him, trusting him to keep her safe.

He pulled away, kissing down her jaw. Heat pooled inside Aesara and her breathing picked up. Every sensation was so new to her, and despite her typical fear, she wanted him—wanted what Vance had to give her.

Vance let his hand slip down the links of her corset, fingering the clasps, but never opening them. Aesara was about to tell him to just open them when he jerked back with a yelp.

Aesara sat up on her elbows. "What? What happened?" Her heart raced in her chest, afraid that she did something wrong.

Vance sucked on the tip of his finger, and when he pulled it out briefly, Aesara could see the blood welling from a cut.

She tilted her head to the side in confusion. "You cut yourself?" she asked. "On what?"

"I didn't cut myself," he growled. "Your damn bird bit me!"

Aesara swung her head around to look at Sono, who chirped and blinked at her before hopping forward and rubbing against her. Aesara couldn't help it—she laughed. It was a loud, from the gut, laugh.

Vance glared at her without malice. "Oh, you think that's funny, do you?"

He launched forward, grasping at her skin where it was bare. Aesara laughed uncontrollably as he tickled her, wriggling and writhing trying to back away from him.

"Stop, stop! I can't breathe!"

He didn't stop. Aesara gasped for breath, trying to control her laughter. She managed to grab hold of his wrists and pulled them away from her body. There was no force pulling back as Vance let her catch her breath.

"You have a beautiful laugh," Vance said, his warm breath fanning against her skin.

Aesara stared at the cabin ceiling, the weight of Vance on top of her comforting.

"My father used to play with me all the time. We would wait in the garden for my mother and scare her." She chuckled at the memory. "You should've seen her face. There was one time she was carrying a new flower—I think it was a violet—and when we jumped out, she dropped it. There was dirt *everywhere* on the pathway. Of course, Mother cleaned it easily and threw it on Father instead." Tears welled in her eyes as the happy memory faded from her mind. "But then she left us and my father turned into what he is now."

"I remember your father when he was fair," Vance whispered. "He did what he could for Tecrane despite the land's challenges. But I fear losing your mother did things that cannot be undone. The dead weigh heavily over many."

Aesara nodded before resting her head against Vance's shoulder. She looked at Sono before her eyes shifted to her mother's letter that rested on the floor.

Aesara lifted her head and sat up, Vance moving with her.

"What is it, Princess?" he asked, shifting off her.

She picked up the letter and pulled the riddle from her pocket, comparing the two.

"Vance…if my mother knew the secrets of the Coves and how to get there, do you think she shared those details with my father?"

Vance frowned, shifting so he could look over her shoulder. "I imagine so, if their love was as true as we were led to believe. Why?"

"Because I think he's going to try and bring her back."

CHAPTER
Twenty-Eight

Aesara paced the cabin as Vance sat at the desk, looking between the riddle and the letter.

"It makes sense," Aesara blurted. "You said yourself that the dead weigh heavily on people."

Vance pinched the bridge of his nose in frustration. "Say you are right. Where did he learn dark magic? How is he getting to all these places seemingly without ever leaving the castle? And what in the Silver are *we* supposed to do about it?"

Aesara thought it was glaringly obvious what they were supposed to do. She stepped forward, slamming her hand on the map, right over Sodaya.

"We go to Sodaya. I'm still the Crown Princess of Tecrane. If I can get an audience with King Onuphrius, I can tell him everything and—"

"And what, Princess? All you're doing is telling him that your people can't be trusted."

Aesara clenched her fists, trying to rein in her anger. "No, I'm going to convince him to go against my father. Call upon the other kings of Gilan for a meeting. If there's enough against my father, he can be removed from the throne peacefully."

Vance raised an eyebrow. "And you think your father will accept that? That he'll go *peacefully?*"

"Well, no," Aesara said, thinking carefully about her next words. "If he refuses to give up the throne to the next heir, the kings have the right to forcibly remove him."

"And why do you think they haven't already done that, hmm?"

Aesara closed her eyes, frustration and realization leaking from her every move. "He has them in his pocket."

Vance snapped his fingers, a smile on his face. "He has them in his pocket. Exactly, my dear. What we need to figure out is who he has and what he has on them."

Aesara thought back to the letters they'd intercepted and the information they'd picked up along the way.

"He has King Sol. Well, I think he's killed King Sol and replaced him with one of his men. It's the only thing that makes sense with the fake betrothal and all the greenroot. Isamund is a dead country. There hasn't been a king there in over thirty years. The only kingdom left would be Sodaya, which certainly hates my father."

The information settled in as she realized that her father had been slowly but surely coveting enough power to take on Sodaya. Every move he made was carefully crafted. He had been planning this for years.

Aesara let out a weak laugh. "We never stood a chance, did we?"

Vance watched her carefully as he spoke. "Your father has always been cunning. But I think we might have a chance if we go directly to the source. If we take out your father —"

"We would surely die," Aesara said, interrupting. "Trying to attack my father now would be suicide. He is the *king*, Vance.

Compared to him, we have nothing. We are nothing. Don't you get it? I have been fighting this battle for ten years. You cannot win against him alone."

"But you were scared before. And you didn't possess the skills you do now." Vance stood and walked around the desk. He clasped Aesara's hands in his, making hers look small. "We could do it, Aesara. You and I, together."

Aesara wanted to keep her hands in his forever, wanted to agree, but she knew he was wrong. She pulled her hands from his.

"I am still scared. I never stopped being scared. I only grew to work through my fear. I made him angry because if he couldn't see what he had become, by G'iv, I was never going to let him forget. I want my father off that throne, but I will do it when I know I have a chance."

Vance threw his hands in the air and huffed. "You are so stubborn. I have been around for *centuries*, Aesara. He may have a kingdom, but I have time. Not even he could wield my sword. Doesn't that mean anything?"

Even Aesara could see him growing anxious, like he needed reassurance that he was still right. Aesara hadn't seen him in such a state before and she didn't know if she should comfort him or not. Without knowing what the right decision was, she opted to speak the truth.

"It does mean something, but I know my father. Haven't you wondered about the deal he made with you? Don't you think it's odd that all he wanted was to hold it?"

Vance shrugged. "He reacted the same as anyone did."

"He was testing himself, Vance. If what I think is correct, he's been dabbling in dark magic since my mother died. He wanted to know how powerful he had become."

Vance placed his hand atop hers. "But he has not become more powerful than me."

"No, of course not." Aesara did not say aloud her fear that in the months they'd been at sea, King Ciran may have become as powerful as Vance, if not more. "I still think it would be better to go in with a plan—with allies."

Reaching forward, she pressed her hand against his cheek. The rough stubble there scratched against her palm, and the stranger who had saved her from the thugs flashed through her mind—the gold of his magic seared in her memory. She took a step back in shock and wished she knew his name.

"Princess? Are you all right?"

Aesara blinked, the stranger's face disappearing from her vision and morphing back into Vance's. She nodded and placed her hand against his cheek once more, thankful no memories assaulted her.

"I just don't like seeing you this way. You're a lot of things, Captain Vance, but unsure isn't one of them."

Vance placed his hand atop hers and leaned into her touch.

Aesara covered her slip-up well with the truth, but she couldn't stop herself from wondering why she suddenly thought of the stranger. He had saved her, yes, but he was rude, coarse, and extremely brutish. He had manhandled her, for G'iv's sake.

But he was handsome. He even gave Vance a run for his coin.

Aesara wanted to shake her head at herself. Since when had she become so vain?

She pulled herself away from Vance, leaning against the desk.

"So," she started, "if we're not going after my father straight away, what is the plan?"

Vance looked her up and down appreciatively, and, for the first time since they had gotten closer, she didn't know how she felt about it.

He moved closer but didn't touch her. "Sodaya has the resources to oppose King Ciran. They have an army, food, and ships, not to mention control over the Coves."

Aesara cursed at herself. "*Of course.* They have control of the Coves! That's why my father wants a war with them." She swung around the desk and shuffled the maps, searching for the one that pinpointed the path to the Crystal Coves.

Everything made sense at that moment. With Aesara out of the picture, her father was able to do whatever he wanted in the castle without anyone to question him. She was the only one who would've been able to speak against him. Ever since her mother died, he had blamed her.

Aesara had been young, barely seven, when she snuck out of the castle to play with some of the villagers' children. Unfortunately, the season for the Rose Fever had begun. Aesara had thought she was safe playing with the boys since the fever only affected women, but what her naïve young self didn't realize was that the men could still pass it along.

Her mother had insisted on taking care of her and, as everyone predicted, caught it herself. Aesara was young; she easily got over the fever. Her mother, however, had not been so lucky.

With Aesara gone and an intense motive, Aesara didn't doubt her father would reach the Coves. If her mother had shared the pathway in, the world was in terrible danger. The Coves stored incredible power inside each crystal and gem. They served as amplifiers to the magic one already possessed; if you had enough of them, even someone without obvious magical abilities could use magic. For someone who did have magic, Aesara could only imagine what kind of power they would possess. It was for this reason that the Coves were protected and guarded to prevent anyone from going in and taking whatever they wanted.

Sodaya had taken responsibility for this and, so far, they had done their job. They did not use the crystals for themselves, nor did they allow others to use them.

Aesara looked at Vance with determination. "We have to go to Sodaya. Make them see reason."

Vance braced himself against the desk, the muscles of his forearms on display. "That's if they don't kill us on sight, isn't it, Princess?"

"We make me look the part. We sail this as an emissary vessel from Tecrane. According to the laws—"

"According to the laws, your father is a madman, and they can do whatever they believe is right to protect their kingdom. Remember, Aesara, you're apparently betrothed to King Sol."

Aesara wanted to break something. Her father had thought of everything to make it difficult for her to oppose him. It was never easy in the castle, but now it was even harder.

"It doesn't matter," she said. "We have to try. I didn't do enough in the castle when I should have. I *have* to do what I can now, even if it's not the best plan."

Vance studied her for a moment, walking around the edge of the desk to stand by her side. He took her chin between his fingers, lifting her face to look up at him.

He looked at her with a gentle expression. "I have found that I don't like arguing with you. I like making your skin flush for other reasons. We'll go to Sodaya, but the second there's trouble, I'm turning this ship around and getting you out of there. I don't want to lose you. I *can't* lose you. It's not often I find myself drowning in love. Deal?"

Aesara couldn't help the waver in her voice when she answered, "Deal."

He dipped down and kissed her again. Before she could deepen it, though, he pulled away, ducking out of the room and shutting the door behind him. She could hear him shouting orders, rerouting the crew and ship.

Love… Vance had said love. Aesara didn't know what to think or do. For so long she had wanted a man's love, but now that she had it, she wasn't sure.

Aesara looked at Sono. "What am I going to do?"

The crow didn't have any answers, though. He simply swooped onto her shoulder and made himself comfortable.

On the deck, the crew ran about, changing the direction of the ship. Aesara dodged the frenzy and made her way to the helm to stand next to Vance. He eyed the crow on her shoulder.

"I see he's not leaving."

Aesara chuckled. "No, it doesn't appear so."

She had just leaned against the railing when he pulled her back against his chest. She cocked her head at him.

"Vance?"

"Say it," he whispered.

"Say what?"

"Say you want me." His voice was desperate, as if she was the only thing keeping him stable.

For once, she didn't have to think about what she was going to say. "I want you, Vance."

He let his head fall against her shoulder and groaned. "You're going to be the death of me, I swear, Princess. When this ship is steady, I'm locking you in my room, and I don't give a damn who knocks on the door."

Heat pooled in Aesara's belly, and all she could muster was a nod.

He moved to kiss her once more when Sono interrupted, squawking wildly. Vance grumbled and reluctantly released her.

"If I can't have you now, will you find Byrd for me? He should be around here somewhere."

Aesara nodded and headed down the stairs, her mind still in a daze from what Vance had said. The crew had started to calm down with everyone in their rightful position. Six waved at her from the crow's nest. She waved back, wishing he was on the deck with her. She wanted her friend close by now more than ever.

The sun shined down and warmed Aesara through her clothes. Aesara took a moment to herself and sighed peacefully. She tilted her face toward the sky, breathing in the salty air. She had begged and begged to be back on land, but land had only provided attempts on her life and sleepless nights. At least on *The Promisea* she knew she would be safe.

She frowned as a cold draft blew in and a shiver wracked through her, making the content feeling dissipate. In seconds, the sun was blocked from the sky and a dense fog floated in, covering the ship so completely Aesara could barely see the crew next to her.

Six shouted from the crow's nest, but his voice was lost to the wind. Aesara breathed out a white breath and heard someone step behind her.

"We just left the port. I didn't think there were any islands this close?" she asked.

Byrd stepped beside her to look over the ship. For a while, he didn't say anything, and then, "There aren't. The sea has seemed to...move."

Aesara frowned, worried by how much time he was taking to think about his words, how carefully he was choosing them. Someone only did that when they didn't want the other person to react in the wrong way.

"That doesn't make any sense," Aesara said. "The sea can't just move." She paused and looked at Byrd. "Can it?"

"There are some things that cannot be explained by the use of logic." Byrd looked at Vance at the helm. Aesara followed his gaze. "This is something our captain learned a long time ago."

Aesara opened her mouth to speak when she was thrown forward. Rocks hidden in the fog rutted against the ship. Vance quickly spun the wheel, guiding the ship away, only to have more rocks appear.

When Aesara looked behind them, there was nothing but fog. She could not see the lights of the port or land at all. It was as if they had never been there at all.

"How can he see?" Aesara asked, her voice just above a whisper. The crew remained eerily silent, and she didn't want to be the one to break it.

Byrd answered her, unbothered by his volume, "He can't."

Aesara snapped her head to watch Vance direct the ship through the treacherous rocks, praying that G'iv would guide his hand.

In the midst of her prayer, a soft whisper flitted through the fog. Byrd and the crew stood at attention and shifted nervously on their feet. The breeze took the whisper by Aesara's ear, and the language it spoke was unfamiliar to her. She frowned and shuffled through her vast knowledge of languages and still came up empty handed. The language on the wind was entirely new.

Behind her, a splash broke her concentration. She and the crew ran to the starboard railing to see one of them thrashing in the water, struggling to stay afloat in the shifting waters. Phantom hands tugged at his body, trying to pull him under.

One of the crew members yelled, "Man overboard!" They rushed to fetch a rope, but Aesara stood still, unable to tear her gaze away.

"Leave him," said Vance. Aesara shifted to look at him.

He faced forward and kept his eyes on the water ahead of him. He didn't spare a single glance to the crew or the drowning man. The crew looked at one another, skeptical, but followed their captain's orders.

Aesara had never seen this side of Vance. She had seen him captain the ship, yes, but this was different. He watched the waters as if expecting something to pop out of them.

Aesara looked back at the drowning man as they slowly passed him. He sank into the sea, his hand still reaching for help. Aesara cringed, hating herself for not doing more to help him, but the sea was unfamiliar territory for her still. Would she have survived if she had gone after him?

Another whisper floated through the ship. Byrd put a hand in front of a sailor walking to the edge and shook his head. The sailor looked confused but went back to his station.

"What's going on?" Aesara asked.

She did not get an answer. Instead, the ship jolted forward and Aesara fell with it, landing on her hands and knees. She slipped a little on the misty planks but rose to her feet.

"Why have you come here?" asked a woman's voice, her tongue gentle and sickly sweet.

Aesara started. She looked around, but the only woman on the ship was her.

"Watch yourselves, men," Vance said, still focused. He spared Aesara a glance, but nothing more.

The woman laughed, her voice circling the ship. Aesara whirled around, trying to follow it.

"Come now," she said. "I will take care of you."

A wind passed through the ship, giving a phantom caress to the crew. Aesara shivered, revolted by the feeling. She watched, confused, as the crew walked toward the railings of the ship as if they had no control over their bodies.

Vance slammed his fist down on the wheel. "Enough, Morana! Show yourself to me."

Fear rang through Aesara at the name Vance spoke. Ice spread to her hands, an involuntary reaction to the fear spreading through her body.

No, she wasn't ready. She couldn't fight her yet.

The wind became still. The whispers stopped. The fog cleared a path, and the sea-witch appeared. Her skin was a sickly green that sparkled in the light, and her tail faded to an obsidian. Scales covered her from tail to chest, and around her fish-fin ears rested a tall black crown of shells that spiraled into points. She was stunning in a dangerous way.

She raised her arm, and the water rose to make her eye-to-eye with Vance. Despite being the same height, Vance was dwarfed in comparison to the sheer size of her. Her tail alone was the size of him.

"You dare speak to me in such a way, *Captain Vance?*" Morana spat his name out through daggered teeth.

Though Vance appeared unafraid, Aesara saw his hand twitch.

He ignored Morana's question and asked his own, "How long have you been following me?"

"Long enough."

Vance chuckled. "I figured you were close by when the currents started to change. I was just hoping I was wrong."

Aesara wished she could appear as unafraid as he did, but the more Morana inched forward, the more Aesara inched back.

Morana hissed, "You've had your time. I want payment."

"I want more time."

Morana scoffed at his words. "I let you sail freely, I let you have the sword, and you think you can demand whatever you want?" She chuckled darkly, circling him. Water splashed across the ship as she moved. "I think not. I gave you the power you possess, I can just as easily take it back."

Aesara's mind reeled. Vance had said she'd cursed him, forced the sword upon him, but the way Morana spoke... Aesara clenched her hands into fists, stiffening her body as she glared at the captain.

She had given him so much of herself and he had *lied* to her. He was no better than any of the other men in her life.

Aesara marched forward, uncaring that the seawater seeped into her boots, making her socks squelch when she walked.

"You dirty, rotten liar!" she screamed. "I trusted you, and this whole time, you were *lying?*"

Aesara could feel Morana's questioning gaze, but she kept her focus on Captain Vance. He remained calm, letting Aesara scream at him.

"Go back to the deck. This is between the sea-witch and me. No reason for you to get involved," he said, completely ignoring her accusations.

Aesara nearly lost it. "Excuse me?" The wind whipped across the ship, violent in response to Aesara's anger. Morana lifted her head, sniffing the air curiously. "No reason for me to get involved? I am the reason, you bastard! You think I don't know my family's history?"

His eyes widened and he grabbed her by the shoulders, leaning in close. "Shut up, right now."

Aesara tilted her head, a wicked smile on her face. "What's wrong? Did you think I was that naïve?" She shoved him off her, pressing her ice-cold hands against his chest, leaving bits of frost stuck to his clothing.

He glared at her. "You don't know what you're doing. Get back down to the deck."

Aesara crossed her arms. "No."

Vance closed his eyes in frustration, doing his best to keep his hands to himself. "Aesara, I swear——"

"Aesara?" Morana interrupted. She slithered forward, pushing herself between Vance and Aesara. "You are the princess?"

Aesara glared behind the witch as she answered, "Yes."

Morana sniffed her. Aesara did her best not to move, even when water dripped on her.

"Why are you here?" Morana finally asked.

Vance stepped forward. "King Ciran made a stupid deal, that's all."

Morana snarled at him, snapping her tail and throwing him backward. She turned her attention back to Aesara. "You said he lied. Tell me, what has he lied about now?"

With Morana in her face, Aesara's bravado started to die, but she was too far in to back out now. "He said you killed his captain and crew, leaving only him. That you cursed him with the sword."

Morana paused before laughing. It was a wet sound, like she had water in her throat. "I did not *curse* him," she said when she finally regained composure. "He came to me. He brought his captain and his crew to my doorstep, promising them a bounty worth a lifetime. And they did receive it. Too bad their lives were cut short by yours truly."

She shifted to reveal Vance, who was getting up from where he had smacked into the railing. His eyes connected with Aesara's, guilt and regret obvious in their dark depths. Aesara couldn't tell if it was for her or the crew he'd slaughtered, and *that* made her fury burn even brighter.

Morana slid around her, encircling her with her tail. "Your precious captain butchered them all for the power I gave him, for the sword that never misses, that grants him eternal life. He would be the most powerful, but I told him the price would be high. He said it would never happen, and yet, here we are."

Aesara chuckled, the sound empty to her own ears. "It's me, right? The thing that would never happen."

Morana moved behind her. Aesara couldn't see what she was doing, and it made her restless.

"Tell me, Princess Aesara, do you love him?"

The question assaulted her. It wasn't something she had ever expected to be asked. She wanted to come to terms with it on her own. Aesara didn't know what love meant. Her mother had never explained it to her before she passed, and her father had certainly never tried.

She knew that when she looked at him, her heart beat a little faster, and when he touched her, her skin flushed. He made her mind go fuzzy when he kissed her, and she knew she never wanted him to stop. But the stranger entered her mind again. Could he make her feel the same way? The anger slowly dissipated, the red turning into something blue.

"I don't know," she answered honestly. "I don't know what it means to love."

Morana hissed, her forked tongue slipping between her lips. Vance looked at her with sorrowful eyes, as if she had said the wrong answer.

"If you do not love him, then his debt remains." She whipped her head to look at Vance. "In fact, you've been the wielder of that sword for far too long. Let's make it a little harder for you, shall we?"

Aesara's eyes widened, and she tried to step forward, but Morana's serpentine tail curled around her legs, hindering her from moving.

"Wait," she called. "I said I didn't know, not that I didn't!"

Morana swung her attention back to Aesara. "It is a yes or a no question, little falcon. Do you or do you not love him?"

Anger rose in her, a smoky smell rising from her hands as the frost melted to be replaced by small licks of flame. "It is not as easy as yes or no, witch. The only love I've ever known was taken from me when I was young. You ask me a simple question that does not have a simple answer. If you want to know if my heart races when I'm around him, then yes. If you want to know if I lose all common sense when he invades my personal space, then yes. If you want to know if I like it when he touches me, then *yes!* But if you want to know if I love him, then I do not know!"

Aesara could see a glimpse of the prideful smirk across Vance's lips, but she didn't have time to concern herself with him. She had to worry about the sea-witch in front of her.

Morana narrowed her eyes. "Fine," she said slowly. "Then I will give you time to figure it out." She uncurled herself from around Aesara and, despite her size, slithered to Vance in one swift movement.

The sea around them shifted, rocking the ship. Aesara struggled to keep her balance, and her hair whipped back and forth as the wind picked up. Water splashed onto the deck, and with it came horrific sea creatures. It was as if someone had taken two or three different types and sewn them together to create something entirely new. They screeched as they boarded and immediately started attacking the crew. Screams quickly filled the air as the ship turned into a battlefield.

Byrd roared next to Aesara, pulling a crab-like creature off his back and ripping one of its legs off. Blue blood splattered across Aesara, but in the flurry, she did nothing to wipe it off.

She had to find a way to stop this. Looking toward Vance and Morana, her heart nearly stopped. Morana grabbed Vance by the throat, her claws digging into his skin, drawing blood.

Aesara pushed her way through the fighting, trying to reach them before it was too late. She would not have more death on her hands. The sea creatures parted for her—Aesara did not have time to question why.

A sailor raised his sword to kill one of the creatures. In her fury and fear, Aesara launched herself at him, knocking him off balance. They rolled across the deck until Aesara was able to wrestle his sword from his grip. She stood over him and put the sword to his throat.

He looked at her with fear, and Aesara shook her head. She slammed the sword into the wood next to his head. "Killing them will only make it worse."

A sea creature next to them clicked its pincers and moved on.

Aesara looked at Vance once more. Morana dug her other hand into his chest, clawing to his heart. Vance's eyes were wide, and his mouth gaped open as she pushed her claws deeper.

Aesara sprinted toward them, slipping only once. "No!" she screamed.

Morana stilled. "No? What do you mean 'no?'" She ripped her claws out and let Vance fall to the ground with a thump. He groaned in pain as blood spilled from his wounds.

"I mean no," Aesara said, standing her ground despite the fear coursing through her. "I may not have the strength to fight you, but I will try." She met Vance's gaze. "I keep my promises."

Morana blinked in shock before laughing. "You are funny! I like your nerve." She leaned down, picking Vance up by the throat. He dangled, his knees just a few inches above the ground. "For her, I'll change your payment. I want the blood of the one who cursed me. You bring me this and your debt will be considered paid." She threw him across the helm.

He groaned as he tumbled to Aesara's feet.

"That isn't fair payment," Aesara objected. "It was a royal mage who cursed you, one whose name has long been forgotten. If he does have any heirs, it would be impossible to track them down."

Morana hissed, "That is my price for his life, little falcon. Should he return to the sea without it, the sea will claim him as its own. He will return his lives to me."

She looked between Aesara and Vance before whistling. The sea creatures stopped their attack instantly, diving overboard and back into the deep sea below. As their queen, Morana left last.

"Love has the same cost as magic, little falcon," she said. "Even those without both are beginning to pay the price." Leaving Aesara to ponder her riddle, she dived into the sea, taking the murky magic and fog with her.

The sun returned in a brilliant fervor, nearly blinding Aesara. The ship overlooked the glistening waters once more; not a single wave rippled out of place. Aesara breathed in the salty breeze, something she didn't think she would miss.

Vance groaned. Aesara ran to him, grabbing his arm to help him up. He shoved her off him, causing her to stumble. He leaned against the wheel instead, eyes ablaze.

Aesara frowned, hurt by the anger in his eyes. She had saved his life, done everything in her power to help him. *Why was he angry?*

"You ruined everything," he growled.

Aesara blinked. "I saved your life! I saved all our lives. What do you mean—"

"I needed that debt paid off!" He lunged for her, and Aesara dodged as he had taught her. He fell forward, panting, and swung around with a finger pointed at her. "You were supposed to help me pay it off, but no! You couldn't admit that you loved me."

Aesara's world stilled as she realized what he meant. "It was all fake," she whispered. "You never meant any of it."

"Of course I didn't!" He paced the deck. "You think I would fall in love with someone like you, a spoiled princess from a castle? It's you and the other high-blood bastards that make sailing hard. You tax the ports, tax the goods we carry, you even tax the letters we carry *for* you!"

Each word he said stung worse than the last. "I thought—"

"You thought what, Princess? That I actually cared?" He let out a dry laugh. "You were the means to an end, that was all. And now, thanks to you, I have to sail to land to find this—this *heir* that might not even exist."

Aesara winced when he said princess, the pet name hurtful now that she knew the malice that hid behind it. "What was the price?" she asked, her voice a whisper.

Vance stopped pacing. "What?"

"What was the price?" Aesara enunciated each word clearly, practically yelling them at his face.

"You want to know—all right, fine. Morana saw no love in my heart. She said that if I could find someone who would love me despite my black heart, my debt would be paid. When your father offered me you..." He whistled. "I knew he had no bastard sons. Siofra was the only one he ever gave himself to and that was how it would always be. I also knew you had never been given true experiences outside the castle. I figured if I could give those to you, then you would easily fall in love with me. I would get laid and my debt would be paid."

He spread his plan out in front of her, each step presented clearly. An invisible hand squeezed her heart, threatening to make it burst.

"How did you know I would fall in love with you?" Aesara asked, trying to focus on that rather than the more hurtful aspects of his plan. She was trying to spare herself from any more heartbreak, but it didn't matter. Her eyes still watered.

Vance scoffed. "You said yourself you didn't know what love meant. Of course you were going to fall in love with me."

Aesara blinked, and the first tear slipped down her cheek. "I see. So, what now, Vance? What's your grand plan?"

Vance took a deep breath and turned away from her. He walked to the wheel, steering the ship to the right.

"I do what I should've done in the beginning." He looked past her. "Byrd."

Aesara heard steps behind her, and her eyes widened. She darted to the side, but Byrd grabbed her before she could get far. Panic seized her as the ship's railing came closer.

"Stop, stop!" she cried, twisting her hand to look at Vance. "What are you doing?"

Vance looked straight ahead, as if she weren't worth his time. "The witch wouldn't take you," he said, his voice flat and uncaring. "Maybe the sea will."

Her body was lifted, and she kicked against Byrd's grip. Six scrambled down from the crow's nest.

"Captain, wait! You can't do this!"

Vance snarled at him, "Unless you want to join her, you'll mind your tongue."

Six looked at Aesara with fear and worry. Aesara shook her head. "Don't," she whispered. "Don't waste yourself on me."

He opened and closed his mouth before facing Vance. "At least let her go on her own accord. She deserves at least that much."

He looked between them for a moment before spitting, "Fine."

241

Byrd set her down on the deck, and she wobbled at the sudden need to balance herself. He walked away easily, but she could've sworn she saw a bit of remorse in his eyes. Six ran to her.

"I'm so sorry, Aesara. I didn't…this wasn't what I thought would happen. I didn't know his plan, I swear." Tears welled in his eyes.

Aesara hugged him tightly. "It's okay, Six. It's okay. Just make it out of here, all right? Promise me that you will."

Six nodded. "You would've made a great queen."

Aesara smiled sadly. "You were a great friend, Six. Thank you."

Aesara watched as the crew shoved a wooden board out the side of the deck for her. She glanced at Vance, who still avoided her gaze. She let go of Six and walked to him.

"You know, I think I could've," she said, laughing sadly through her tears.

"You could've what?" he snapped, refusing to look at her even then.

"Loved you." She didn't wait for his response, instead walking away and down to the prepared plank. She swallowed as the wind gently rocked the plank back and forth.

Byrd stepped behind her. "I warned him. And I tried to warn you."

Aesara smiled. "Yes," she said. "Many did. I was a fool not to listen." She turned to face him. "I don't suppose I'll ever see you again, Byrd, but know that I hated every second I was in your presence."

Byrd blinked before letting out a boisterous laugh, tilting his head back and holding his stomach. "For what it's worth, I hope you survive this," he said when he finally caught his breath.

"Me, too," Aesara said with a chuckle. "Me, too."

"I granted your wish! Don't take advantage of my kindness," Vance yelled from the helm.

Aesara took a deep breath and turned to the sea. She did not want to jump. But there were many things she didn't want. She walked to the end of the plank and stared at the water below.

She turned to face the crew. Vance had made his way down from the helm and stood front and center. He bore an expression that Aesara couldn't make out. It wasn't quite sorrowful, but it wasn't quite hateful either. *So, he did feel guilt, after all.*

She smiled. "I hope you find the heir." Vance's face shifted to one of shock. "Maybe being free will give you your heart back."

He stepped toward her. "Princess, wait."

For the second time in her life, Aesara jumped into the sea.

CHAPTER
Twenty-Nine

She hit the water hard, her body already aching. Water filled her mouth, and she kicked her feet frantically, trying to reach the surface. She broke through finally, gasping for air.

She wanted to call for help, to beg for them to come back for her, but she knew they wouldn't. A wave washed over her head and dragged her down. She pushed to reach the surface once more. The ship sailed further away from her as she struggled to stay afloat. Through her panic, she realized she needed to make herself lighter. She gasped, taking in a gulp of air, and dove under the water. She unlaced her boots and ripped at her corset, breaking the buckles. She was sad to see it go, one of the reminders of kindness in the world sinking to the bottom of the sea.

She kicked up and took a breath, staring at *The Promisea*.

It should've been called The Ship-Full-of-No-Good-Rotten-Scumbags-That—

Her thoughts were interrupted by a splash in the distance. Aesara frowned, squinting against the sun to see what it was. It looked as if one of the lifeboats had been released. A few moments later, she saw someone jump in after it.

Without hesitation, Aesara swam until she reached it. She pulled herself in, winded and exhausted, and looked for the sailor that had jumped.

"Six!" Aesara cried, her heart in her throat.

He was floating toward her. She would curse him for his foolishness after he was safely in the boat. She reached out and grabbed him, trying to pull him in with her. She managed to pull him up by his shoulders, but she didn't have the strength to pull him further.

"Come on, Six," she said, gritting her teeth. "You've got to help me."

She lost her grip, and he splashed into the water. Panting, she looked at her hands to see them stained red. Horror filled her as she snapped her head to look at him. He was sliced open from chest to stomach, his entrails spilling out and bleeding into the ocean around them.

Aesara screamed and fell back into the boat, rocking it. She curled into the fetal position, refusing to look at the water.

He killed him. He killed him. He killed him.

Tears fell freely as the image ingrained itself in her mind forever. The man she thought she could trust, perhaps love, had *slaughtered* her only friend simply for helping her. The thought hurt more than she wished, but she couldn't tell if that was because he'd murdered someone or because he hated her.

It was for that reason, that confusion, that she held her legs tightly, whispering prayers. Her breathing was labored, and she stayed there until she was sure Six was gone, until the sun began to sink in the sky. She had seen dead bodies before. She was no stranger to the dead, but they had always seemed at peace. There had been no peace for Six, and knowing Vance, his soul would not see peace either.

How she *hated* that damned sword. Her tears of despair turned to tears of malice. She would destroy it. She would free the souls within it. If she could do nothing else, she would do that.

When she finally arose, his body was gone and so was the ship. Aesara was completely and utterly alone. Her face felt tight from the tears she'd cried, and she scrubbed at her face, trying to wipe the feeling away. She sniffled, refusing to cry again, and grabbed the oars with one hand and the ring still chained around her neck with the other.

"G'iv be with me. Strengthen me so I do not fear. I have no need to be afraid, for You are with me and will not forsake me." She took one last deep breath and began to row.

HER MOTHER USED TO SAY THAT BIG DECISIONS DIDN'T ALWAYS LEAD to big events. But as Aesara looked across the vast ocean with nothing in sight except dark and thunderous clouds, she wondered if maybe the same could be said of the opposite. Small decisions didn't always lead to small events. Her magic would do her no good out here—not only had she tried, but she didn't have a clue which direction to go.

Aesara had thought the choice was clear. She would've helped Vance find the mage's heir, not because she needed his help, but as his friend. Aesara clenched her fists and slammed them into the bench in front of her, welcoming the pain. She screamed into the wind, letting it take her heartbreak somewhere else. She screamed and cried until her throat was raw, until she had nothing left to give. She had given everything to him—*everything*. Even now, she gave herself to him. More tears threatened to escape, but she sniffed, blinking them away. She had shed enough tears over a man who likely shed none over her.

Aesara looked across the endless water that gently rocked her small boat. Blood stained the wood from where Six had fallen against it. She winced as his broken body flashed through her mind.

So many thoughts flashed through her mind—about Vance, Morana, Six, even herself. It was as if a dark cloud covered her thoughts and she could only see the negative. Aesara liked to think she was good at seeing the positive, but right now, sitting in a small rowboat in the middle of the ocean with no sense of direction, she didn't think she was good at anything.

She had once thought she could save Tecrane, stop her father from taking over the Coves and decimating the kingdoms around them.

Aesara blew out a breath, wanting to laugh at herself. Who was she kidding? It had taken her weeks—months—to figure out the truth.

She paused, sitting up straight. *But she had figured out the truth.*

No one else knew except Vance, and he wasn't likely to keep his word in helping anymore. No one was going to stop her father. No one was going to see it coming.

No one except for her.

Grabbing the oars, she started to row. She would make Six's sacrifice worth something. She didn't care that she didn't know where he came from or his favorite color or his favorite time of day. If he could give his life without knowing hers, why couldn't she do the same? As a slight breeze blew across her face, she mumbled under her breath, whispering a prayer.

THE RAIN BLEW IN STRONG AND HARD UNTIL A STORM CAME UPON HER several nights later. Aesara shivered, the cold seeping through her clothes and into her very bones. She watched her arms row, knowing she was doing it but feeling nothing in her blue fingers.

She tried to flex them against the oars' handles, but she couldn't tell if she was doing anything. It was her body against her mind. She had tried to use her magic to create a bubble around herself, but it had only lasted for a few moments. Her body was too weak to keep the barrier up for long.

She licked her lips, swallowing the rainwater. The cracked skin was rough against her tongue, the taste of iron potent. She took hard, quick breaths, as if she couldn't get enough air.

But there was plenty of air! Aesara wanted to scream, but nothing came out but a hoarse sigh.

She missed the ship. It could handle storms like this. Her rowboat was not as well suited. Waves crashed over her, and she struggled to keep the boat upright and afloat. She was so tired of fighting—fighting the water, the air, her own body. She wanted to be done.

"I'm trying!" she cried into the wind. "I don't know what You want me to do! Please, tell me. Am I supposed to continue? Is this Your way of telling me to give up?"

She would. She would release the oars into the water and let the ocean swallow her if that was what G'iv wanted. But Aesara found she did not want to. With everything she had been through, by Silver, she wanted to *live.*

A wave hit the boat, knocking the breath out of her and yanking one of the oars from her grip, sending splinters into her palm. She hissed in pain and grabbed her hand, releasing the other oar without thinking.

"No!" She hadn't meant to let go; it was instinct to clutch the area that was in pain. She tried to catch the oar, but it was too late. It belonged to the raging sea. Aesara sat up straight, the weight of what she'd lost bearing down on her.

Eyes wide, she looked across the tremendous waves rising and thundering down. Lightning flashed in the dark sky, and fear washed over her as a wave formed above her, larger than all the rest.

There wasn't much for her to do, she knew that. So, she did the only thing she could think of.

Aesara's lips moved faster than her mind, mouthing a prayer she could not say aloud. It would make the situation too horrifying, her fear too real. Instead, she planned her next move. If G'iv had wanted her dead, He'd had many chances to do it. She would not let the sea take her now.

Aesara waited until the last possible moment, right before the wave fell on top of her, and then she jumped into the water.

Her body already numb to the cold, she didn't notice the freezing waters. The boat splintered to pieces above her head, and though she tried, she could not breach the surface. The pressure of the crashing wave held her beneath the water.

Aesara kicked and kicked, fighting for air. If this was to be her end, she would go down fighting tooth and nail, there was no doubt in her heart.

Her head broke through the surface, and she gasped, only to be shoved underneath once more by another wave. Over and over, she repeated that cycle. She'd find the surface only to be pushed back under again until her legs were weak and she could no longer move her arms.

She kept her eyes open as she sank beneath the surface. The water was a brilliant blue, lighter than it should have been in the storm. It shimmered in front of her, begging to be touched. Aesara did what it wanted.

Reaching up a hand, she let her magic flow through her. Green light exploded around her, and ice flooded her body. Her limbs stiffened and she slowly stopped moving altogether, the ice freezing her from the inside out.

As she slowly lost consciousness, she gave a little bit of herself to the sea, letting it seep to her very core. That was its tithe, and eventually all would pay it.

CHAPTER

Thirty

Aesara opened her eyes to darkness. She blinked, but there was nothing in front of her, just the pitch black.

She took a step forward, her bare feet stepping in water about an inch deep. It was thick and viscous, like she was walking through syrup.

A spotlight shined in front of her, with Lord Avery in its center. Aesara tried to call to him, but her voice made no sound.

Instead, Lord Avery spoke, his voice echoing. "War has been threatened. We are going to lose."

Aesara tried to tell him what she knew, that he needed to get away from her father, but the more she tried to speak, the louder Lord Avery spoke.

A second spotlight appeared, its pedestal weather-beaten, black water stains dripping down its sides. Vance stood atop it, staring at Aesara with blank eyes. Aesara glared, trying to keep her focus on Lord Avery. She needn't concern herself with Vance—there were larger matters at hand.

"Don't think for one second that I need you to survive." Vance's voice spoke over Lord Avery's, and Aesara nearly collapsed. His words affected her—his voice affected her more than she thought it would've. She tried to keep her eyes on anything but him, but she couldn't. Her eyes found his, and they were just as emotionless as the last time she saw them.

Aesara's eyes watered, and she started to sink to her knees. She knew he didn't deserve her tears, that she had cried enough already, but she couldn't help it. The heartbreak was still too fresh in her mind, and whatever was happening to her knew it.

A third spotlight illuminated herself as she appeared in Kimi's shop.

"Uncertainty is a core feature of humanity," she stated.

Uncertainty was all Aesara felt. Every time she felt motivation to continue, something came to tear it down.

She questioned herself every waking moment, and now she could not even rest, trapped in her own mind.

Aesara wondered when it all would end—if it ever would.

Their voices overlapped, each one pounding against Aesara's skull. She wanted to tell them to stop; she wanted to run away, but everywhere she moved, they followed.

Aesara collapsed to the ground, slapping her hands over her ears to try and drown them out, but it was no use. They were inside her head. She couldn't escape.

Make it stop. Make it stop. Make it STOP!

A hand touched her shoulder gently before a body enveloped her.

"You will always be the princess to me," Carina whispered in her ear. Her voice broke through the pounding, its softness louder than the others, yet gentle against Aesara's raging emotions.

A second pair of arms wrapped around her, Six's arms. *"Your time will come, Aesara."* His words rose over Vance's, the encouragement brighter than the spotlight, his hope higher than the pedestal Vance placed himself upon.

Aesara felt the vibrations as the column toppled, crumbling under the weight of something heavenly. She hiccupped as her tears turned from something haunting to something hopeful.

A soft kiss was placed against her head, and Aesara smiled through her tears as her mother spoke. *"I will always be with you."*

Aesara sat up with a jolt, gasping for air as warmth returned to her body. The dream had felt so real—as if they had been right next to her. Aesara hugged herself before quickly drawing her hands back. She looked down at herself, seeing bandages wrapped in several places.

Her memory was foggy, but she remembered her boat sinking. Everything after that was a blur. Had she washed ashore and been found?

She looked around the room she was in. It was a small healer's cabin. Potions and bottles lined various shelves, and Aesara recognized some from her time with Carina. Other than that, there was nothing discernible about where she was.

She swung her legs around the side of the bed. If she didn't know where she was, then it wasn't ideal to stay. Aesara took a deep breath, preparing herself to stand, when a crow cawed, swooping above her and landing next to her.

Aesara tilted her head, nearly crying at the sight as the crow tilted its head back.

"Sono!" She picked him up and brought him to her face, nuzzling him into her cheek. Sono cooed softly, nuzzling her back. Some of the nervousness left her at something familiar.

"I'm glad you're awake," a voice said in the dark. "He's been pestering me since I brought you here."

Aesara stiffened, looking to the corner where the voice came from. His accent was thick, as if Tecranian wasn't his first language. She didn't recognize the voice, but Sono seemed to believe the man was a friend. Aesara took a small comfort in that fact, but still kept her guard up.

"Who's there? Who are you?" Aesara asked, trying to put on a brave voice, though truth be told, her body still ached and she wasn't sure she could stop anyone from doing anything.

The man stood, the stool he sat on scraping against the ground. Aesara squinted until he stepped into the light. He had dark skin and short black hair. Robes of various blues draped over him in a simple way to allow for mobility and breathability in the hot and humid air.

Curses flooded through Aesara's mind as she gazed at him. Her mouth dried and her tongue stuck to the roof of her mouth as he spoke.

"I am Vassilis Chavalon, healer of the people and Crown Prince of Sodaya. The question is, who are you, *Tecranian?*"

Aesara's heart dropped to her stomach and her lungs failed to work. Her mind raced with the possibilities of what could happen, of what she could say. She could tell the truth. She could tell him that she was the Princess of Tecrane, that the war was false, but would he believe her?

She thought of the many lies that had flooded her world up to this point. Aesara didn't know that she cared if he believed her or not. She wanted the truth and that was what she would give.

"I am Princess Aesara Virral of Tecrane, sole heir to the throne and…" She faltered, laughing as tears formed in her eyes. "Oh, G'iv, it's all rather stupid, isn't it? I'm sitting here trying to prove myself to you, but it doesn't really matter. You'll either believe me or you won't." She sniffled, blinked away some of the tears, and looked at the prince directly. "I have vital information about the war. It's not what anyone thinks it is. I want to stop it and I know I cannot do that alone. I ask that you help me or set me free so that I might still try. That is my truth and all I have to offer."

Prince Vassilis stared, as if he wasn't sure what to do with her. He opened his mouth, closed it, opened it, and then closed it again. He did nothing to hide the emotions playing on his face.

"I must admit," he started, "I do not know what to do with this information. You give it freely with emotion, which makes me believe it is the truth, and yet, I must wonder if you play me for a fool." He clicked his tongue. "If you are who you say, there is much to consider."

"If you help me, I will tell you everything I know," Aesara offered. "But if you will not, I beg of you, please just let me go. I will not return."

Prince Vassilis put his hand to his mouth in thought. "You said you want to stop the war, correct?"

Aesara nodded.

He took a deep breath and sat on the stool. "Lucky for you, I am more trusting than my parents and want to stop this war as well. Talk, friend."

Friend. That one word made Aesara's shoulders ease and the ball of nerves in her stomach untangle. Her hands on Sono loosened, and she leaned against the wall of the cabin. She opened her mouth, and she talked.

The End

www.ingramcontent.com/pod-product-compliance
Lightning Source LLC
Chambersburg PA
CBHW060311260626
47160CB00007B/2569